WHAT OTHERS ARE SAYING ABOUT
## *THE STAMPED IMAGE...*

Riveting!

> Mike Spicca, Vice President, Private Bank,
> FSNB Chicago, Illinois

Two thumbs up!

> Dr. Oranu Ibekie, President, CEO, First Med,
> Schererville and Merrillville, Indiana

Stunning!

> Dr Sylvester Nwokedi, Physician,
> Los Angeles, California

Must-read list!

> Dr. Valentine Ozoigbo, President, ValCee Medical
> Corporation, Memphis, Tennessee

Thought-provoking!

> Jack Weichman, CEO, Weichman and Associates,
> P.C. Munster, Indiana

What can I say? You did it!

> Dr. Chideha Ohuoha, Adjunct Assistant Professor,
> Uniformed Services University of the Health
> Sciences, Bethesda, Maryland

Eye-opener!

Dr. Ayo Gomih, Attending Urologist,
Olympia Fields, Illinois

Spectacular!

Attorney Jewel Harris, Jr. Lyle and Harris Law Firm,
Gary, Indiana

Page-turning mystery!

Eke Okeke, Engineer, Philips Corporation,
Andover, Massachusetts

A pulsating thriller!

Dr. Paul Nyongani, General Surgeon,
Valparaiso, Indiana

# THE STAMPED
# IMAGE

To my Dear Friend

Dr M. A. Rahman

Enjoy it

Thanks a lot

Dr Arekene

ADOLPHUS A. ANEKWE, M.D.

# THE STAMPED
# IMAGE

TATE PUBLISHING & *Enterprises*

Published by Tate Publishing & Enterprises, LLC
127 E. Trade Center Terrace | Mustang, Oklahoma 73064 USA
1.888.361.9473 | www.tatepublishing.com

Tate Publishing is committed to excellence in the publishing industry. The company reflects the philosophy established by the founders, based on Psalm 68:11,
*"The Lord gave the word and great was the company of those who published it."*

Book design copyright © 2008 by Tate Publishing, LLC. All rights reserved.
*Cover design by Jacob Crissup*
*Interior design by Lindsay B. Behrens*

Published in the United States of America

ISBN: 978-1-60462-510-3
1. Fiction    2. Science Fiction    3. Religious    4. Thriller
08.01.07

# ACKNOWLEDGMENTS

First of all, I give thanks to Mary, the blessed Virgin, our mother, on whose inspiration, guidance, and under whose watchful eyes the completion of this project was made possible.

To my wife, Angela, who has endured countless hours of lost husband time without complaining, her encouraging words still echo in my ears.

To my children, Ife, Emeka, Anthony, and Adora; the latter two would take turns sitting on my lap many a time while some of the typing was in progress.

Thanks to Sherra Stubbs, she typed the original draft of the manuscript and the subsequent corrections that followed.

To Ellen Beck, she reviewed the raw material and guided it into a manuscript that was worthy of presentation for publication.

To my brothers and sisters, Godwin, Obi, Marci, Felicia, Mike, Theresa, Cecelia, and Ben, they lent their support and encouragement.

To my staff at Broadway Medical Corporation, especially Carla Toney and Rose Graddick, Mary

Hernandez, Gloria, Kim, Ebony, Dorothy and Deloris, who have been with me all these years and have tolerated my constant, nag for perfection, and Dr. Mary Okam-Ubanwa, my partner.

Also, thanks to Mr. Ed Charbonneau, for his insightful foreword.

Finally to Dr. Richard Tate and the Tate Publishing staff who accepted my original manuscript with such encouraging words and devotion. The Lord will truly bless them.

# FOREWORD

I have known Dr. Anekwe both as a professional physician and as a distinguished member of our medical staff.

Once in a while a book comes along that makes me stop and think. In *The Stamped Image,* Dr. Anekwe took medical science to a whole new level, to an area beyond our ordinary imagination.

Imagine for a second the discovery of the real location in the body where the number 666 can be found among those chosen.

The prospects and questions raised by *The Stamped Image* are exciting and provocative to say the least. This discovery in the body of the actual location of 666 is not your everyday discussion.

I have read a lot of books in my life, but *The Stamped Image* actually challenged me on a personal and professional level. I thought to myself, *What I would do if The Stamped Image was actually a true story?* I really do not have any good answers.

*The Stamped Image* brought issues to the limelight in such a succinct way that it provokes as well as entertains.

I especially like the part where the author asked what you would do if you are looking at the devil in the face and at the same time have the mechanism in place to do something. That's intriguing.

*The Stamped Image* showed evil in its raw form, the type of evil we face here on earth on a day to day basis.

The other interesting aspect of this brilliantly written book is the dynamics at play throughout the chapters of the book: human emotions; Christianity; conscientious objectors; morality; and most interestingly, the interplay between government and religion.

This book will keep you on constant emotional high, and I highly recommend it.

Ed Charbonneau,
State Senator, Indiana

# PROLOGUE

### SIGNUM MAGNUM

A great sign appeared in the sky—a woman, clothed with the sun, the moon under her feet, and on her head a crown of twelve stars. She was pregnant with child, and she wailed aloud in pain as she labored to give birth.

Then another sign appeared in the sky. It was a huge red dragon with seven heads and ten horns, and on its heads were seven crowns. The dragon's tail swept away a third of the stars in the sky and hurled them down to earth.

The dragon stood before the woman, who was about to give birth, ready to devour the child that was almost out of the birth canal. This child, a son, her first male child, is *destined* to rule all the nations with an iron rod.

The child, however, was rescued from the dragon, and taken up to the Almighty and His throne. The woman herself fled into the desert, where she would be taken care of for years to come.

A war broke out in the Kingdom. Michael, the valiant rescuer, and his soldiers battled against the dragon. The dragon and its disciples, fought back, but they were defeated and chased out of the Kingdom because there was no longer any place for them.

The huge dragon, the ancient serpent, also called the devil, which will deceive the whole world, was *thrown down to earth,* and all its disciples were thrown down with it.

There was a big rejoicing in the Kingdom, and a voice could be heard proclaiming that the false accuser is gone, but *woe to earth* and the sea for the dragon has come down to them with great fury, knowing that it has but a limited time.

When the dragon saw that it had been thrown down to earth, it pursued the woman who had given birth to the male child. The woman, however, was taken to a place in the desert to be cared for, far away from the dragon. But the dragon, still in pursuit, spewed a torrent of water out of its mouth after the woman, to sweep her away with the current. The earth, in an effort to help the woman, opened its mouth and swallowed the flood made by the dragon.

The dragon, who was the serpent, became very angry with the woman and went off to wage war against the rest of her offspring.

The dragon commanded a beast to come out of the sea. The beast had ten horns and seven heads. On its horns were ten crowns, and on its heads were blasphemous names. The beast looked like a leopard with bear's feet and a lion's mouth.

The dragon gave the beast its power, along with great authority. A mortal wound on the beast's head was easily healed in the presence of earth's inhabitants. Fascinated by it, the inhabitants followed after the beast. They worshiped the dragon because it gave its authority to the beast.

The beast then started uttering proud boasts and blasphemies against the Almighty. It blasphemed His name and His Kingdom, and all those who dwelled in the Kingdom.

The beast was also allowed to wage war against the other inhabitants who were not followers, in order to conquer them. The beast was given authority over the conquered tribes, people, tongue, and nations. The conquered people, especially those who were destined to be conquered, worshiped the beast.

A second beast was commanded out of the earth. It had only two horns like a lamb, but spoke like a dragon. It wielded all the authority of the first beast and made all the conquered inhabitants worship the first beast that came out of the sea.

It was then permitted to breathe life into the first beast's image so that the beast's image could speak and have everyone else who did not worship the beast and the dragon put to death. It forced all people, the famous and the unknown, the rich and the poor, the free and the imprisoned, to be given a *stamp image* of the beast in their body, so that no one could buy or sell except those who had the stamp image of the beast's name, or the number that stood for the beast.

*Wisdom* is needed here. One who *understands* can *calculate* the number of the beast, for it is *a number that stands for a person.* That number is 666.

—Modified from the Revelation to John.

# INTRODUCTION

Did Dr. Regina Dickerson and Dr. David Abramhoff make a shocking, Holy Grail discovery—the actual location of 666 in the body?

Dr. Dickerson from San Diego and Dr. Abramhoff of Chicago, working separately, discovered a new position in the human chromosome called HLAb66 found only in people with wicked intent.

While Dr. Abramhoff believed that this is a special marker seen in those individuals destined for violent behavior, Dr. Dickerson, a Catholic physician, on the other hand, meticulously analyzed and proved that this is the true location in the human body where the number 666, the stamped image, the mark of the beast, is located.

A simple blood test was all that was needed for detection. Initial tests of incarcerated criminals for HLAb66 were positive in those who were convicted of bizarre and evil crimes. America's notorious killers all tested positive. Further testing, however, showed this phenomenon to be worldwide.

The race is on. The questions are endless. Dickerson and Abramhoff proved beyond reasonable doubt that all HLAb66 positives are destined for mayhem.

But what is the trigger? Studies showed that two or three percent HLAb66 positives are found in the normal population; what will become of them, the government wants to know?

The difficulties and challenges posed by this important discovery suddenly became front and center of a national debate. Opposition to the discovery was fierce. The United States government was thrust into a state of quandary as it debated whether to impose mandatory testing on all Americans.

Other nations joined in the debate. Religion was thrust into the mainstream of politics. Dr. Dickerson's life came under serious danger.

# CHAPTER ONE

Dr. Regina Dickerson was sitting on the aisle side at St. Stephen's Catholic Church on Mount Pleasant Street in La Jolla, California, listening to Father Yarderos delivering the sermon on this cloudy Sunday morning.

It has been one of those Sundays in San Diego. Dickerson woke up late, then accidentally turned off the ocean wave sound for the backup alarm. The sound of water rushing fiercely toward the reef always fascinated her. She spent countless weekends at the Hilton Hotel in La Jolla, with a special view of the Pacific Ocean, just to be able to watch the water waves rushing to shore.

That same sound of water rushing to shore on her alarm clock has always been successful in waking her, no matter what time she went to bed. Yesterday, however, Dickerson was up late at the laboratory, preoccupied while attempting to isolate an elusive HLA Antigen. She has been working on this particular HLA for almost two years, and multiple gel test runs have yielded mixed results.

"In the letter of St. Paul to the Corinthians from today's second reading, St. Paul teaches us one thing," Father Yarderos' piercing voice interrupted Dickerson's deep thoughts, "that there are people who rejoice at others' misfortunes. We see this every day in our daily life, especially in this competitive world. Mind you, there is nothing wrong with competition—after all, competition is the fabric of American society, but the Lord will not take kindly to those who glee when their neighbor is suffering. Whatever happened to Christ's teaching of loving thy neighbor as thyself?"

Immediately Dickerson thought about Dr. Peter Millons. *That jerk.*

She remembered the conversation they had Friday when Millons appeared to be rejoicing at her misfortune.

"How is Manuel?" asked Dr. Peter Millons in the crowded doctor's lounge at the University Hospital.

"Peter, I've told you for the tenth time, we are no longer together," Dickerson responded while still flipping through the morning newspaper.

"I didn't know you're divorced."

"We are not divorced yet, but we are planning on it."

"I like that guy; I thought it was a marriage made in heaven." Millons smiled sarcastically.

"Well then, you should have married him."

"Come on, Dickerson, I am strictly pusa-bagged," answered Millons, using the new California subtle slang for a non-homosexual male.

"Whatever that means, and for your wife and children's sake I hope you remain that way."

"I thought you are a Catholic?" Millons persisted.

"So…and…?"

"They don't believe in divorce, do they?"

To mask her fury and obvious anger, Dickerson sipped very noisily the hot coffee she was holding, and then replied, "You know what, Peter, if they sell brains at Sears, yours must have been purchased from the Idiot Department."

She got up to leave to head back to finish rounds with the residents.

"Well, I am still married." Millons was hoping to sneak in the last word.

"You call that marriage?" Dickerson retorted, in obvious reference to the rumor circulating around the hospital that Mrs. Millons enjoyed one-night stands with young residents.

Dickerson couldn't help but ask how Millons could be so naïve, or that he just surreptitiously chose to ignore it.

Driving home from church, Dickerson thought about her life.

Here she was, a forty-something, beautiful medical doctor, and one of the top research scientists at the University of California, La Jolla Medical School; no children, no obligations, yet her life appeared to be in shambles.

She got along very well with her patients. She had long figured out that her patients were the key to her success. Treating patients the way you like to be treated, regardless of the patients' status in life, she thought, was the key. She could communicate with patients in ways no other doctor could.

Those difficult, know-it-all, internet-educated, question-every-test patients were her most treasured, because she delighted in explaining to them in her most simplest verbiage the hard-to-comprehend medical terminologies and tests, and patients loved her for that. They knew they could talk to her and be able to get an understandable answer.

Her marriage to Manuel was wonderful for a while, but lately a major crisis had erupted.

Manuel was the senior sales representative for Novartis Drug Company in the San Diego region. Mike Smith, the drug representative who normally calls on Dickerson, brought his senior manager along in one of his details.

Dickerson always liked to challenge the drug reps, as they are called, on the merits of whatever article they quoted in support of the use of a particular drug. Dickerson, a published researcher herself, loved these exchanges. That day, however, Manuel volunteered to answer all Dickerson's questions.

The exchange was a little testy at first, but finally, Manuel asked, "Can I invite you to an evening of a medical conference at the Hilton Hotel in La Jolla, sponsored by University of California, Los Angeles Medical School? The conference may shed light to some of your concerns."

Dickerson accepted.

At the conference, Manuel was surprised to see Dr. Dickerson drink as much as she did, without getting drunk, but eventually the conversation turned personal.

"Are you from San Diego?" asked Manuel.

"No, I'm from Vermont," explained Dickerson, "a little town called Bellows Falls."

"I have heard of that town," said Manuel, excited.

"How?" asked Dickerson, looking at Manuel askance.

"When we were at the company headquarters in New Jersey for training, one of the guys came from that town, and they used to tease him by calling the town…"

Dickerson did not let Manuel finish, for she has heard that joke several times.

"Fellows Balls," Dickerson finished, as a matter of fact. "Yeah, we know."

"I'm sorry, go ahead," Manuel urged.

"After my medical school at Tufts University in Boston, Massachusetts, and residency at St. Elizabeth's Hospital in Boston, I did a fellowship in Immunology and Genetics at San Francisco General Hospital. From there, I was hired in San Diego."

"You like it here?" asked Manuel.

"Yeah, I love it."

"What do you do for fun?"

"Oh, nothing, I had my marriage annulled after sixteen months, because my ex-husband who was not Catholic, refused to convert, and like a typical man, no offense intended, also refused to zip-up his pants." Dickerson paused. "Since then I have buried myself in my work and I am near a breakthrough in a new HLA-antigen and its linkage that I have been working on."

"That sounds interesting," said Manuel.

"Yeah, it is."

"Do you like Mexican food?"

"Living in San Diego, of course I love Mexican food."

"What is your favorite Mexican restaurant?" asked Manuel, leaning on the table.

"Let me think," Dickerson closed her eyes for a second, "Cantina Mania Don Bravo Restaurant."

"That big restaurant located on University Drive?" Manuel's face lit up.

"So you know it?"

"Yeah I do," answered Manuel, "but let me tell you, the best Mexican restaurants around here are in Tijuana."

"You know, that's one place I have never visited around here."

"You haven't been to Tijuana and you live in San Diego?" Manuel sounded surprised. "You should go."

"I will, one of these days."

"I will take you whenever you are ready," Manuel freely offered.

That was the beginning of a short, but romantic, courtship that cumulated in marriage six months later.

Dickerson's marital problems started about two years ago when she stumbled upon an HLA antibody found on a young, drug-addicted prisoner under police hold at the Veterans' Administration Hospital.

He was arrested for public intoxication and also alleged brutal strangulation of two homeless men. The prisoner died less than twenty-four hours after admission, and Dickerson was given a blood sample for analysis and evaluation of a possible genetic explanation of the sudden death.

On the gel test studies of the HLA, a nice band rested on the B locus at position sixty-six.

*This is new!* she thought.

No previous tests had clearly defined this band, although Dr. Abramhoff, writing in the July issue of the Journal of Immunology, talked about predestined behaviors that he claimed could be traced to the HLA B locus.

*What is this drunk predestined for?* Dickerson asked.

Is he destined to kill somebody? Or is he just predestined to be an alcoholic?

Does this HLA type make people kill?

When Dickerson called her friend, Marie Pinkett—Pinky, for short—the lead detective with the San Diego Police Department, the conversation was initially about marriage, with Dickerson trying to convince Marie about getting married and how wonderful it would be for her career.

"You have been telling me that for a long time," answered Pinkett.

"And I will keep telling you until you do it."

"When I do, you will be the first to know."

"Listen," began Dickerson, "I need to talk to you about the Pedrosa case."

"What about it?" Detective Pinkett asked.

"I was running a test on his blood sample the other day, you know, the HLA-test."

"Yes, yes."

"There is this peculiar band on HLA B locus that is puzzling."

"What is the B locus?"

"It's just the nomenclature we use to differentiate the HLAs."

"Okay, go ahead."

"Well, this is the first differentiation using our specialized solution that improves detection."

"What does that have to do with Pedrosa?"

"Plenty," continued Dickerson, "because I was thinking that if I perform more testing on more individuals I can make a reasonable deduction."

"Reasonable deduction?" inquired the detective. "What kind of individuals are we making this reasonable deduction about?"

"Well, Mr. Pedrosa is a hardened…more like a hardcore criminal; alcoholic with multiple run-ins with the law, murderer, and God knows what else."

"And you are saying…"

"If I can start a program with your department to do blood work on all inmates as part of the booking process, maybe I can run more tests to determine the significance of this finding on the B locus," Dickerson finally blurted it out.

"Oh, I don't know." There was resignation on the detective's voice. "I think we might be infringing on inmates' rights here, because, whatever you do with it, some smart lawyer will likely challenge you in court."

"I am not planning on publishing any article on this, at least not yet," Dickerson informed her. "Whatever I find, it will remain within the scientific community, and will be labeled as the so-so B-locus antigen associated with certain groups of people."

"You have to be careful now," warned the detective, "because you do not want to be accused of discriminatory labeling."

"Hush up, trust me, I know. I am acutely aware of that. What I am doing is simply making an association," Dickerson explained. "Once an association is made, then we can ask the government, or whoever, for a wider study."

"I don't know, I just don't know. I have to think about that and see if I can actually handle it," the detective replied.

### 666

Detective Pinkett, an Oklahoma University graduate in criminal justice systems, had been with the San Diego Police Department for seven years. She had seen it all, ever since being promoted to lead detective five years ago.

"You do have a natural instinct to analyze clues, especially in a crime situation, don't you?" a lieutenant colleague once asked.

"Oh, I don't know," answered Pinkett.

"I will say one thing—at least you are better than our former boss."

"Thanks for the compliment, Lieutenant."

A short but well-proportioned woman with dark hair, she had often been accused of acting like a man. She was always neatly dressed and her hair always well groomed.

"The gun of yours, isn't it Smith and Wesson 4911PD, the lightweight thing?"

"No, Lieutenant, that's a 1911PD, and yes, that's the lightweight thing."

"Are you sure? I just looked at one a month ago."

"I am absolutely sure, because I bought it."

"What is it with you and the Sherlock Holmes novels? You've read every one of them, I heard."

"Are you coming on to me, Lieutenant?"

"No, no, not at all," stammered the lieutenant. "I'm just…"

"That's okay," interrupted Pinkett. "Yeah, I love Sherlock Holmes. Most of the cases I have seen have some resemblance to a Sherlock Holmes novel. That man was a genius."

The police department, even though they gave her a hard time at the beginning, had come to accept her as one of their own and had actually attributed the lower crime rate in the city as emanating from her ingenuity.

She owed few people few favors, and that's why when she asked the police chief for permission for the blood sampling, she encountered no obstacles. The only stipulation was that Dr. Dickerson and the university would be the responsible party for everything that had to do with blood handling. Dickerson, of course, saw no problem with that, and as a matter of fact, her staff at the Immunology Department volunteered to handle all that.

# CHAPTER TWO

A cold January wind was blowing all over Lake Michigan, freezing everything and anything in sight. The traffic on Lake Shore Drive remained at a standstill.

Taking a sharp left onto Jackson Street to avoid the endless delay, Dr. David Aaron Abramhoff drove down to the less crowded Michigan Avenue, and turned north toward the Magnificent Mile on to Chicago Avenue.

He flashed his identification card to the car lot attendant before driving into the parking garage.

"Good morning, Dr. Abramhoff," greeted the broad smiling garage attendant.

"Good morning, Mr. Johnson," replied Dr. Abramhoff, stern as the winter weather.

"It is freezing, Doc."

"Yes," was all Dr. Abramhoff could answer.

He parked his car at his designated parking space on the second floor of the five-story building. The garage, connected to Richard C. Needleman's Medical building, felt warm.

The so-called "RCN Medical Building," a sprawling twenty-two story towering medical complex, housed Chicago's Loop University Medical School, the LUMS;

the university hospital; and several other medical department, including the Department of Immunology and Genetics.

Dr. Abramhoff, chairman of Department of Immunology and Genetics, nonchalantly strolled into the Needleman's building.

The highly expensive marble floors were the pride and joy of Dr. Abramhoff, having been instrumental in the final construction phase of the complex.

The main hallways were lined with the most expensive paintings Chicago had ever seen.

Dr. Abramhoff wielded a lot of power and influence. A tall, gray-haired, solidly built Chicagoan in his mid sixties, he always wore brand-named dark blue suits. He was trained at the University of Chicago Medical School. After finally choosing to settle for Immunology and Genetics, he had always been fascinated with the immunological aspect of brain function. A microbiologist and theorist at college, he strongly believed that people who perform purposeful acts have been genetically programmed at birth to do so.

According to Dr. Abramhoff's theory, most people usually realize what they were programmed for, early in life, then pursue this path and become good at it, while others miss it completely. The later folks, according to Dr. Abramhoff, will spend the rest of their lives lamenting on what they could have been if they had acted at the appropriate time.

He concentrated his research on the histo-compatible antigens, especially the human leukocyte antigens, otherwise known as the HLA. Several diseases in the body were pre-programmed through this HLA, and it was only fitting that purposeful behaviors were also pre-programmed, theorized Dr. Abramhoff.

"Good morning, Dr. Abramhoff," Sabrina, the beautiful secretary, greeted as Abramhoff walked into the office.

Abramhoff, always pleased to see Sabrina Marley in the morning, nodded first and then proceeded to take off his winter coat.

A slim and beautiful woman, she carried herself well. She became the most efficient secretary in the entire medical complex, and she virtually ran Dr. Abramhoff's office.

"Have you heard of a certain Dr. Hood?" tested Dr. Abramhoff one day.

"Yes sir. He is the orthopedic surgeon recently recruited by the department of surgery," Sabrina answered without hesitation.

Everyone knew that if something needed to be done around the campus, Sabrina, not Abramhoff would do it, and 99% of the time, it would be done correctly.

"Are you related to Bob Marley?" A question frequently asked of Sabrina.

"Just because we are both from Jamaica does not mean that all Marleys in Jamaica are related to Bob Marley," Sabrina always responded with a smile.

"I will say one thing, you have lost your entire Jamaican accent," complimented a co-worker.

"That's from living in United States for thirty years," Sabrina graciously responded.

"Good morning, Sabrina," Abramhoff finally replied. "What's on my schedule today?"

Setting a cup of coffee down for Dr. Abramhoff, who strolled behind the big L-shaped oak desk and settled down, Sabrina began, "Today you have a class at 9:30 a.m. at the Meridian Hall, room 470 for the second-year medical students; a meeting at eleven a.m. with Dr. Ashutt Achampi to…"

"I like how you say that," interrupted Abramhoff. "It sounds like you are saying 'A short H and P,' but a little faster."

Sabrina grinned, but quietly continued.

"You and Dr. Achampi are to go over the CDC grant. Then you have a lunch meeting with the immunology faculty at noon; laboratories from one to three; interview residents from 3:30 to four p.m.; then meet with the Pfizer Senior Representatives at five to seek sponsorship of our project at Kankakee Psychiatry Hospital."

"That's a full day's work," commented Abramhoff.

"Yes, sir, but you can handle it," Sabrina responded.

*I admire her sense of confidence,* Abramhoff thought to himself.

"What class am I teaching?" asked Abramhoff.

"Oh," said Sabrina, flipping though the schedule book, "the HLA antigens."

"Good topic," declared Dr. Abramhoff, nodding his head.

"Yes, sir," concurred Sabrina, heading off to her office.

The medical students were always in awe of Dr. Abramhoff. He exuded such power and influence that he was one of the most feared and respected professors at the university. Abramhoff had shown no qualms flunking students from his classes, because as he explained it to the dean, students better realize the purpose for which they are here or else the school would be putting out graduates who have no purpose in life, and according to Abramhoff, eventually turn out to be bad doctors. The dean agreed.

Entering classroom 470, there was immediate silence from the students. All eyes were glued on him. Abramhoff believed that the second-year medical students were a little bit more knowledgeable than the first year. That's why he never wanted to teach first-year students.

"Since this is the first day of your second semester, this is what I would like you to do for the rest of the semester," Abramhoff began without lifting his head from the spreadsheet that he rested on the marbled podium. "I will assign readings for the next upcoming classes, and in every session, we will discuss the featured readings to solidify our understanding of them."

When he lifted his eyes eventually, he surveyed the 124 students sitting in silence.

After what seemed like an endless silence, Abramhoff continued, "Ask questions if you do not understand any paragraph in the chapter, or chapters, so that you can get proper explanation." He opened the laptop computer and pushed on a key, "I will call on you periodically with my own questions. Do not come back and tell me you forgot to read an assignment. That's unacceptable."

Pushing another key, big HLA letters appeared on the screen behind the podium.

"Let's begin with the basic understanding of the HLA," Abramhoff started teaching. "As you may have learned, the nucleus of every cell in the body houses the DNA. In the DNA, there is a region called the chromosome. Each organ of every species normally has a characteristic number of chromosomes. Humans have forty-six chromosomes. Because of their complexity, the chromosomes are numbered into areas. The HLA are found at chromosome area six."

Abramhoff paused to have a drink of water. He then pushed on the remote control and continued. "Class-I HLAs are grouped into A, B, C, and D as shown here," Abramhoff stated, pointing to a graphic table on the screen. "The most versatile of them is B."

He pushed on the remote again and showed a picture of the HLA with its B locus. "Different positions on the B locus have been attributed to various diseases and behaviors. The research is on to find out the exact location for behaviors, such as criminality and wanton senseless acts, because I believe that locus does exist on the B."

After forty-five minutes of basic teaching, Abramhoff returned to his office, took off his white coat, and went into the corner bathroom inside his office.

He was out in less than five minutes to the sound of Sabrina knocking at the outer door.

"Come in," answered Abramhoff.

"Dr. Abramhoff, Dr. Achampi is here," announced Sabrina.

"Oh, bring him in," answered Abramhoff.

Dr. Ashutt Achampi, a recently transferred second-year oncology fellow from Duke University Medical School in North Carolina, admired Abramhoff and worked very closely with him. Abramhoff, on the other hand, respected his quick sense of deduction.

"Good morning, Dr. Abramhoff," greeted Dr. Achampi.

"Morning, Ashutt," replied Abramhoff. "Did I say it right this time?"

"Yes, you did, sir," Dr. Achampi said with a nod.

"So, where we are with the Center for Disease Control grant?" inquired Abramhoff.

"That's the one for the link between HLA-B60 and Burkitt's lymphoma?" Achampi clarified, then frowned and sat down across Abramhoff's desk.

"Yes?" Abramhoff looked curiously at Achampi.

"The CDC did review the application but may be wavering on the price tag."

"So we might not get the five million we asked for?"

"Probably not; they may however, approve one of two only."

"How do you figure that?" asked Abramhoff, who was not accustomed to rejection or reduction when it came to grants.

"I strongly believe that Burkitt's, especially when it comes to West African type of Burkitt's, is a rare form of lymphoma not common in the general American population," stated Dr. Achampi. "I believe, therefore, they may be leery about the five million."

"Continue to pursue and persuade them anyway, and oh, don't forget to use my name to make contacts at CDC, and see what you can achieve," instructed Abramhoff.

"Yes, I will do that," answered Achampi.

"I do have a late meeting today with Pfizer representatives," informed Abramhoff. "I will see how much they can help."

666

Since the Loop University Medical Center in Chicago was instrumental in the development of their now famous anti-impotent drug, Abramhoff surmised that Pfizer would want to be part of the Kankakee project and maybe, farther down the road, develop a drug that could arrest the progression of the bad HLAs.

"Good evening, sir," greeted the Pfizer representatives upon being ushered to the office.

"And you are?" asked Dr. Abramhoff.

"I am Deborah Bond. I am the senior project manager for Pfizer for the Midwest district."

"Nice to meet you, Miss Bond," greeted Abramhoff with a smile.

"And you?" inquired Abramhoff of the gentleman accompanying the business-dressed lady to the office.

"I am Roger Ezra. I am the national grant specialist, what you may call the overseer."

"So you are Miss Bond's...boss?" asked Abramhoff.

"Yes and no," answered Mr. Ezra. "She has the authority to approve, but in complex projects it comes through me for reference to headquarters."

"So I am talking to the right people?" inquired Abramhoff.

"I would say you are," answered Miss Bond.

"Okay, then," began Dr. Abramhoff, balancing himself in the middle of the black leather cushioned chair, "what we are trying to do at the Kankakee Correctional Institute is to study all hardcore criminals, especially those who have committed heinous or fallacious criminal acts." Abramhoff used both hands demonstratively to emphasis his points.

"We believe that these individuals have an HLA marker, like a genetic stamp that predisposes them to criminality, just like HLA B27 predisposes someone to get ankylosing spondylitis, you know, the disease of the spinal joints, and just like these diseases, we do not know yet the trigger mechanism for manifestation."

"If we can research these people and find a common marker, could you imagine the potentials? Drugs for early identification, gene therapy, and so on and so forth?"

"That's something new," Miss Bond uttered.

"I will agree with that," Mr. Ezra concurred.

"So are you guys on board?" inquired Abramhoff.

"Well, how much money do you think you will need?" asked a nervous Miss Bond.

"Well," answered Abramhoff, "you know I have to initiate a laboratory for genetic isolation and identifications. We have to recruit inmates even if we might have to pay the institution, medical assistants, research technicians, equipments, office computers…I think 20 to 30 million dollars may be appropriate."

"Twenty to thirty?" asked a perplexed Miss Bond.

"What Ms. Bonds is trying to say," Mr. Ezra immediately came to the rescue, "is that…for an amount like that, it definitely must go to the corporate office in New York for final consideration."

"Yes," Miss Bond said, who finally composed herself, "even if we approve the amount, the company will not issue that kind of check without corporate input."

"So what do you think our chances are?" Abramhoff asked.

"Good, I would dare to say," commented Mr. Ezra, looking at Miss Bond.

"How about excellent, then I will be happy," Abramhoff joked.

"With a little push, I think it will go a long way," commented Miss Bonds, still non-committal.

"So will you guys push it then?" asked Abramhoff.

"I will get to work as soon as I receive the proposal from you," Miss Bond answered.

"When can I hear from you all?" inquired Abramhoff.

"Give us about a week or two after we receive the proposal to be able to make all the necessary contacts," said Ezra.

"That's fine," concluded Abramhoff, rising from his chair.

"Good-bye, sir," echoed both Miss Bond and Mr. Ezra, picking up their bags and heading toward the door.

# CHAPTER THREE

Driving cautiously between fifty and sixty miles per hour on Route 21, Stella appeared exhausted. She just disembarked from Savannah International Airport on a United Airline flight that was delayed in Chicago.

Stella Montgomery had already figured out what to prepare for dinner when she got home, counting on the fact that she would be home before her husband.

Here it was, 7:30 p.m., and she had quite a distance to drive to get to home on Ogeechee Road. Because of the traffic jam on Route 95, Stella sat in her motionless car and reflected on her trip to Chicago, and the visit to the Oak Lawn facility.

She was most impressed with the exclusivity of their project. The special crate arrived through United Parcel Services to section E of the Oak Lawn facility for medical research.

Dr. Hamish K. Shah, the medical director, was very cordial. He assured Stella of the high level of security for their project, and the difficulty anyone would have in attempting to divulge them of information.

He showed Stella the processing labs, the deep freeze, and the dedicated group of loyal employees.

Finally, Dr. Shah asked whether she was happy with the money she made on the last delivery. Stella was certainly pleased with the $250,000 she received from Dr. Shah for their latest business deal. She couldn't wait to get home and show the check to Martin.

When Stella finally reached home, she backed the Toyota Highlander into the garage.

Inside, Martin was playing with Trianna and Joseph. Lisa, grouchy as usual, was sitting at the kitchen table writing in her secret diary, which nobody had read, but everybody wanted to read.

"Hi, honey," greeted Martin as Stella entered through the garage door into the kitchen.

"Hi!" answered Stella, putting her suitcase down between the kitchen and the living room door.

"How was your trip?"

"Brutal! Between the snow storm in Chicago and the traffic, I thought I would never make it home."

"I know. They were talking about the storm in Chicago on TV. I was surprised they let the plane fly."

"That's why I like parking the car at the airport for those short travels."

Trianna and Joseph were leaning against Stella's business suit, waiting for attention.

"Hi, kids!" Stella greeted the children. She leaned down and gave each one a bear hug.

"Hi, Mom, nice to have you home," said Trianna.

"We missed you, Mom," Joseph added.

"What were you doing in Chicago, Mom?" inquired Lisa, not bothering to get up from the kitchen table where she was sitting.

"Well," answered Stella, "I went to Oak Lawn, Illinois, a suburb of Chicago to visit Dr. Shah. He is the Chicago affiliate of my company."

"What's affiliate mean?" asked Lisa.

"Somebody you do business with who stays somewhere else."

"Dinner is ready, honey," said Martin in an attempt to break the icy conversation.

"Who cooked?" asked Stella, diverting her attention to Trianna and Joseph.

"Dad!" answered Joseph, pointing accusingly at Martin.

"What are we eating?" asked a hungry Stella.

"Spaghetti and meatballs," answered Martin.

"Yummy, let's eat, I am starved." Moving her luggage to the stairway, Stella sat down at the dining table.

Dinner had become routine at the Montgomery family. Stella would ask the kids about school. Trianna would be happy to tell all about Mrs. Parker, the mean English teacher, who delighted in giving them daily homework. Lisa, on the other hand, usually remained quiet at the dinner table, answering questions sparingly, only when asked.

Ever since Tom's death, Lisa had not been the same.

Tom and Lisa were buddies. Separated only by twelve months, they looked like twins, especially when they were playing.

*I think Lisa must still be in mourning or is hiding something, and besides, what's up with that diary, anyway? Lisa is only eight years old, and since when do eight-year-olds keep secret diaries?* Martin, always suspicious, wondered.

After dinner Lisa went quietly to her room. She had her own room since Tom's death.

Two years ago, Tom, the oldest son, died of unexplained natural death. What surprised Lisa the most was that Mom and Dad insisted on not burying Tom. They sent his body to this crematorium in Oak Lawn, Illinois, for cremation. Now they had another white crystal jar in the living room with Tom's ashes in them.

*Why would Mom and Dad keep ashes of dead people in the house?*

Lisa suspected that something was not right, especially before Chris died.

Chris had a fever, coughing, and was not feeling well. Mom refused to take Chris to see the doctor, explaining that she had been to the doctor many times before with the same complaint and all she ever got was Tylenol and cough medicine.

The night Chris died was strange to Lisa. She had gotten up in the middle of the night to use the bathroom and heard some quiet commotions coming out of Chris' room.

Lisa decided to investigate to be sure Chris was all right. She slowly pushed open the door after quietly turning the knob so as not to wake Chris in case she was asleep.

What she saw had been on Lisa's mind since that day, three years ago.

Dad appeared to be holding a pillow over Chris' face. Just then, Stella saw Lisa. She quickly came to the door and escorted Lisa out of the room.

Stella was frightened when she saw Lisa. Closing the door behind her, she led Lisa back to her room.

"What's wrong with Chris?" inquired Lisa.

"She is not feeling well, and Dad was checking her out," answered Stella, taking a deep breath.

"Will you take her to the doctor, Mom?" pleaded Lisa.

"Yeah, first thing in the morning," reassured Stella.

Lisa was satisfied, Mom tucking her to bed after a visit to the bathroom.

Lisa was happy. She wanted her older sister to get well so they could go to the Creek Side and watch the boys play. The boys always acted silly, but were fun to watch.

"Why was Dad holding down the pillow over Chris' face?" asked Lisa, out of curiosity and fear.

"No, honey, Dad was removing the pillow from Chris' face, because Chris has a habit of sleeping with the pillow on her face, and Dad was making sure she was not suffocating herself," explained Stella.

Her death was ruled an accident by the county coroner. The explanation, though plausible, still weighed heavily on Lisa's mind.

Lisa, although she was only eight years old, considered herself the brightest kid in her class. She had been acknowledged for her analytical mind. She was the one other kids came to for advice when they were having problems. Lisa somehow always managed to come up with workable solutions.

Being a popular girl at school, Lisa tried so hard not to be analytical at home, usually taking things at face value, especially from Mom and Dad. But Mom's explanation about the pillow incident was very unsettling for Lisa, and she made many entries about that in her secret diary.

"I am really worried about Lisa," Martin pondered aloud from the bathroom while changing into his pajamas.

"She is okay…she is just a very smart kid, and smart kids tend to be less playful," Stella answered.

"Well, how come she has never been sick?" inquired Martin.

"That I don't know, because with Tom, he had the severe case of the allergy. Shawn had the…I think they call it 'gastroenteritis,' but he was vomiting and was very dehydrated. Yeah, with Shawn you didn't have to press the pillow hard at all for him to stop breathing."

"I know Chris was a hard one. She tried to struggle and choked, my, oh my; I thought she would never die."

"You know, I believe it was the noise that either woke Lisa up or made her open the door."

"I told you to always lock the doors behind you."

"I simply forgot that night."

"I still think Lisa saw something," insisted Martin.

"Even if she did, I explained to her that you were removing the pillow off Chris' face," reassured Stella.

"Did she buy that?"

"Oh, I am sure she did."

"Hmm…by the way, how much money did they pay for Tom again?"

"It was $250,000 cash, plus a percentage of whatever price they sell each organ."

"So, we made almost a quarter million with Chris and nearly as much with Shawn," Martin surmised.

"Actually, Dr. Shah said next time we might cash in more than three quarters of a million dollars. Do you believe that?" Stella picked up a copy of *Money Magazine*, nodded her head three times, and climbed into bed.

"That's great, but why is that?"

"He explained that there is a bidding war from five millionaires for one kidney, the other for the liver, and I forgot what the rest are, but when they are sold we might net $750,000 plus."

"I'm confident the next one will fetch us over one million." Martin tightened his pajamas.

"I pray. Then we will be the millionaire next door, just like in the *Money Magazine*."

"You know sometimes I wonder how they legally sell these organs without state or federal detections."

"These guys are genius," explained Stella. "I don't know the exact details, but somehow they do."

"That's amazing," Martin noted, letting out a sneeze.

"Bless you."

"Thanks."

"Quite a few centers, like the prestigious Lake Shore University in downtown Chicago, do escape federal audits, and they are one of the best and frequent clients of the scientific research facility. This is a multimillion approaching billion dollar operation."

Stella shook her head, in puzzlement at the amount.

"I am happy we are getting some of that money," exclaimed Martin.

"I am also."

"I am still worried about Lisa."

"Why?" Stella finally descended down to earth.

"Being smart and all, never sick, she could fetch us well over one million, then we will have only two kids left, like we originally planned."

"Be careful; let's not be greedy, hasty, or irrational, so says Dr. Shah. Yeah, she is smart and all and she keeps that diary. Who knows what's in it?" said a worried Stella.

"I have made several attempts to steal it. Even the other kids cannot get to it, let alone find it. I am really tempted to force it out of her."

"No…no, I don't think we need to go that far," Stella frowned.

Lisa could not sleep well that night.

"Mom came back from Chicago looking all excited, even though she got stuck in a snowstorm in Chicago," Lisa wrote.

She did not understand why Mom took trips to Chicago soon after Shawn and Chris' deaths. What is this place in Oak Lawn, Illinois, and what do they actually do there? Do they have anything to do with Tom, Shawn, and Chris' cremations?

Lisa was acutely aware that the entire family wanted a peek at her diary, a secret she had kept since age four, protecting the diary by sometimes even hiding it in her underwear while she slept.

Lisa also had figured out that whenever one of them got sick for over two to three days that was when they invariably died, usually in their sleep.

Lisa knew this girl, they said she had a blood cancer, but she died in a hospital.

Lisa made a vow that she would never be sick, because if she ever got sick, she would not live. She worried about Trianna, who had been coughing lately.

Mom took her to the doctor twice, and the doctor said both times that she had a cold. She seemed to be getting better though.

"Dear diary," Lisa resumed her writing with the doors locked. "Mom came back today from Chicago, happy. She showed Dad a piece of paper that looked like a check, and Dad yelled 'Yes.'

"When I asked what it was they both said it was nothing, except that Mom got some donation for her company from the research center in Chicago.

"I wonder how much it was for Daddy to be that happy. Trianna has been sick lately, I wonder if she is going to die also.

"Kim, at school, said that I should tell Mom and Dad what I am thinking, but I am afraid to tell them. I also made Kim today to swear on her granny's picture never to tell anyone, and she did.

"Next time when any of us gets sick, I will have to figure out a way to see or hear what my parents plan to do."

Two weeks later, Lisa noticed that Trianna started coughing again.

This time, she had some runny nose that clogged her up at night, making her mouth-breathe all night long. She had been waking up with sore throats, but somehow managed to feel better as the day went by.

Lisa, who had been watching Trianna closely, documented her everyday symptoms, at least hoping that Mom would take her to the hospital.

*If she dies there,* Lisa thought, *she will die in a hospital under the care of doctors and nurses.*

# CHAPTER FOUR

Late afternoon Thursday, the weather became unseasonably cold in Savannah, Georgia.

*It is quite an unusual temperature for March around here,*
thought Lisa.

It had rained all day. The sun had not been heard from
or seen for almost twenty-four hours. The wind was blowing aimlessly, and water was everywhere. The temperature
dipped to an all-time low of almost thirty-three degrees.

A lot of children did not attend school because of the
cold weather, preferring instead to stay home sick. Lisa
made sure she bundled herself up for school. She took
some Theraflu cold tablets that morning without her
mother's permission, as a guarantee not to get sick.

She was a little sleepy at school, but that did not deter
her determination to remain alert.

Recently, she had become increasingly suspicious that
something would happen in the next coming days.

Arriving home from school, in her usual quiet mood,
Lisa declined supper.

She alleged that she did not feel well, maybe from
overeating at school.

Joseph, sitting at the dinning table, was eating a peanut butter and jelly sandwich.

"I don't know about that girl," observed Martin, as Lisa headed to her room to change.

"Don't worry about her; she is being her usual self," defended Stella.

"Should we then go ahead with Trianna tonight?" asked Martin, eyebrows raised.

"I don't see why not," a confident Stella confirmed. "I will check on Lisa early, prior to joining you to make sure she's asleep."

"When you come in this time make sure you lock the door."

"I will, I will."

Four hours later, after watching some primetime network shows, Lisa took permission to retire early.

"Are you okay?" Martin asked. "You have been awfully quiet."

"Just minor stomach cramps," replied Lisa, making a sick face. "I'll be fine in the morning."

"Do you want me to come and tuck you to bed?" asked Stella with a broad smile on her face.

"No, Mom," Lisa smiled back. "I'm going to check on Trianna and see how she is doing, and then I'm going to bed."

"Don't you have any homework today?" Stella continued, attempting to loosen Lisa up.

"Nope," Lisa replied, shaking her head negatively. "Too many kids were sick, so they decided not to give any homework."

"Okay, sweetheart," replied Stella absentmindedly, watching television with Martin.

Lisa climbed upstairs and headed to Trianna's room. At the top of the stairs, she turned to take a second look at Mom and Dad appearing engrossed at the television.

Stella, aware that Lisa was watching them, uttered: "Goodnight," without turning her head.

"Night," Lisa whispered back, then proceeded to Trianna's room.

Trianna was asleep, but as soon as Lisa entered the room, she woke up, and coughed two or three times.

"Hi, Te-Te," Lisa smiled broadly.

"I don't feel too good," answered Trianna, rubbing her nose.

"I know. You'll be okay. Mom is supposed to take you to the hospital tomorrow," reassured Lisa with concern. "The doctors will make you well."

"I hope so," replied Trianna through another cough.

Lisa then listened intently to be sure she did not hear any footsteps.

"I am going to put this machine under your bed to protect you," explained Lisa, slipping a twelve-hour miniaturized tape recorder under the bed.

"They said that if that stays under your bed all night, you will feel better in the morning."

"Thanks, Lisa," appreciated Trianna, repositioning her head on the pillow while letting out yet another cough.

"I will let you get some sleep." Lisa pulled the cover closer to Trianna's chest.

"Good night."

At about 10:45, Lisa remained awake in awkward anticipation.

*What if my plan fails?*

*What if Mom and Dad decided not to do anything tonight?*

*What if Mom finds the tape recorder?*

She realized she should not have told Trianna about the tape recorder in case she blurted her mouth to Mom. Too late now.

Lisa decided to get up before six in the morning to retrieve the tape recorder so nobody else would discover it accidentally.

"Lisa…Lisa?" a gentle knock at the door proclaimed.

"Come in," Lisa answered with a faked sleepy voice.

Rubbing her eyes pretentiously, Lisa feigned a yawn.

"I'm just checking on you before we go to bed."

"I'm okay, Mom. I feel a lot better already."

Lisa did not want to give any indication or excuse for her parents to come after her.

She already figured out a plan to scream as loud as she could if Dad came after her with a pillow. To be sure that the next door neighbors could hear her scream, Lisa had started leaving the east end window ajar every night, a week after Chris's death.

Sometimes, Lisa thought she was getting a little paranoid, but her deductive reasoning always convinced her that she did not want to be the next victim.

At exactly 3:33 a.m., something woke Lisa up. She looked around the room frightened, but there was no one there.

Did the alarm go off accidentally?

Lisa sat up in bed. It was still raining outside. Lisa could hear the raindrops through the east end window. The chilly room sent shivers through Lisa's bones. She got up, and put on her jeans and her school blazer over her night gown. She took her diary from under the pillow, tucked it in her blazer pocket and set out to check on Trianna.

She inadvertently picked up her cell phone like she usually did on her way to school.

Arriving at Trianna's room, Lisa noticed dim lights emanating under the door.

She tiptoed, cat-like, to the door and listened.

Mom and Dad were in the room whispering. Lisa could not make out what they were saying.

A muffled moan could be heard, and then it suddenly stopped.

Lisa sat on the floor, thought for a minute, and then decided that she would take a chance. She got up, turned the doorknob gently to slowly open the door, but only to discover that the door was locked.

Just then Lisa heard Mom ask, "Is she dead?"

"I think so," Martin answered.

Lisa gasped. Frightened, she let the doorknob go.

The knob closing sounded like a big gong in the silence of the night.

Realizing what just happened, Lisa took off running.

Instead of running down the stairs like she usually did whenever she was in trouble, she ran to Chris' old, now empty, bedroom.

She quietly opened the window and climbed outside on the roof. She had since figured out that this was the only window close to the drain pipe that she could easily use to climb downstairs to the back of the house.

Martin and Stella were downstairs in the living room looking for Lisa.

When the doorknob snapped, they knew immediately that it was Lisa.

By the time they opened the door, Lisa was nowhere to be found. They both immediately ran downstairs to the living room, instinctively thinking that Lisa was hiding in her usual hiding place. Not finding her there, Stella barked with clenched teeth, "Lisa!"

No response.

"Lisa!" Stella barked a second time.

"Let's check her room. She might still be up there," instructed Martin between heavy breaths.

"Yeah," Stella agreed.

As they hurried their way to the stairs, there was a thud outside. When Martin and Stella finally gowned and went outside in the rain, they saw what appeared like a little girl they presumed to be Lisa, running down the street approximately two to three blocks away.

She was talking on a cell phone, while occasionally looking behind.

Savannah Police Chief, Elijah Goodwin, initially doubted Lisa when she came to him about five weeks ago with an incredible story about her parents being responsible for killing their children. The county coroner had previously cleared Mr. and Mrs. Montgomery of any wrongdoing in the death of their children. His detectives had interrogated them previously and had found no evidence of foul play. But Chief Goodwin became intrigued by this intelligent, detective-oriented young female. His main regret now was that Lisa did not inform him earlier that she suspected something might go down tonight.

"Why didn't you tell me about your suspicions yesterday? We might have been able to save your sister's life," Chief Goodwin queried.

"I'm sorry," Lisa sobbed. "I had a strong feeling that they might, but I wasn't 100 percent sure."

"How did you come up with planting a tape recorder there?"

"Because my parents talk too much," Lisa sniffed, "and I know they will have something to say while in the act."

666

The police recovered Trianna's body, still in the bedroom. The tape-recorded conversations, mostly whispered, were incriminating enough for a conviction.

Mr. and Mrs. Montgomery were found guilty of first-degree murder in the deaths of their four children.

They were spared the death penalty, but were given four life sentences with no possibility of parole, because they agreed to cooperate with the federal investigation of the Oak Lawn, Illinois operations.

# CHAPTER FIVE

"Coming home late again? I hardly see you anymore since you started working with those prisoners," said Manuel eight weeks into the study.

"Yes, I know," said Dickerson, sitting at the kitchen bar stool, hands clasped beneath the chin, looking guilty.

"We haven't even been to Tijuana in a long time."

"But you have, haven't you?"

"What do you mean I have?" asked a surprised Manuel.

"Come on now, twice you told me that you took some doctors to Tijuana to entertain them," Dickerson reminded him.

"Oh, yeah," answered Manuel quickly, looking into the kitchen cabinets for sardines.

"That's okay by me, honey, because I know that's part of your job," Dickerson said while looking for a Corona in the refrigerator.

"Well if you had been home, I see no reason to take those doctors to Tijuana," said Manuel, playing the blame game.

That surprised Dickerson. *What is Manuel upset about?*

She realized that she had been working late hours at the university to finish her project because she planned to present her findings at the American College of Immunology and Genetics, scheduled to meet next month in Florida.

Manuel did call on several occasions to check on her, and Dickerson did not appreciate that, but to reciprocate, she did at times call Manuel to see how he was doing.

A week later, it was about 11:30 p.m. Dickerson had been working late at the laboratory and had totally lost track of time. She made significant progress and worked longer hours looking for that elusive band on the gel electrophoresis.

Tonight, however, on the third trial using the new analytical solution, she was so overjoyed to see the elusive band finally separated on its own. Leaving the two technicians behind, she dashed out of the laboratory to rush home and share her joy with her husband.

At the corner of Geneses Avenue and Noble Drive, Dickerson was about to run the yellow light when she noticed a squad car parked at the curb on Noble drive. She stopped as the light turned red.

*What a difference a simple solution makes,* Dickerson thought.

All she needed was to add 5 percent dextrose solution with the ethylene benzoic prior to the gel electrophoresis run. It clearly defined position sixty-six and, just like that, eliminated the other fuzzy positions, especially the one at position sixty-eight.

"Yes! Yes and yes," shouted Dickerson pounding her right fist on the lab table.

*There may be a connection after all between some criminals and the HLA,* she thought.

Face glowing, she turned to the two techs and literally shouted, "We did it…yes, we did it!"

She rushed to each tech and planted a kiss on their cheeks before dashing out the door.

Fumbling with the keys and finally opening the door, Dickerson suddenly realized Manuel was not home. She dialed his cell phone, but only got the voicemail.

Just then, the phone rang. She rushed to the phone, mistakenly thinking it was Manuel.

"Hi, honey, listen, there…"

"Hello!" said a sobbing female voice on the other end.

"Hello," Dickerson answered, wondering whose voice that was.

"Is this Dr. Dickerson?" asked the stranger.

"Yes, who are you?"

"My name is Jennifer; I am a friend of your husband," said the strange voice.

"What happened? Is he okay?" Dickerson's mind rushed to some traumatic event.

"Yes, he is…I think."

"Oh, thank God," Dickerson breathed a sigh of relief.

"I should just come out and tell you," sobbed Jennifer.

"Tell me what?"

"I am a drug rep with Ortho-McNeill in Southern Los Angeles County, and I don't know how to say this," said Jennifer, trying to calm herself down.

"What do you mean…how to say, what? Come on with it," Dickerson demanded. "Just go ahead and say what's on your mind."

Dickerson was already thinking Manuel was caught doing something unethical for one of his doctor friends, and in the process probably lost his job.

"I have been seeing your husband for six months," started Jennifer.

*Oh no,* thought Dickerson, *not again. Please God, let it not happen again.*

"You mean you have been seeing him or sleeping with him," Dickerson shouted, breathing heavy and obviously angry.

"Yes, we were sleeping together," confessed Jennifer.

"So, why are you calling me?"

"I just wanna get it off my chest, because we are not seeing each other anymore."

"You mean he dumped you."

"Yes, for that tramp, Janice…"

"Excuse me! Who is Janice?"

"The girl he is sleeping with now. She works for Bayer Pharmaceuticals."

"Did you love Manuel?"

"We were supposed to be getting…" There was a pause on the other end, and then, the phone went dead.

"Hello, hello!" Dickerson was screaming to a dial tone.

That was the beginning of the end of Dickerson's second marriage.

# CHAPTER SIX

It had been two weeks since Dickerson's divorce was finalized. Because she had a pre-nuptial agreement, and the fact that Manuel finally pleaded no contest, the whole process was executed quickly and painlessly.

Back in the laboratories, she had been able to test the nearly 106 processed inmates.

Of those, only four clearly showed HLA B66 differentiations on gel electrophoresis.

One was a forty-six-year-old man who drove the family's van with all his six children in front of an oncoming train in an attempted mass suicide. The second and third cases were similar, in the sense that they were both involved in multiple killings during armed robberies.

The final four included the bizarre case of a husband who, even though he did not believe in Christ, claimed that his born-again Christian wife was possessed by the devil. So while she was sound asleep in bed one night, he doused the entire bed with gasoline, and then set it on fire. She later died in the hospital for burns sustained to over 90 percent of her body.

Dickerson called Detective Marie Pinkett at home early Sunday morning to discuss her findings.

"Hello, Doc," Pinkett yawned, "good morning."

"Did I wake you up?" asked Dickerson.

"Not really," Pinkett yawned again, "I need to get going."

"So, what's happening in the criminal world?" asked the doctor, trying to strike a conversation nonetheless.

"A lot," answered the detective. "How about you, any good news?"

"Quite a bit."

"Well?" Pinkett asked, prompting the doctor for more information.

"Okay. We've tested about 106 inmates so far," Dickerson rattled in obvious excitement. "Out of that, guess how many tested positive?"

"I don't know, how many?" Pinkett was unprepared to guess this early in the morning.

"Four tested positive," answered the delighted doctor.

"Is that a good thing or a bad thing?" asked the puzzled detective.

"Very good thing," proclaimed Dickerson. "Four out of 106 in science is a poor result, but looking at it differently, it points us in the direction and type of clients we need to focus our attention on."

"Go ahead, I am listening," a very curious Pinkett urged.

"We were testing all your departmental bookings: petty thieves, rapists, larcenists, arsonists, purse snatchers, shop lifters, traffic violators, and so on, only to find out that the high probability of positive HLA tests are those who commit ferocious or heinous crimes," explained the doctor.

"You mean—" began Pinkett.

"I mean," Dickerson continued, still excited, "Let's look at the four positive tests; one is that train accident that killed his family. The other two, with no remorse, killed six people between them, and the last guy set his wife on fire. What does that tell you?"

"That you are looking for people who commit or have committed serious crimes," suggested Pinkett.

"That's exactly the kind—those that have committed serious but more gruesome crimes. Maybe like the infamous celebrity from Savannah, Georgia, what's her name…Stella Montgomery and her husband, who suffocated their own children to sell them for body parts. I will bet my last dollar that they test positive," Dickerson theorized.

"Well, my suggestion is to go down to the federal prison in Lemon Grove, select the prisoners that match your description, and then test them," suggested Pinkett.

"That, my friend, is a brilliant idea, and that's where you come in," Dickerson exclaimed.

"You are not asking me to…" Pinkett started in disbelief.

"Yes, I am," interrupted Dickerson.

"You're gonna owe me plenty for this," demanded the detective.

"I know; I know, I will take you out to dinner," Dickerson suggested.

The next couple of weeks, Detective Pinkett made several trips to Lemon Grove and met with Superintendent Thomas Strickland.

After several communications between him and Pinkett, Dickerson was only allowed to collect limited data pertaining to incarceration records and blood drawings.

Dickerson spent only two days going through the records of the prisoners. She selected about one hundred inmates who she thought might qualify, according to her specifications. Dickerson purposely selected the number one hundred, for her ease of mathematical calculations.

She was so pleased with Pinky's effort and work that she again promised her dinner at her favorite restaurant in La Jolla. An offer the detective accepted.

When Dickerson met Mr. Strickland, the superintendent, she was rather taken aback. He was a tall, heavy-set, no-nonsense kind of guy in his late fifties, who was more concerned about rules and regulations than the study outcome in general. His stipulations were that the testing be done only when the inmates came to the infirmary complaining of illnesses, which happened very frequently. He wanted all contacts concluded as soon as possible and recommended that the entire inmates' testing be done in about three to six months.

"I don't think that will be a problem," Dickerson answered. "My medical staff will draw the bloods and take all the necessary precautions. We will come with all the required containers to transport the blood samples."

"So you will have someone to pick up the blood?" asked the superintendent.

"Yes, we will," answered Dickerson. "One of my staff members or me will come and pick them up."

"We have to issue you and one or two of your staff members a medical security pass so that as soon as each arrives, a detail officer can escort that person to the medical unit of the building," instructed the superintendent.

"No problem."

Superintendent Strickland then took Dickerson to the medical facility building. As they approached the heavy steel guarded entrance, Dickerson nervously reached into her purse to light a cigarette.

"Please, no smoking in here, Doc," cautioned the superintendent.

"Sorry," Dickerson apologized, then, putting the cigarette away, she murmured, "Darn it."

"What was that?" asked Mr. Strickland with a faint smile over his partially turned face.

"Nothing," Dickerson responded rather quickly.

Entering the medical complex, the entire staff was on its best behavior at the sight of the superintendent.

"Hi, everyone," greeted the superintendent, "this is Dr. Dickerson from the university in La Jolla. She is the one I talked to you all about in the memo I sent. We will be starting our project I hope Monday, if that's okay with you, Doc." He turned to look at Dickerson.

"Monday is fine," answered Dickerson, who was surprised how quickly this whole thing was moving along, as if by some divine intervention.

"You all have her phone number, so as soon as each blood is drawn from the list of inmates I designated, call her and she will come and pick it up. Does anyone have any questions?"

After a little hesitation the penitentiary nurse asked, "What are the tests for?"

Before Dickerson could answer, Superintendent Strickland intervened.

"The state of California has authorized the university to conduct a test, and it is not the policy of the state to divulge any information until the appropriate time."

*How diplomatic,* thought Dickerson, driving back to the campus on the crowded Interstate Route 5.

She decided that whenever the time came to get a state approval for a statewide test that might be the line to use with reporters.

"How did the visit go?" inquired Pinkett.

"Great—that man must have been a general at one time. He commands respect," answered Dickerson.

"He is a good man, and he runs that facility well," defended Pinkett. "He has one of the best run facilities in the entire state."

"Well, he promised to have all my blood tests done in about two to six months," informed Dickerson.

"Trust me, if Strickland promised to have all your blood work done in that time, you will get all your blood work in two to six months," reassured Pinkett.

The last blood sample arrived days prior to the allotted date for the conclusions of the blood draws. Dickerson prepared each sample for analysis—categorized, labeled, and stored each in the nitrogen freezer.

She wanted to run the tests in sequences, so as to minimize sampling errors.

The last sample arrived on Thursday morning at about 10:17 a.m. By Saturday noon, she has finished running all one hundred samples.

"I don't believe this," Dickerson uttered aloud in astonishment.

She immediately called Detective Pinkett to share her information. The detective was out on a crime call, and the department promised that she would call her back as soon as she got back to the station.

Dickerson was so excited she could not contain herself.

She went straight to the dean of the medical school and spent almost an hour and a half going through the details of her anecdotal study and argued for some funding to expand the study. Having obtained full support and cooperation from the dean, Dickerson was just entering her office when the phone call came from Detective Pinkett.

"You're looking for me?" began Detective Pinkett.

"Yes, I was," answered Dickerson with high excitement in her voice, "I have very good news about the blood samples from Lemon Grove."

"Forty of them were positive," Pinkett joked.

"Much better," answered Dickerson, oblivious to the joke, "ninety-two of the one hundred blood samples tested positive for HLA B66."

"Wait a minute, wait a minute," stammered Pinkett. "Ninety-two? That's pretty good. Are you sure about the testing?"

"Yes," answered Dickerson. "Because I ran each test four times, just to be sure of what I was looking at, and when all the numbers were re-counted, we had 92 percent success rates."

"What about the eight that was not positive?" Pinkett asked.

"I don't know," answered Dickerson. "I called the superintendent, and all he can tell me was that they were interesting characters."

"Very interesting indeed. What are you going to do next?"

"I am going to incorporate that in the detailed report that I plan to present to the American College of Immunology in Orlando next month."

"Don't you think that may be premature?"

"No. Not really," Dickerson was blunt. "I heard that Dr. Abramhoff in Chicago, another immunologist, may be performing the same test even as we speak."

"Then, go for it. But how can you widen the testing without provoking public outrage or government sanctions?"

"That's the $6 million question," answered Dickerson. "I think if I can talk to Dr. Abramhoff at the meeting, and we might find a way to collaborate and in the process, we will be able to formulate something."

"Keep me posted, please, this is becoming more intriguing than I thought."

"You aren't kidding," Dickerson agreed, thinking about all the possible scenarios concerning the use of such data.

While on one hand, she did not want to infringe on inmates' civic rights and jeopardize Detective Pinkett and Superintendent Strickland's positions, on the other hand, this information had explosive scientific advancements that to conceal it would be an injustice to the entire scientific community and the criminal justice system in particular.

She decided to hold off all further pronouncements until the meeting in Orlando, Florida.

# CHAPTER SEVEN

Tapping his left index finger against his two lower incisor teeth in a melodic, pensive fashion, while in the interim, constantly suckling and chewing on Brach's Hi-C fruit snacks, Bill was trying to create a nonsense circuit overpass against the newly designed security-code password being developed by Saturn Microsystems.

"I can do this," Bill said aloud.

A systems analyst for Saturn Corporation, Bill Stockton's job was to check and visualize every imaginable hacker plan against any new security system developed by Saturn.

"I can do this," repeated Bill, not realizing that his voice carried.

"I know you can, Bill," a perturbed voice answered from the next cubical.

Bill was working on the new software system, Saturna-10. The new system was supposed to be hacker-proof, and Saturn had invested nearly $2 million on its research and development.

"Are you going to lunch, Bill?" asked the same voice some time later.

"No, go ahead. I have my Brach's here, I'm okay."

At about 4:30 p.m., Bill finally thought he had something.

419naWAYO, the 241 computations, was the latest nonsense code Bill tried. Suddenly a message appeared on the screen.

"Heck, yes," Bill shouted, pounding a clenched right hand on the palm of his left hand. "Who is the king of ace, now?"

"Are you talking to yourself again, Bill?" asked the same perturbed voice.

"Heck yes," Bill smiled. "At least I don't answer."

He had cracked the super sensitive code that was supposed to be impenetrable.

He entered the code in his palm pilot and shredded the notepad with the 240 other different computations he had tried.

"Any luck?" asked George, the supervisor, as he entered Bill's cubical.

"Not yet," answered Bill with his sardonic, half-faced smile, "I have about ten codes that came close, but so far, the system appears tamper-proof."

*If Bill was unable to crack the security system working from the inside, no one can,* thought George.

"I know you have been working hard at this so why don't you go home, tomorrow is another day," George offered.

"I think I will do that," Bill answered.

"See you tomorrow," George waved.

"Thanks Mr. Dobbs, see you tomorrow."

Bill left the Saturn building, located at the corner of Piedmont Avenue and Ellis Street overlooking the busy Interstate 75/85 in downtown Atlanta, Georgia.

Driving home, Bill thought of what could be accomplished if only one person could crack the security of Saturna-10.

*It will be virtually impossible to track the source of the intruder, without having to recall the entire Saturna-10 system.*

The launch of Saturna-10 was very successful.

George Dobbs was very pleased, and Bill received a $27,000 bonus with another 100 shares in the company's common stock.

Bill knew that, with the 419naWAYO code, he could roam around Saturna-10 at will, totally undetected, because the code overrode all point security checks.

Sitting at home, at the newly constructed and sprawling community of Whispering Oaks neighborhood, in East Point, Bill logged on to Saturn-10, entered his code, and with a DSL speed he was roaming the entire Internet.

He immediately went to his favorite site, and headed straight to the chat room. There were 120 people in the "hurt-me" site.

Bill followed the various conversations, his face already in the half-smile. He then singled out and tracked Silva2782 for a while.

"I need a real man to bite a real hard job," typed Silva2782.

"Hey, Silva2782, try me," typed in three responders.

Bill saw what he wanted.

"Silva2782, bet I can bite you and you'll explode."

"Bet y'can't," responded Silva2782 after a few other messages.

"How much y'wanna bet?" typed Bill.

"One thousand."

"Y'on. D'ya wanna try me?"

"I don't even know ya."

"Would you like to?"

"Why, you might be a freak?"

"You are mine for 1k."

There was a brief rapid other entries.

Bill could have lost a response.

"Si12782, do you want a private chat room?" offered Bill.

"Okay," answered Silva2782.

Once in the private chat room, the exchange turned personal.

"What do you do?" asked Silva2782.

"I work for a reputable computer company in Atlanta," answered Bill. "How about you?"

"I am a cocktail waitress in East Chicago, Indiana."

"Are you married?"

"No, are you?"

"Me? No."

"How old are you?" asked Bill.

"I'm thirty-three, and you?"

"Thirty."

"Atlanta must be a beautiful city."

"Would you like to visit?"

"I don't know, I have to work, and I don't have the money for traveling."

"I can send you a ticket."

"Y'owes me $1,000 already."

"Oh, yeah, you'll get that."

"I have never been to Atlanta before."

"Atlanta is a beautiful place; I will show you around."

"I have three days off next week."

"That's fine."

"Okay."

"What name shall I put for the ticket?"

"Silvia Loopier. What's yours?"

"Bill Stockton."

"Okay, I have Thursday, Friday, and Saturday off…, I am sorry, it is in two weeks."

"That's okay; the ticket will be for Thursday night, to return on Saturday night. Is that okay?"

"That would be perfect."

"What city in Indiana you fly from?"

"No, we fly from Chicago."

"That's easy, O'Hare then."

"You aren't freakish, are you?"

"I have a very reputable job with Saturn in Atlanta."

"You sound cute."

"I think I am; you'll see."

"I will start packing tonight."

"You will not regret it," concluded Bill.

Bill picked up Silvia at Hartsfield Atlanta International Airport. She was booked with American Airline leaving Chicago at 7:39 p.m. arriving at 11:45 p.m.

*She is not a bad-looking gal,* thought Bill when Silvia arrived wearing their pre-arranged red blouse, light blue jeans, short pants, and a red umbrella on the left hand.

One visible butterfly tattoo could be seen on her left leg; she had four earrings on each earlobe.

A brunette, about five feet seven inches tall, slim upper body with a slight heavy thighs and legs, *and she carried herself well,* Bill observed.

Bill was not expecting an educated girl but was surprised at her intellect, especially working as a cocktail waitress.

"I called Saturn," said Silvia after formal introductions.

"Why?" Bill was visibly surprised.

"Just to see if you really work there," said Silva.

"What did they tell you?" inquired Bill.

"Ah, don't worry, I just asked if Bill Stockton works there," explained Silvia.

"They didn't tell me you called," probed Bill.

"No, because when she said, 'May I ask who is calling,' I told her it was nothing and hung up," reassured Silva.

*Smart girl,* Bill thought. She left no traces.

"Here we are," Bill pointed out his car at the short-stay parking area, after picking up her two small lightweight suitcases from the baggage claim area.

"That's your car?" exclaimed Silvia in admiration of the maroon-colored Lexus ES 300.

"Yeah, that's my car. You like it?" asked Bill, while noticing the admiration.

"I love it," said Silvia.

*First man I have dated that drives a decent car.*

The drive to Whispering Oaks was rather quiet. Few exchanged conversations about East Chicago, Indiana; the Luckiest Luck Casino where she works; and about Atlanta. She surprisingly confided to Bill that she did not tell anyone of her escapade to Atlanta, fearing that her co-workers might make fun of her.

"I'm very shy and sensitive, but my one love is to roam the web," she confessed.

Arriving at about 12:30 a.m., they encountered few motorists on the road.

Bill parked the car in the garage next to the Toyota Highlander.

"You own that car, too?" asked Silvia.

"Yeah, in case the Lexus breaks down," answered Bill.

"The Lexus cars don't break down," said Silvia naively.

"Sometimes they do," Bill said.

Sitting in the comfortable leather cushioned loveseat in the living room, Silvia was really impressed with the house decor.

"Tell me something about you," begin Bill.

"Well, I attended Indiana University Northwest in Gary, Indiana, for three years, then my parents got divorced and my dad refused to pay for my tuition anymore. I had to leave school and work to make enough money to go back to college. A cocktail waitress, especially at the Casino, can make a decent wage, you know, and I think after one more year, I will have enough money to complete college."

"That's admirable," Bill commented. "Do you have relatives, friends, roommates, or a boyfriend?"

*He is really inquisitive,* Silvia observed.

"Relax; like I said, no one knows I am here. I live alone in a one-bedroom apartment in Hammond, Indiana. I work all day. I have been only on four Internet dates before. I didn't care for them. My sister and I don't get along. She lives in Minnesota. The last time I talked to my parents was a year ago."

"You really a loner?" inquired Bill.

*She volunteers information a lot.*

"Yeah, you can say that," answered Silvia.

*Perfect,* thought Bill.

"I am a loner too. I'm the only son. I was born in Tuscaloosa, Alabama, went to school at Clark University here in Atlanta, and got a job here working for Saturn," Bill narrated.

"Do you want something to drink?" Bill offered, not wanting to say more.

"What do you have? I need something to relax me."

"You name it," volunteered Bill.

"Hennessy, VSOP with orange juice," Silvia blurted out.

"You must like that; it will only take a minute." Bill rose from the couch, bowed his head, and then disappeared into the kitchen.

"Why did you pierce your tongue?" Bill asked from the kitchen.

"Some guys like it like that. I think it's cute," answered Silvia.

"Oh I don't know…it may hurt," said Bill.

"I'll take it off then."

Silvia unhooked the silver metallic ring, pierced through her tongue.

"Better now?" ask Silvia sticking out her tongue.

"That's much better." Bill gave Silvia his half-faced smile.

*That's an odd way to smile,* thought Silvia as she sipped the Hennessy.

She noticed that the drink mix tasted a little bitter.

"M…m…that's different," said Silvia, wiping her lower lips.

"I added a little tonic to bring out the flavor," said Bill, intently watching Silvia.

"Yeah," agreed Silvia, not wanting to appear like an alcohol novice.

Noticing Silvia's eyes closing, Bill went over to the music box, pushed a button, and a slow jazz music filled the room. This was the moment Bill had prepared for.

# CHAPTER EIGHT

At work, Bill was happy to hear that yesterday's sales figures had pushed Saturn Microsystems net worth to nearly the one billion dollar mark, and that helped push Saturn Microsystems stock to $63 per share.

The systems analyst departments were very thrilled.

In reciprocation, George asked Bill if he could entertain a party in his house. Taken back a little, Bill unwillingly agreed.

"I guess that's okay," Bill responded. "I hope folks don't mind goat meat and lamb chops."

"I am sure that will be fine," reassured George. "For once we get to taste the cooking that you have been bragging about."

"Next Saturday, okay?" asked George.

"I can accommodate that," said Bill.

666

It took almost two years for the national media to tie together cases of the vanishing women, as it is now being called.

Initially listed as missing persons, each case somehow reached a dead end in Atlanta.

With no new leads, most of the cases were filed away.

When a young, ambitious, would-not-take-no-for-an-answer investigative reporter from Channel 5 in Chicago tried to review the files of the missing women, he noticed a developing pattern.

They were in their thirties, living alone, some with college education.

"Two of missing women had told friends that they were going to Atlanta for a date," the reporter mentioned to the station manager. "But when the police in Atlanta were alerted, they denied finding out-of-state dead females.

"They claimed that most of the victims in Atlanta were identified as local, except one forty-five-year-old female whose body was so mutilated and stripped of all IDs that police are still trying through dental records to identify the body."

When the composite report made national news, the Federal Bureau of Investigation finally took over the cases. After thoroughly investigating all the cases, the FBI finally took a special interest in Saturn Microsystems. Arriving in Atlanta and briefing George on the investigation, the FBI wanted to talk to Bill.

Detailed analysis of Silvia's Internet chats failed to identify who she had her last conversation with. But with the help of the local phone company, Silvia did place a call to Saturn Microsystems here in Atlanta the last day she was seen at work.

The FBI privately interviewed all the phone operators at Saturn Microsystems who worked on the day when Silvia called.

It was getting late in the day; Bill was notified by George that the FBI would like to schedule an interview with him first thing tomorrow morning at eight o'clock sharp.

"What's it about?" asked Bill with his usual smile.

"I don't know, but my hunch tells me that it might have something to do with those missing girls," George confided.

"Do they think somebody here has something to do with it?" the half-face smile on Bill's face disappeared.

"Don't worry about it," reassured George. "I think they are looking in the wrong place."

"Thanks," Bill answered.

"Don't forget, eight a.m.," reminded George on his way out of Bill's office.

Next morning, Bill did not show up for his interview with the FBI.

By 8:10 a.m., local police in conjunction with federal marshals were dispatched to Bill's house.

After several knocks at the door that failed to illicit any response from within, the door was busted open.

Bill was found sitting in the basement shower, cold as ice, a sawed-off shotgun on his lap. There was blood mixed with whitish pasty material all over the bathroom wall, and Bill's face was totally unrecognizable from the bullet wound.

# CHAPTER NINE

It was a beautiful, hot and muggy autumn evening in Cicero, Illinois.

The sun was a little rusty in all its background shadows, unsure whether to rise or set, even though the time on the First Suburban National Bank building showed exactly six o'clock in the evening. In Cicero, the southeastern section had been called a gorgeous neighborhood, especially toward the end of summer.

There were cars parked on both sides of the narrow street in this middle- to higher-income section of town.

At 87th Street near Kedzie Road, a child, trying to cross the street, caught Joanne's eyes. Joanne couldn't understand why this little, happy-looking three- to four-year-old boy was trying to navigate the street alone.

"Where are the parents?" Joanne asked herself.

*Where is this boy going?*

*Who is he playing with?*

The child skipped and hopped, periodically looking between the cars, while singing an inaudible song.

Joanne saw no one around. The street appeared deserted. In the distance, Joanne saw a silhouette, and within seconds, heard the humming of an oncoming vehicle.

The car must have been traveling at quite an excessive speed, because the acceleration was getting louder and louder.

The child apparently did not hear the car, Joanne surmised, because just as Joanne delineated the make on the car, the boy veered between the red Ford Escort and the blue Nissan Pathfinder parked some distance south of the junction of 87th Street and Kedzie Road. Joanne immediately knew what was about to happen.

She screamed at the top of her lungs, "Hey, kid! There is a car coming. Don't cross the road yet."

Twice she yelled, but the kid appeared to be ignoring her. Just as the child cleared the parked cars, on came a Toyota Camry at an excessive high rate of speed. The car must have been traveling at least sixty miles per hour on a posted thirty-five miles per hour speed zone.

Just then, the boy looked at Joanne and gave her a closed-mouth, sad-faced smile.

"I have seen you before," Joanne said to herself aloud.

The squeaking of the brakes, the shrieking of the child, and the strange buzzing sound coming from the distant steel mills became deafening, and then, silence.

Joanne woke up from a strange dream to the buzzing of the radio alarm on the nightstand.

It was Monday morning in Chicago.

Joanne had spent the whole weekend arguing with Doug's parents, so much so that by Sunday night she was tired. They were here for the weekend, visiting their grandchildren.

Dick and Valerie Stead made their quarterly trip from Beloit, Wisconsin, to Chicago for their usual aggravation visit on the pretense of seeing their grandchildren. What made things worse, Joanne believed, was that Doug, her own husband, always sided with them.

"That really is very frustrating," murmured Joanne, face flustered, as she walked out of the bathroom, heading toward the kitchen.

"Good morning," Doug's voice pierced the silence of the morning and startled Joanne.

"Yeah," Joanne replied, hardly opening her mouth, and not in the mood for any conversation, especially with her husband.

"That was a wacky weekend."

"If you say so," replied Joanne with a loud yawn.

"Come on, honey, what was that supposed to mean?"

"What was what supposed to mean?" Joanne snapped, her voice stern, her face serious and sarcastic.

"Ouch!" Joanne bellowed as she turned on the coffee maker.

Doug, standing at the edge of the beautifully marbled kitchen counter, said with a small grin. "You knew exactly what I mean."

Spreading her hands in an effort to try and minimize the situation, Joanne appeared mystified. "No, I don't know what you mean," she replied.

*Not this morning,* she thought. All she wanted to do was to get the kids ready for school. Alexis and Isipe were still asleep in their respective rooms.

Joanne made a move toward the kids' rooms in order to get them up and ready for school.

"Honey," Doug interrupted, pretending to realize the source of the contentions. He asked, "Are you still angry at them?"

"You know what," Joanne retorted, with a serious angry look on her face, "your parents are the most irritating individuals I have ever met. I think they take personal pleasure at exploiting...manufactured weakness, so that they can have reasons to justify...and especially in your case, their point that Stella would have made a better wife for you."

"What? Where did that come from...and...what does Stella have to do with this?" Doug appeared genuinely baffled, even though he knew that was coming.

*Joanne tends to do this whenever she is really upset,* Doug thought, *and that is one of her faults. She never accepts the fact that she is good at what she does.*

"Oh, so you don't see what they are doing?" asked Joanna, fumbling to put on her slippers with one hand while she balanced herself on the dresser with the other clenched hand. "Of course you don't. You are too busy agreeing with them and of course, the laugh is on me."

"What is this 'of course, of course,' thing?" asked Doug, face puzzled and serious.

Doug, who was an attorney, never appreciated it when opposing lawyers used the phrase "of course."

He always interpreted that phrase as a backward way of minimizing his arguments.

"They are not doing anything," continued Doug, who started walking toward Joanne to hold her hands. "Do you think that my parents have the power to disrupt this marriage?"

"Yes, I do," snapped Joanne, wrenching her hand back, her voice rising.

"Well, if you think that, then you are severely mistaken," with an equally raised voice Doug responded.

With a sense of rejection, and not wanting to make any more peace, Doug headed to the bathroom.

"You are always naive!" Joanne shouted, angrier that Doug was walking away. "And why do you always walk away whenever you start losing an argument?"

"Hi, Mom," greeted two voices, coming out of the two adjoining bedrooms.

Alexis and Isipe, Doug and Joanne's two children had been sleeping in their respective bedrooms but were apparently awoken by their parents' arguing again.

"Hi, Dad," said Isipe, acknowledging Doug as he made his way back into the kitchen.

Alexis was rubbing her eyes like she normally did every morning, while Isipe yawned.

"Cover your mouth when you yawn, sweetheart," said Joanne, in a much calmer voice, even though she was still breathing hard.

"Yes Mom." Isipe covered his mouth and finished the rest of the yawning.

"Come on, kids, let's get ready for school," Joanne urged the children.

"I thought you said we are not going to school today," Alexis, always the smart one, reminded Joanne.

"When did I say that?" asked Joanne, her composure almost regained.

"Last night after dinner, remember? You came to help me do the dishes," Alexis responded as she sat on the high stool and leaned over the counter top.

"No, sweetheart, I was probably upset," Joanne clarified, managing to inch out a smile.

"Like you always are," Doug could not help that one.

"Drop dead," muttered Joanne as she reached over to lead Alexis out of the kitchen to the bathroom.

"What?" Alexis asked, reaching over to grab Mom's hand.

Joanne took a deep breath, paused for a moment, then looked at Alexis and said, "Nothing sweetheart, your Dad is upsetting me as usual."

"Dad, stop upsetting Mom!" demanded Alexis, sensing her mother's uneasiness.

"I do not," pleaded Doug, as if trying to win his case in front of a jury. "Your mother is the one with the problem."

"So I'm the one with the problem, huh?" Joanne asked. "I suppose you are the one with all the answers, aren't you? You know what, you'll see."

"See what?" asked Doug, standing at the door to the master bathroom, face perplexed.

"You will see," reiterated Joanne.

Doug brushed it off as one of Joanne's little tirades and went into the master bathroom to shower, shave, and dress for work.

Doug, who just got promoted to junior partner at Lloyds and Benson's Law firm, one of the most prominent law firms in Chicago, worked long hours. Joanne resented the fact that Doug spent more time at work than at home. Joanne, on the other hand, had been accused by her friends at the Johnson's Pharmaceutical Company in Niles, Illinois, of being overprotective of her children.

Joanne also was recently promoted to the position of senior sales supervisor.

"Good-bye, honey; bye, kids," Doug waved, leaving for work in haste.

He was already dressed in his blue business suit, briefcase in hand, walking out the door.

"I have an eight o'clock meeting with Donald Stallman—you know, the guy on TV, who was accused of murdering his wife," Doug said, trying to leave the house on what he thought was a reconciliatory note.

"What are you…?" Joanne was about to bark.

"I was only joking," Doug interrupted immediately. "My goodness! You can't even appreciate a joke anymore. He is being accused of embezzlement."

With that, he closed the door behind him.

Joanne wanted to do something to Doug right there and then, but before she could make any move, Doug was already out the door, no mention of breakfast or coffee, no good-bye kisses to her or the kids. Feeling thwarted,

Joanne was engulfed with rage. She cursed at everything and anything in her path.

Alexis and Isipe were busy in their rooms getting dressed for school. It was look-your-best-day for the seventh and eighth graders at Wicker Park Middle School. Joanne had promised the kids that his year they would be the best-dressed kids in the entire school.

"Hey, Mom, you like?" asked Alexis, feeling rather good in her new clothes.

"You look…okay," answered Joanne, somewhat absent-minded.

"I think I don't look badly either," Isipe said, wanting his own accolade.

"You look like a gentleman."

Joanne was trying to put on the best face possible, all the while lost in reverie.

"You know what, kids, let's not go to school or work today," suggested Joanne out of nowhere.

"What?" exclaimed Isipe with that puzzled look on his face.

"Let's all go for a ride in the boat on the lake."

"Are you serious?" asked Alexis.

"Yes. It is a beautiful day for a boat ride. Come on; pack a few things and drinks. Let's go have fun on our boat."

Doug and Joanne Stead were members of the Navy Pier Yacht Club, and they owned a medium-sized boat, which they had used on few occasions to sail around Lake Michigan.

It was during one of the boat rides almost eight years ago that the first Stella-implicated arguments between Doug and Joanne occurred.

While enjoying the scenic skyscrapers, Doug had quipped, "This is like the good old days."

"What good old days?" Joanne had inquired.

"Oh, never mind."

"Please, tell me."

"Okay, I want you to promise me you won't take this wrong."

"I won't."

"Well," Doug had begun, "about eight or nine years ago, Stella's parents took us on a boat ride along the lakeshore. It was a wonderful experience. There was champagne, hamburgers, and beers. It was on a hot summer day just like today."

"You miss that, don't you?" Joanne had suggested with a curious urge on her face.

"Yeah," Doug had replied, nodding his head haphazardly.

"Was it better than now?"

"What do you mean, better than now?" Doug had asked, suddenly realizing the course of the conversation.

"I mean, would you rather be there, than here?" Joanne had wanted to know.

"Be where?"

"Be in the boat with Stella."

"That's ridiculous. I am here with you, am I not?" Doug had asked.

"Yeah, but your heart was there, otherwise, you would not have brought it up," Joanne had argued.

"You promised you would not be upset."

"I'm not upset. I just wanna know."

"Can we drop this?" Doug had gotten up immediately and walked toward the deck.

That was the beginning of several serious arguments about Doug's previous relationship with Stella. Even Joanne agreed that most of their arguments were about how Doug's parents fell in love with Stella's parents, how the marriage did not happen because Doug loathed Stella's abrasive behavior and her standing up for herself.

"Okay, Mom, we are ready to go sailing," Alexis interrupted Joanne's thoughts.

"Pack your school bags with your shoes and clothes in case we dock at Navy Pier to go shopping," instructed Joanne.

"We did already," Alexis yelled with a surprised look on her face.

"Oh, yes!" Joanne answered.

In less than forty-five minutes, they arrived at the yacht club members-only parking lot. Safely parked, they headed to the boat with backpacks, one suitcase, and a cooler filled with cans of Diet Seven-Up and Sierra Mist.

Joanne's plan was to dock at Navy Pier for lunch, then shop for new clothes for Alexis, sneakers for Isipe, and fine jewelry for herself.

These were the rare occasions when Joanne could splurge on herself and the kids, knowing full well that

Doug would have something to say against the whole idea.

"I brought some orange juice and doughnuts," said Joanne.

"I'll have some," Alexis was quick to respond.

"I will do that too, then the Sierra Mist later," said Isipe.

Joanne reached into the cooler she brought, while gingerly steering the boat against the gentle summer Chicago wind.

"Here," Joanne said to Alexis, "pour one for you, and one for Isipe."

"The doughnuts are in the plastic container, at the corner."

Both Alexis and Isipe had their fill and were satisfied. With their life jackets on, they started comparing which skyscraper was better looking and which one they would like to own if wealthy.

Within minutes thereafter, Isipe yelled from the washroom, "Mom, I am sick."

"What's the matter?" inquired Joanne with an anticipatory look.

"My stomach is upset and I am gonna throw…" Isipe could not finish his sentence before a projectile vomit mixed with blood spewed out of his mouth.

With that, he fell to the ground, curled himself into a fetal position, and grabbed his throat as if something was choking him.

With a little whimper, "I need a doctor," he turned blue, starting with his finger tips then traveling to the neck.

He struggled to breathe to no avail and passed out. Joanne ran to find Alexis. There on the bathroom floor was Alexis, covered with blood-soaked vomit, while blood droplets dripped from her nose. Her entire body had turned dark blue.

"I declare," said Joanne, quivering but composed, "that cyanide worked as quickly as they said. Those guys at the Genome Laboratories are something else."

With that, Joanne drank the rest of the orange juice then plunged into the cool waters of Lake Michigan.

# CHAPTER TEN

The campaign for the governor of Illinois had suddenly become very contentious.

It pitched the Democratic State Secretary Edger Jones against the Republican Congressman Milton Roderick.

Mr. Jones ran as a strong Secretary of State, and advocated liberal sentences, like home monitoring, for petty criminals so as to avoid overcrowding in state prisons.

Mr. Roderick, on the other hand, campaigned on stronger and longer prison terms for all criminals, promising to rid the state of Illinois of all criminal elements, and also to restore ethics in government.

Mr. Roderick won the election, and on January 2 was inaugurated governor of the state of Illinois.

Dr. Abramhoff supported Mr. Roderick during his campaign, especially on the criminal issue. He donated a substantial amount of money to the campaign.

During one of the gubernatorial campaign stops in Chicago to highlight Mr. Roderick's support for reform in Illinois run-away medical malpractice insurance premiums, Dr. Abramhoff had an opportunity to discuss with him the Kankakee Project.

The gathering was at the Sheraton Hotel overlooking the Chicago River in downtown Chicago.

"Hello, Mr. Congressman," began Abramhoff, noticing Mr. Roderick alone momentarily at the bar table.

"Hello, Doc." Mr. Roderick smiled, and then shook Abramhoff's outstretched hand. "I am grateful for all your efforts. Folks like you will make this a successful campaign."

"You know I am in total support of your stand on crime," continued Abramhoff.

"Thank you," replied Mr. Roderick, reaching for the gin and tonic that he ordered.

"Actually, my department at the university is currently designing a project in Kankakee to study relationships, if any, between hardcore criminals at the maximum security prison and genetics."

"That's good," agreed the congressman. "Care for a drink?"

"No thanks. What I mean is that we are looking to see if there is a genetic tendency to criminality just like there is a tendency to, say, diabetes, cancer, and some bowel diseases."

"Are you implying that there may be a link between criminals and inherited genes?"

There was a curious look on the congressman's face as he reached for his second sip of the drink.

"Not real inheritance, per say, but people with criminal intent...I mean those individuals may be predestined to commit crimes, just like Joanne Stead, that Chicago woman that poisoned her kids, and that fellow in Atlanta," stammered Abramhoff.

"Now that's really interesting," responded Roderick, letting out a slight cough. "You mean that these individuals were supposed to commit terrible crimes?"

"Actually…yes, what we are looking for is to develop a testing mechanism to determine who therefore is going to commit these terrible crimes, just as there are now testing mechanisms to determine who will develop arthritis, diabetes, or breast cancer." Abramhoff finally regained his composure. "Once that is done, who knows, we might invent a better cure for criminals."

"How do you intend to develop this test?" asked Roderick.

"There are two areas we are focusing on. One is the DNA, which we clearly know is not yielding good results, but an area known as human leukocyte antigen, HLA for short, has taken a whole new meaning and new research interest."

Abramhoff appeared more comfortable.

"Human leuko-what?" asked a confused Roderick.

"In medicine we call it the HLA," simplified Abramhoff.

"So you think there is, or may be, a link between this…this…?" started Roderick.

"HLA," Abramhoff assisted.

"This HLA and criminals," concluded the congressman.

"Yes." A look of excitement lighted Abramhoff's face as he perceived that Mr. Roderick was finally getting the picture. "And we intend to prove just that."

"What do you need from me?" asked the congressman as he finished his drink.

"We have requested federal help to start a pilot project at Kankakee Federal Penitentiary," answered Abramhoff.

"I was just wondering," continued Abramhoff, "if the state of Illinois can champion this project, and if the research pans out, imagine the national attention it can garner and subsequent federal funds it will attract."

"Could you imagine what that would do to my career and to the state government?" Congressman Roderick expressed his thoughts aloud.

"How do you perform this test again?" asked Mr. Roderick.

"One second," gestured Mr. Roderick to an aide motioning at his watch.

"What test?" asked Abramhoff.

"This HLA thing," queried Mr. Roderick. "Do you draw blood, shine a light in their eyes, urine test, or spit test?"

"Oh!" answered Abramhoff with a smile. "The project would involve identifying the hardcore and twisted criminals, and start with them. We will draw their blood, isolate their leukocytes, identify the antigen areas, and using chromatography, map out their HLA."

"Too much technicality for me," responded the congressman, as he dropped five dollars in the glass jar collection bowl. "Bottom line is what?"

"The blood drawn to find an area or areas on the HLA that may be the commonality between these criminals," answered Abramhoff.

"And if you do?" asked a highly curious Roderick.

"Most likely develop a test for it," said Abramhoff.

"Now help me again," continued Mr. Roderick. "What would the test do?"

"Well," continued Abramhoff, "with the testing, we can then identify individuals who are predisposed or pre-destined to become criminals."

"People who are predestined to become criminals," reflected Mr. Roderick. "Do you realize the implication of this both nationally and internationally?"

"I do fully realize the implication, sir," said Abramhoff with a certain amount of authority.

"Okay, I'll see what I can do if I am elected governor," assured Roderick, heading toward the ballroom.

"You will be elected governor, trust me on that," affirmed Abramhoff.

"I will hold you up to it," smiled Mr. Roderick as he walked off with the aide.

6 6 6

Two months after the inauguration, Dr. Abramhoff asked Sabrina to place a call to the governor. Two hours after the call was placed, the governor called back.

"Hi, Doc," began the Governor.

"Hello, Mr. Governor," greeted Abramhoff. "Congratulations. I told you that you would be governor."

"Yeah, you did say that," the governor agreed. "How is the weather in Chicago?"

"A bit chilly and windy, what else?" answered Abramhoff. "How is the governorship going?"

"We are getting into it," answered the governor.

"Oh, by the way," started Abramhoff, "do you remember our conversations in Chicago about the HLA project?"

"Yes, I do remember," answered the governor, "as a matter of fact, I was talking to my health officer about you and your HLA theory this morning, and he thinks that a meeting might be called for."

"I'm all for that," said Abramhoff, nodding his head in agreement. "Where do you all want to meet?"

"We are scheduled to have a public health meeting in Chicago next week to discuss the possible effect of a flu vaccine shortage on the state, and how to prevent it from happening again," explained the governor, "and I was just wondering if we can meet either prior to or after the meeting."

"That would be great," said Abramhoff.

"Okay, then," responded the governor, "I will have my executive secretary call yours and set things up."

Sabrina scheduled the meeting for nine a.m.; an hour and a half prior to the governor's scheduled meeting with the health officers.

Dr. Abramhoff brought Dr. Achampi with him to meet the governor and also to hear from him.

Entering the Hilton Hotel on Michigan Avenue, Abramhoff for the first time actually thought about the social implications of the testing. He was previously only looking at the medical aspect of the project. How much something like this would advance medical science, but for the first time, however, his attention drifted to the social implication of a linkage, if one did exist.

How would the implication affect the governor?

Would it make the governor popular nationally?

If he became that popular, perhaps he may run for president, and then who knows, he might want to take someone with him from Illinois to Washington for health-related issues.

Abramhoff vowed to work hard at establishing the association in the project.

But what if there were none, then the entire project would be lumped as one of those pork projects that the Governor allocated to his campaign contributions.

Just the thought of that made Abramhoff shudder, because he had never been accused of being a stooge before. *I will have to weigh the consequences when, or if, the time arrives,* he vowed.

The meeting started fifteen minutes after nine o'clock at the State Street Conference room.

"Good morning, governor," started Abramhoff as soon as the governor and his team entered the room.

"Good morning, Doc," replied governor Roderick.

"This is my associate, Dr. Ashutt Achampi," Abramhoff started the introduction. "He is an oncology fellow at our university, and he is going to work closely with me on this project."

"Good morning, governor," greeted Dr. Achampi.

"Good morning to you, Doctors. I hope you all had a good night's sleep?" asked the Governor.

"Yes, thank you, sir," replied Achampi in a joyful haste.

"This is Dr. Mary Jackson, the state health commissioner." The governor introduced a smiling, middle-aged woman in a colorful business suit.

"Dr. Andre Artis is our deputy health commissioner, and Ms. Kendra Morris our executive administrator."

"Good morning," each said, as their names were introduced.

"Please, let's sit down," invited the governor.

There was a brief exchange of further handshakes while everyone helped themselves to coffee and bagels. Sitting down at the east-end corner of the small round conference room table, the Governor began.

"I have known Dr. Abramhoff for...," he looked over at David, "almost fifteen years now," Abramhoff nodded in approval, "at various social functions. We had an interesting conversation last time we met at Sheraton Hotel just prior to the election. He very eloquently briefed me on a project that he has been working on at the Kankakee Federal Penitentiary."

All eyes were now focused on Abramhoff. It was moments like this he felt he was predestined for.

"I would like Dr. Abramhoff to explain to you the project as he explained it to me. Okay, Doc." The governor turned to Abramhoff with a smile.

"Thank you, governor," began Abramhoff, and methodically, without much fanfare, he explained to the panel his belief in the predestination of the human race and that this predestination is somehow tied to our cells. He explained that once an individual was born, he or she was programmed at birth.

"Individual lives are nothing but manifestations of these various programs. Science has successfully decoded the programs for various diseases. The coding processes are located at the HLA site.

"HLA coding is a lot different from DNA inheritance," Abramhoff explained. "In DNA, individuals are just manifesting certain characteristics already existed in the parents, but the HLA coding is novice to each individual.

"I strongly believe that criminality is encoded on HLA site or sites, and a test can be successfully cultivated to detect it or them," he concluded.

When he finished, everyone including Dr. Achampi looked with awe at Abramhoff.

"What do you think?" asked Abramhoff to the audience.

"Fascinating, don't you think?" asked the governor, nodding his head at the health commissioner.

"I am really impressed," Dr. Mary Jackson answered. "If what Dr. Abramhoff is saying is true, this would signal a significant advancement in science with national and international implications."

"You took the words right out of my mouth," added the governor.

"How can the state be of help?" asked Dr. Artis with a shy deep baritone voice.

"Like I explained to the governor," an excited Abramhoff did not wait for the question to finish, "we would like the state to fund the project at Kankakee with any assistance from the National Institute for Health in Washington."

"I don't know how we can do that," reflected Dr. Jackson.

"The trick maybe is to find unallocated money, or discretionary money, and then funnel it through the Health Department. What do you think?" asked the governor, looking at Dr. Jackson.

"Yeah, I think through the Health Department that will give it legitimacy and cover, especially from human-rights advocates and the state legislators," agreed a hesitant Dr. Jackson.

"What will we call it?" the fidgeting governor asked.

"A Health Department Study of Diseases in criminals at the Kankakee Federal Prison," volunteered Dr. Artis.

"Sounds…okay?" grimaced the governor, hands outstretched, looking at Dr. Abramhoff.

"That's fine by me," agreed Abramhoff.

"If, and when, an association is established…, what then? Gene therapy…?" Dr. Jackson asked the open-ended question.

"We will cross that bridge when we reach there," instructed Governor Roderick.

# CHAPTER ELEVEN

At the beautiful and most recently opened Marriott Grande Lakes Hotel in Orlando, Florida, the American Academy of Immunology and Genetics Conference attendees could be seen everywhere.

Dr. Abramhoff arrived Sunday evening at the hotel, driven from the airport by a chartered limousine. He was very impressed with the shiny marble floors, the marble walls, the elegance and ambience of the registration desk area, and how the hotel had that European look to it. The last time he had seen such a beauty was in Switzerland, at the Hotel President Wilson in Geneva. After registrations, he was ushered to his suite on the twenty-sixth floor.

Dr. Dickerson arrived earlier in the afternoon. She was disappointed at the location, mostly because there were no surrounding waterways except for the few small lakes, scattered some distance away from the hotel. She wondered if they were man-made.

Meeting schedules were handed out to all attendees at the registration desk. The registration itself continued all afternoon and well into the night.

The opening remark of the meeting was delivered by the president of the American Academy of Immunology.

He expressed his gratitude for all the attendees, and then systematically went into the day-to-day activities for the next three days.

After the welcome speech and few housekeeping items, Dr. Georgia Chambers, the immediate past president rose to introduce the keynote speaker, Dr. David Abramhoff, who was received with warm applause. Dr. Abramhoff, in a distinguished immaculate blue suit, started lecturing in his usual methodical fashion, with his belief in the concept of predestination.

"It now appears," stated Abramhoff, "that science is about ready to bear that out."

He elaborated his study methods, the protocol, and also the support the Governor of Illinois had pledged, at the state level, especially for his research at the Joliet Correctional Center and the Kankakee Federal Penitentiary.

So far, his focus had been to establish predestined connections between HLA antigen and criminality. The preliminary report concluded that among hardcore criminals there was a fuzzy alignment on the B Locus of the HLA. He was not sure what to make of it, but he hoped that the next presenter, Dr. Dickerson from the University of La Jolla in San Diego, would shed some light on it.

After an hour and a half presentation, and a fifteen minute break, Dr. Dickerson was introduced as the next speaker. Dr. Dickerson gracefully, and with a much clearer understanding, followed on Dr. Abramhoff's presentation. In a step-wise yet studious fashion, she illustrated how the HLA of certain criminals had come to rest on the B locus at position 66. This was achieved using a much-improved chromatographic method.

"We were able to carry out our own studies first at our local police station," Dr. Dickerson stated. "We initially tested all processed offenders and found that the HLA B66 positives were mostly concentrated on hardcore criminals. Armed with that, we solicited the help of the officials at the notorious San Diego Correctional Facility. We selected one hundred maximum-security inmates who have committed heinous crimes and to our greatest surprise, ninety-two of them tested positive for HLA B66."

"I will predict that with further investigations, and more elaborate research, this association may have a 98 percent sensitivity and specificity, and in the right environment we might even find a 100 percent predictive value."

During the question and answer session, just before lunch break, Dr. Abramhoff and Dickerson unwittingly presented a united front from endless questions with technical and social implications. "I was very impressed with both scientific findings," most commented. "What troubles me is exactly how this finding will ultimately be used?" others questioned with great concern.

At the break-out afternoon sessions, Dr. Abramhoff and Dr. Dickerson's small group meetings were standing-room only and the questions continued endlessly.

"There will be a formal dinner at the Florida and Everglade Ballrooms. We will start serving promptly at six p.m.," it was announced at the conclusion of the formal sessions.

Drs. Dickerson and Abramhoff, however, had previously agreed for an informal dinner at the outdoor café overlooking the beautiful swimming pool at the back of the hotel.

"That's a spectacular view," noted Dickerson. "I didn't like this place at first."

The sun was just beginning to set, surreptitiously cognizant of their presence. In a slow-motion dance, the evening sun, which could be seen clearly from the café, gyrated and hid behind two thin clouds, an appearance that could be mistaken for two big sunglasses on a wary, tired face.

"That setting sun is something, isn't it?" Abramhoff joined in equal admiration.

The Grande Lakes could be seen from the various walkways surrounding the circular pool. The water in the pool itself, flowed in a continuous motion, circulating around a central bar area.

"That's a nice swimming pool," Dickerson observed, eyes roving in admiration. "It reminds me of the same style swimming pool at Sandals hotel in Ocho Rios, Jamaica."

Beyond these beautiful outdoor areas, and the Grande Lakes, was a sixteen-hole golf course, meticulously maintained. The water, sprinkling of the golf course, created a miniaturized rainbow across the manicured lawn.

"I knew I should have brought my golf cart," lamented Abramhoff, "but I was in such a rush."

Dickerson was not as disappointed in her admiration as she thought she was when she arrived yesterday. She knew she should have taken a walk around this vast hotel yesterday, but she had chosen, instead, to remain in her room and use the occasion to put a finishing touch to her presentation.

"That was some session, Dr. Dickerson," began Abramhoff when both finally sat down to dinner at the Decanter poolside restaurant.

"Please call me Regina."

Dr. Abramhoff nodded in acknowledgment.

"I did not expect that many hostile questions," expressed Abramhoff with a wrinkled forehead. "I was really surprised."

"On the contrary, I was not surprised, Dr. Abramhoff," said Dr. Dickerson, shrugging her shoulders.

"David, please."

"Okay."

"You realize that we are on the verge of something that may revolutionize the entire judicial system," said Abramhoff, sounding like a judge.

"I am acutely aware of that, but why can't some people see that?"

"Part of it is jealousy, part ignorance, and the rest is simply obstructionism."

After a momentary reflection, Dr. Abramhoff continued, "In Chicago, I met with the governor and the state health commissioner, and there was a consensus on moving forward."

"You have really gone further than I did. I only used the help of our local chief detective and the superintendent of a correctional institute."

"Can I get you all something to drink?" interrupted the waitress.

"Yes, please, club soda," answered Dr. Abramhoff, always the one to take the lead.

"What can I get you, madam?"

"Late harvest white Riesling," said Dickerson, looking at the wine list.

"Thank you, I will be back to take your orders." The waitress headed toward the bar.

"How did the 5 percent solution of dextrose ethylene benzoic acid come up?" Abramhoff asked.

"Actually, we previously used it to clarify and accurately define the genes responsible for the galactosamine disorders."

"Very interesting, but how did you think of using it here?"

"One of my research assistants suggested using it to wash out the impurities in the solution. Guess what? It worked."

"I can't wait to get back to Chicago. The governor will be thrilled."

"How did you get the governor in on this?" asked Dickerson.

"Well, he ran his campaign on a crime reduction theme, and I enthusiastically supported him. In any event, I knew him from his days in Congress."

"That's a nice connection. It may come in handy."

"He has actually given us his blessing and has allocated state funding for more research at the Kankakee Correctional Center."

"That's great," expressed Dickerson with some envy. "How did you pull that off?"

"Are you guys ready to order?" interrupted the waitress while serving the drinks.

"What do you seriously think about these HLA B66 findings?" asked Abramhoff when the waitress finally left after taking their orders.

"I believe that we are onto something, the implications of which neither of us currently is aware; what do you think?"

"I do believe that with the proper legislative action, we might be on the verge of ridding society of all predestined criminal elements."

"How did you surmise that?" asked a bewildered Dickerson.

"Look at it this way," Abramhoff clasped his hands, leaned forward, and rested them on the dining table, "if we can test people and methodically pick out the HLA B66 positive individuals. Can you imagine?"

With a slight hesitation, Dr. Dickerson, in a barely audible voice, advised, "I think we should move more cautiously in that direction."

# CHAPTER TWELVE

Dr. Dickerson returned from Florida tired, especially after three grueling days attending conferences, chairing sessions, and being the focus of the questions and answer periods. The flight from Orlando to San Diego, except for few sheer wind bumps, was uneventful.

She was able to nap for about twenty-five minutes on the return flight. The rest she spent making mental notes to herself. The overriding question on her mind was what Dr. Abramhoff planned to do with the HLA B66 finding. He unwittingly gave her the impression that he was on some type of witch hunt.

*The Constitution of United States does not permit any type of witch hunting, not in this day and age,* Dickerson thought.

But what if Dr. Abramhoff was right?

If, by using HLA B66 in random testing, the authorities could detect and stop a serial killer, how many lives and resources could be saved, and what financial savings would that be to the states, and the federal government? The dominant question, however, was what to do with the HLA B66 positive individuals who had committed no crime whatsoever. Watch them, imprison them, or what?

Dickerson made a conscious decision to stay on the scientific side of whatever argument may arise, and let the elected officials legislate on the social implications of the findings.

Arriving home, she could not wait to call Pinkett.

"How was your conference?" the detective asked.

"Thought provoking," answered Dickerson.

"What do you mean by that?"

"I mean," she answered with a pause, "Dr. Abramhoff is something else."

"What? He's really smart, or just something else?"

"He already met with the governor of Illinois and has obtained funding from the state to conduct studies at a local state prison."

"Oh, really, that's four steps ahead of you."

"I have to think of something to accelerate our project."

"How about collaborating?" suggested the detective.

"I don't know," said a hesitant Dickerson. "He appeared a little pompous, even though he was a gentleman."

"What, is he handsome?"

"You may say handsome," answered Dickerson, "I say studious, late fifties to early sixties, just a little chubby but dressed impeccably."

"Studiously handsome, well dressed, gentleman…"

"Don't go there," interrupted Dickerson.

"Where I am going?"

"I don't have to tell you where you are going. You know exactly where you're going."

"All right," Pinkett gave up, "at least ask him for collaboration."

"I will do that," Dickerson promised.

666

The feast of Our Lady of Guadalupe on December 12 was a celebrated occasion for Catholics living in San Diego, especially the vast majority of Mexicans. Dr. Dickerson, over the years, had made plans to attend the yearly ceremonial Mass, but schedule conflicts with her work always prevented her.

This year, the feast fell on Wednesday. It was a very busy day for Dr. Dickerson at the university, but she promised herself to attend the afternoon festive Mass and for once, observed the carrying of the statue of Our Lady across Locust Street. She had always been fascinated by the story of the Blessed Virgin Mary's apparition to the folks at Guadalupe.

The first reading during Mass was a passage from the book of Revelation. Usually, half paying attention, she could follow most readings during Mass. A process she mastered over the years of attending Masses.

This time however, her whole being sat straight up when she heard, during the reading, "No one could buy or sell except one who had the stamped image of the beast... that number is 666."

The half sleep in her eyes immediately evaporated. Fully attentive now, she listened to Father Sanchez during the sermon saying that the number 666 was not physically written on the body or on the head of anyone, as

Hollywood had made us to believe, but rather: "We as Christians should hope and pray to God for illumination so that we can identify those who are the agents of evil, and in the process, be able to recognize and avoid their temptations. By the same token, we should be aware of God's immense love for us and follow the path it takes to be a good Christian, no matter the cost, so that in the final analysis we shall inherit God's Kingdom and not that of the devil."

Driving back to the laboratory, and all afternoon, Dickerson was consumed with wild thoughts of a possible connection between the number 666 in the Bible, and their bizarre HLA findings. Multiple thoughts raced through her mind.

*Is this a coincidence?*

*Is there a connection?*

*Wait a minute. The number is 666. Our HLA is B66*

*Is there an HLA 666?*

*Nope, wrong nomenclature.*

*What about HLA B666?*

*That's not possible, because the B locus is not long enough to accommodate up to 600 positions.*

*What then, is the significance of HLA B66?*

*Does it have anything to do with the beast in the book of Revelation?*

*And why is it associated with hardcore criminals at the maximum-security prison?*

Arriving home, late in the evening, Dickerson made her way straight to the bedroom. In the drawer of the nightstand she knew there was a family Bible, the new

American Bible. It was given to her during her graduation from medical school by her dad, who usually explained complicated situations to her by quoting a passage from the Scriptures. Dickerson knew the Bible was there, but had never picked it up to read, except today.

The reading was from the book of Revelation, but what chapter? She hardly ever looked at the Missals during Mass. Not wanting to read the entire book, she called the church and later discovered that the reading was taken from chapters twelve and thirteen. She read the entire chapters and, not wanting to stop reading, went all the way to the end of the book. Early the next morning, she called Detective Pinkett.

"Hey, you," Dickerson called Pinkett on her cell phone.

"What's up, Doc?" replied Pinkett.

"What do you know about the number 666?" asked Dickerson.

"What number 666?"

"You know, the one in the Bible."

"Well, it's supposed to be associated with the devil. What about it?"

"I went to church yesterday."

"Good for you. Did you pray for me?"

"I forgot. Listen, the church reading was about 666. I went home and read the book of Revelation, the part that talked about 666," Dickerson's voice rushed.

"Where is this story going?" interrupted Detective Pinkett.

"Just hush and pay attention."

"Yes ma'am."

"As I was saying, after reading the book I thought about the HLA."

"I'm not following, because I don't see a connection."

"Maybe there is none, but what if the 666 in the Bible is B66?"

There was a momentary pause at the other end, and then Pinkett replied, "Okay, let's look at this closely. The Bible says 666, you have B66. I don't see the match."

"I know…I know," Dickerson contended, "but you cannot deny the fact that B66 is, as I explained to you, found in criminals with what might be called 'hellish' intentions."

"Even if they are, are you suggesting that these people are devils…or whatever?"

"I don't know what I am suggesting, because this whole thing does not make any sense."

"Exactly. No match, no connections, makes no sense, case closed."

"Thanks for your help," Dickerson said in exasperation.

"I am the one here trying to be realistic."

"I know you are. There has to be a scientific explanation though."

"When you find out, could you please let me know?" Pinky ended on a sarcastic note.

After that conversation, Dr. Dickerson fixed her customary breakfast of two pieces of toast, one boiled egg, black coffee, and an orange juice. While eating breakfast, she decided to go back to the church library and find out all she could about the book of Revelation.

At the library, not finding any significant answers, except that the book was written using unfamiliar symbols by St. John during the early years of Christian persecution at the hands of the Romans, Dickerson went to work the next day still in awe and bewildered over the possible connections between an ancient revelations and modern-day science.

At the ten a.m. medical rounds, the subject was Ankylosing Spondylitis, a disease affecting the spinal joints. It had a high predilection for HLA B27. Seizing on that, Dickerson began.

"Dr. Pavigoose, what is your understanding of the HLA system?" Dickerson asked the third-year resident; a shy, introverted man who thought Dr. Dickerson always picked on him.

"I think the HLA systems define compatibility," began Dr. Pavigoose, who, even though shy, was nonetheless intelligent, and quick with his responses. A characteristic admired by Dickerson.

"Yes, go on."

"It defines individuality and orchestrates a rejection when foreign tissues or organs are introduced in the body."

"How does it define or mark an individual?" asked Dr. Dickerson.

"Current literatures suggest that individuals with specific and well-characterized HLAs may be prone to manifest specific diseases or characteristics."

"Impressive, Dr. Pavigoose, you've been following the literature."

A faint smile gleamed on Dr. Pavigoose's face.

"What we do know today about the HLAs, especially the B loci, is that it has that uniqueness to single out disease processes in certain individuals." Dickerson eyeballed the rest of the morning round team. "Most importantly, as you will be hearing in the near future, is that B loci may be associated with human characteristics. The telling point, at this time, is that it may predetermine behavior."

"Is it similar to the predestination theory report by Dr. Abramhoff at the Loop University in Chicago?" ask Dr. Pavigoose.

"Something like that," replied Dickerson.

# CHAPTER THIRTEEN

The snow on 61st Street off United States Highway Sixty-five in Hobart, Indiana, looked like a glistening white powder on this early February morning. It was a cold Saturday morning, and it had snowed all night long.

Alexander Andalusia, with great caution, guided the Ford truck he was driving, concentrating on the road in anticipation of sudden ice patches.

61st Street, the second road off Highway Sixty-five to Hobart, was still under a massive reconstruction into a four-lane tarred road.

Alex had been through this road multiple times, and knew where the hidden ice patches might be located. Not that he had not veered off the road once or twice before, but each had resulted only in minor incidents.

He arrived at the Marathon Gas Station to fill up the truck and pick up a shovel.

Looking at his watch in a surprised gesture, Steve, the store manager inquired, "What are you doing up this early, Alex? It's only…five o'clock."

"Hey Steve, good morning." Alex smiled, and stumped his boots on the outdoor carpet to shake off the snow.

"Morning," replied Steve, wondering why Alex did not have a scarf around his neck since it must be at least ten degrees below zero, counting the wind-chill factor.

"I just need to get me little gasoline and pick up a shovel to work on my barn," Alex replied.

"You should have waited for daylight on this God-forsaken day, so that you could at least see where you are going," Steve insisted.

"You know me, early to bed and early to rise."

"I see, I see…says the blind man to the deaf wife," said Steve in jest.

"Early morning sense of humor," remarked Alex.

"No better time!" Steve responded.

"What time do you normally go to bed?" Steve inquired begrudgingly.

"Oh…usually nine or ten at night," Alex gestured with his hand.

With that, Alex picked up a new Winchester shovel, pulled out his wallet, paid for his purchases, and headed home.

"Have a nice day," Steve waved.

Alex resumed the journey home.

Reaching the T-intersection of 61st and Arizona Street, he nearly veered off the road toward the snowy parched fields on the left side of the street.

*Nerves,* Alex rationalized.

Controlling the steering better, Alex completed the turn and made it to the house without further incident. He arrived at the wood-crafted gate entrance to the compound, closed the gate behind him, and then drove straight to the barn. He picked up the shovel and carefully hid it behind the dirt table that he used to cut different shapes of wood.

Alex had a gift at carpentry. He could take a piece of log, set it on the table, and in about three to four hours could carve out a wooden bird or a wooden horse. The barn became a messy collection of Alex's different carpentry work.

Cathy, Alex's wife, on one occasion, ventured into the barn, came out and requested Alex to clean up the barn in some organized fashion, or she would clean it herself. It was a request that brought a very angry look from Alex. Ever since Alex married Cathy some three years ago, he had always considered her a nag. She would nag about this, and nag about that, and Alex hated nagging.

"Between your job and that stupid barn, I don't think you have enough time to get me pregnant," Cathy angrily responded during one of their exchanges.

That was really hitting below the belt, Alex thought, and since then he had vowed to put an end to that.

"Wake up, sweetheart," said Alex, nudging Cathy.

"W…hat?" came a sleepy voice under the jumbled bed covers.

"I need for you to help me at the barn," Alex requested.

"What time is it?" inquired the sleepy voice.

"About five thirty," replied Alex.

"What the heck are you doing in the barn this early in the morning?" asked Cathy.

"You're the one that asked me to tidy up," replied Alex.

"Can't this wait till daybreak?" asked Cathy.

"It ain't gonna take that long, and I need for you to help me make a decision," answered Alex.

*That's odd!* Cathy thought to herself. Alex had never before asked her to help him do anything, especially in the barn.

How many times had he yelled at her for messing around in the barn, "*snooping around*" he called it. Cathy thought the barn was off limits, a place where Alex took out his frustrations by making useless wooden caricatures.

Her curiosity awakened; Cathy got up and bundled herself with her thick nightgown, then followed her husband to the barn.

"This way, honey," Alex directed her to the eastern corner of the barn facing the hay.

As she turned to inquire what the hay had to do with the pile of junk on the other side, Alex swung at her with the shovel right on the forehead.

Cathy did not even have time to scream. She fell to the ground severely wounded, blood pouring out of her right eye.

Alex, smirking at the face, and realizing Cathy's motionless state, finally stopped swinging the blood-soaked shovel and sat on the pile of hay to catch his breath.

Rest over, Alex starting digging on the eastern corner of the barn. He took care not to disturb the old digs.

At ten a.m. there was some noise at the front of the compound. Alex, almost finished with the four-foot-deep hole, peered out the closed door of the barn to see who it was.

It was the mailman putting the mail in the mailbox.

Alex intently watched the mail truck drive away without incident. He picked up Cathy's limp body, dragged it into the hole, and neatly laid her down like a corpse in a coffin, hands across the chest. He covered the body with an old blanket that he purposely left in the barn, then proceeded to fill up the hole with dirt.

Alex then picked up seven piles of hay and laid them neatly over the new dig. Task completed, Alex went into the house, took a shower, cooked scrambled eggs and bacon, turned on the television, ate, and made plans for the evening at Judy's Crab house on Route 30.

# CHAPTER FOURTEEN

Judy's Crab house had been a popular Hobart fast food diner with a flair for the extraordinary. Decorated by different old paintings on the wall, it boasted collections of old memorabilia of popular movie stars. Everybody loved Judy's place. It became a popular eatery, not just because the foods there were well prepared and tasted good, but also the waitresses were something to behold.

Low cut, short-sleeved shirts, with cleverly exposed cleavage, must have been a requirement for waitressing at Judy's Crab house.

Lots of single women dined out there with their friends, most wanting to be picked up for a date. At 5:30 p.m., Alex walked into Judy's place. He sat at an end table close to the door so he could see every woman coming in. He ordered king crab legs with mashed potatoes off the dinner menu. Some female customers came in, but none were good enough for Alex. Alex settled in his chair, waiting for dinner to arrive.

Mona and two of her friends came through the door. Mona immediately noticed Alex. Mona had been a friend of Alex and Cathy for sixteen months, ever since they met at the Super K-mart shopping store in Portage, Indiana.

"That will be $67.23," said the petite, five-feet-eight-inch-tall cashier.

"Are you paying for it?" Alex asked Cathy.

"Yeah I am," grumbled Cathy. "Who else is gonna pay for it?"

"You folks from here?" asked the cashier.

*What a beautiful smile,* thought Alex.

"Yes," answered Cathy, searching for the wallet in the handbag, "This is Alex, my husband, and I am Cathy."

*She is too pretty for this job, and what a body.* Alex was still in his thoughts.

"I'm Mona," replied the cashier.

"Hi, Mona," Alex was quick to greet.

"Are you gonna help with the bags?" asked Cathy, noticing the admiration from Alex.

Since that first encounter, however, Mona and the Andalusia family had become good friends. Mona made frequent visits, and Cathy was always willing to help Mona.

"Hi, Alex," greeted Mona.

"Hi, Mona," answered Alex.

"Where is Cathy?"

The look on Alex's face told Mona immediately that something was wrong.

"What happened?" asked Mona, as she pulled a chair and sat down.

"Hey Mona, are you coming?" one of her companions asked.

"You guys go ahead and order; I'm gonna talk to Alex for a few," said Mona.

"So, tell me…what happened?" Mona pulled closer to Alex while looking at him straight in the eyes.

"Cathy left me," Alex replied in a sorrowful voice.

"Why?" asked Mona, resting her right hand across her chest.

"Well, she called me a slob, told me to clean the barn, the kitchen, the house, or she's gonna leave."

"That's not fair."

"That's what I thought," Alex replied hastily.

"I thought the…the two of you were getting along fine. I never imagined that there was any animosity or friction between the two of you."

"Cathy has been kind of depressed lately. She blames me for us not having children, and I think that started it all," Alex answered, his face lowered as he looked intently at the table.

"I don't know what to say."

"There isn't…anything to say."

"Where did she go?" a teary-eyed Mona asked.

"She went back to New Jersey. That's where her folks are from."

"Yeah, I know."

"Your friends will be offended if you don't join them in a minute," Alex suggested.

"Can I drop by to see you just for a few?" Mona asked.

"Anytime, I am by myself now," Alex responded.

"How about tomorrow, say two p.m.?" suggested Mona.

"Two would be perfect because that would give me time for church," replied Alex, acutely aware of Mona's religious beliefs.

A faint smile lit up Mona's face at the mention of the word church.

At exactly two p.m. Sunday afternoon there was a knock on the door.

"Who is it?" Alex asked formally, knowing full well who it was.

"Alex, it's me."

Opening the front door, Alex smiled and invited Mona in.

The house was as Mona remembered it. It was the same old country farm house sitting on a five-acre lot. There was a horse barn to the west of the house. That barn had been left unattended since there were no more horses there after Alexis' father's death six years ago.

A small stream from the little Calumet River could be heard running several feet behind the house. Green grassy plains around the stream gave the appearance of an old English country setting near a vineyard. A wooded garage still stood near the end of the stream as it left the lot.

"Hi, Alex," Mona smiled.

"Come in," invited Alex.

"I made some tuna sandwiches with potato chips. There is also Pepsi; I hope you like them."

"Oh that's nice; I am starved," replied Mona.

"Come on then," invited Alex, leading Mona to the kitchen.

Sitting down at the dining table looking around, Mona was surprised how Alex kept the house relatively clean.

"I have not seen you guys in two weeks," Mona commented.

Alex just shrugged.

"So how long has Cathy been gone?" Mona continued to make conversation.

"Oh, about ten days ago," replied Alex, scratching his forehead.

"You have not heard from her since?"

"She told me she's never gonna come back. As a matter of fact, I got served divorce papers while she has leaving."

*That does not make any sense,* Mona rationalized. *Why would Cathy leave like that without telling anyone? That's very unlike Cathy. Maybe she was embarrassed that her marriage was failing.*

Mona could understand that; after all, she left her husband, took the kids, and moved back to Hobart.

"You know that I am your friend as well as Cathy's," Mona said.

"I know," answered Alex. "That's why I am really happy you are here, because these past few days have been brutal, and not having too many friends makes it more difficult."

Mona felt special. She placed her hand on Alex's shoulder in comfort. Immediately, Alex grabbed the hand on the shoulder and squeezed it, then artfully led Mona to the bedroom.

Six months after that encounter, Alex married Mona.

Mona's children, Misha and Berth, were so disapproving of the union that they refused to move to Hobart with their mother, choosing instead to live with the grandparents in Valparaiso, Indiana.

Like a hummingbird in midsummer night's dream, Mona was in love again. Even though Alex's divorce papers had not been completely finalized or even shown to her, arrangements were being made for an October wedding.

A private wedding was planned at the courthouse in Crown Point, Indiana, at the justice of the peace.

"Are you sure this is what you want to do?" asked Alex for the sixth time in the past two weeks.

"Yes! Yes! Yes!" answered Mona. "Don't worry about my parents and kids; they will come around."

"Do you wanna have kids?" asked Alex.

"I don't know! I have two already," responded Mona, guarding her answer, acutely aware of Alex's sensitivity of being fatherless. "And you know I am thirty-eight years old, but if you seriously want a child, I'm willing to try."

"I can't wait for you to be my wife."

Mona smiled briskly.

"What are you going to do with the whole compound?" Mona asked.

"Oh, I don't know," answered Alex. "Maybe sell it and move to Chicago."

"Oh please, not Chicago," implored Mona. "Maybe to Munster, at least it's close to Chicago."

"I buy that," responded Alex.

After the wedding, Mona moved in with Alex. During the first six months, they were happy being married.

Shortly, however, Mona began to notice that all was not well with Alex. For one thing, he would not let her roam, inquire, or tidy up that darn barn.

He claimed that the barn was his parents' hiding place and that he usurped it for his own private use, and no matter how messy it might be, he knew where everything was.

"I respect that," agreed Mona.

"Thanks," said Alex, delighted.

The next week Alex came home one day from working at the Johnson Mobile Electric Company. When supper was finished, Alex went to the barn to retrieve a hammer, which he wanted to use at the compound gate.

He noticed that the table to the west corner has been moved slightly and the dust on top of it has been cleaned. He quickly dropped the hammer and went back to the house.

"Have you been in my barn?" Alex demanded in a menacing voice.

"What do you mean *your* barn? I thought we were married."

"Yes, my barn," Alex re-affirmed. "I told you to keep off that darn barn."

"I only went in to look for the hammer," Mona answered in an innocent manner.

"Did I not tell you to leave that barn alone?" Alex demanded.

"I know you did, but…"

"Aren't no *buts* here; I told you that's my family's secret place."

"I am sorry," apologized Mona.

"Don't you ever do that again!" Alex commanded.

That was the beginning of a six-month back and forth bickering between them, mostly initiated by Alex with eventual apology by Mona.

Mona, sensing that this marriage was not exactly the way she had envisioned it, initiated routine daily phone communications with her family.

Soon, she made up with the kids, then with her parents. She would on occasion drive to Valparaiso to visit and would be gone most mornings before going to work at the Super K-Mart where she still worked as a cashier.

"You seem to be getting a lot closer to your family than this family," Alex asked one day when Mona returned from a trip to Valparaiso.

"They are my family. I can't completely ignore them," Mona responded.

"So what do we have here, a non-family?" Alex looked at Mona with clenched teeth.

"You are my husband. My parents and children are my flesh and blood," Mona said as a matter of fact.

Alex did not like that at all; in fact, he demanded an explanation from her.

"There is nothing to explain. We are husband and wife, and they are my father, mother, and children," Mona restated.

"You are trying to squeeze me out of the picture because I have no children."

"Don't be ridiculous!"

"I am not," Alex insisted.

Two days later, Alex asked Mona to drive his Ford Escort to the store for gas and to pick up some toilet paper.

Mona wanted to drive her own car but Alex insisted that the Escort needed gasoline and that he had to finish fixing the leak in the kitchen.

The smell of gasoline warned Mona that something was wrong with this wretched old car. She cranked the engine up anyway, put the car in drive, and then started toward the bend leading to the gate. She approached the sharp bend, halfway between the house and the gate. At the bend, an unprotected deep ravine made winter driving a little treacherous.

Alex and Mona were used to the bend, but to a stranger it could be a little dangerous.

"What happened to the brakes?" asked Mona as the car was cruising to the bend at a higher speed than normal.

She tried again to brake, but to no avail. At the bend, she panicked and lost control, and the car rolled into the ditch.

The quickness of the entire incident took Mona by surprise.

After a temporary loss of consciousness, she woke up to an excruciating pain on her head, and blood running down her nose. She appeared pinned to the steering wheel, because all attempts to move were very painful and fruitless. She heard some noise on the road. Realizing Alex's footsteps, she attempted to scream while coughing.

"Alex, please help me!"

There was no response. She felt some drizzling, and the strong smell convinced Mona that the gasoline must be leaking. Suddenly the entire car was engulfed in flame.

Mona could have sworn that she saw Alex throw a lighted match at the car. Breathing became difficult for Mona. She could feel and smell her skin burning. That was less painful than the hunger for air.

Alex ran to the house and called for help. The Hobart Fire Department arrived in approximately seven minutes, extinguished the flames, and pulled out Mona's charred body from the wreckage. The incident, after brief investigation by Hobart Fire Department, was ruled an accident.

# CHAPTER FIFTEEN

Months went by, and Alex met Chrissie at The Red Grape Bar and Grill in the Miller section of Gary, Indiana.

Chrissie was a tough gal, Alex surmised.

She liked Alex's muscular body a lot. Chrissie worked out at the Curves in Merrillville, Indiana, and had long admired muscular men.

"You look rather muscular," commented Chrissie, openly admiring Alex's physique. "Do you work out?"

"You might say that," Alex smiled. "I do a lot of physical labor, and in my spare time I lift weights at the Hudson Campbell Center."

"I can't stand stale men, you know, those pencil pushers who do no manual labor," Chrissie pointed out. "For a country girl like me, I like my men meaty."

After six months of courtship, Chrissie agreed to marry Alex.

"I read about what happened with your ex. She drove the car into that ravine and it caught fire, and she died in the blaze?" Chrissie started while both were sitting at the dinning table one evening.

"Yeah, that's about it." Alex did not want to discuss the incident any further.

"You know I am always here for you," said Chrissie matter-of-factly, while tapping on Alex's shoulder.

For months, Alex and Chrissie argued about the barn. Chrissie soon convinced Alex that she was no stranger to arguments.

"I would like to go in the barn and build something too," demanded Chrissie. "My parents are from Minnesota, and when I was a child my dad would let me use the barn all the time."

"Not this barn."

"Tell me, why not?"

"Because it is a family treasure passed down to me by my dad."

"I don't buy that for a second," answered Chrissie. "Barns are not family treasures. Houses, cars, paintings, boats are family treasures. A barn is just a construction farmers use to store hay and do odds-and-ends jobs."

"Trust me, this barn is different."

"What makes it so different?"

"I was told by my dad, that's what." Alex was getting upset.

"Do you believe everything your dad tells you?" Chrissie asked.

"Yes, I do."

"Well, I don't."

Six days later, Chrissie's hunger and her curiosity for the barn, reached a critical level that she forgo the consequences and promenaded into the barn. As she entered the barn, there was Alex sitting on a pile of hay, shovel in one hand, and hammer in the other.

"What are you doing here?" Alex wanted to know. "I thought I told you not to come in here."

"Yeah you did, but I cannot resist," Chrissie explained.

"You are one heck of a curious wench!"

"I have been called worse than that before," Chrissie proudly proclaimed.

"Well do you know what happens to curious cats?"

"Yeah, yeah, they get killed," replied Chrissie, looking curiously around not noticing Alex surreptitious moves toward her.

Alex must have swung multiple times at an unsuspected Chrissie. He did not count.

When Alex finally stopped swinging the hammer, he noticed to his surprise that Chrissie was still breathing.

He picked up the shovel and with one heavy swing smashed Chrissie to death.

When the fire department finally put out the fire on the barn, nothing was left.

Alex denied knowledge of the origin of the fire. He told Fire Detective Ben Torres that Chrissie must have gone into the barn with a lamp, as there was no electricity in the barn. She must have tripped and fell and set the barn on fire.

Combing through the barn, Detective Torres noticed a body that had been burned beyond recognition. Forensic analysis confirmed that it was Chrissie, and she might have started the fire, but the multiple holes on her head were beyond explanation.

Alex was taken to the Hobart Police Department for questioning, and he of course denied ever hitting his wife. Alex, sounding believable, gave all sorts of plausible explanations.

In the end, Officer Torres decided to take a second look at the barn, a couple of days later. Walking on the grounds, in what was once the barn he tripped over a softly covered manhole.

Picking himself up, he noticed that the soil where the hole existed was lower than the rest of the ground.

The local newspapers called it a gruesome discovery.

Four bodies were discovered in a dig at Alex's barn site. His father, his mother, Sophia Busby, a twenty-four-year-old hitchhiker believed missing ten years ago, and that case remained unsolved, and Cathy.

The jury found Alex guilty of murder in all five counts. Alex avoided the death penalty on an insanity plea. He was instead sentenced to multiple life imprisonments at the State Psychiatric Hospital in New Lisbon, Indiana.

# CHAPTER SIXTEEN

Abramhoff entered his office early Monday morning, and, for the first time in weeks, exhibited a happy smile.

*Whatever happened in Orlando must have been good for him,* thought Sabrina.

Abramhoff hardly smiled on Mondays.

Being at the position, and the person he perceived, Abramhoff always maintained that serious look and would only respond when spoken to. He did not generally initiate a conversation.

"How are you this beautiful morning, Sabrina?" Abramhoff inquired with a smile.

"Fine, sir," a flabbergasted Sabrina responded. "Your trip must have yielded dividend."

"Dividend is not the word," said Abramhoff. "It was a fantastic weekend. I think this is the beginning of my whole life's theory, and the proof of that theory is now at my fingertips."

"What theory is that, sir?" asked Sabrina innocently.

"That of predestination," said Abramhoff with a stir in his eyes as if Sabrina should have known by now.

"I'm sorry, sir."

"Not to worry, Dr. Dickerson from San Diego came up with the right mixture of chromatography in order to isolate that HLA gene. We have been after this locus for a while, and we had great difficulty isolating it."

Sometimes, Abramhoff talked to Sabrina like he was talking to one of his colleagues. Abramhoff expected most people around him to understand and follow his logic at all times. Sabrina, the mistress of deduction, always sensed which direction her boss was shifting his argument, and always picked up bits and pieces of the heavy medical terminology, and used them to urge him forward.

Abramhoff, on the other hand, acutely aware of Sabrina's limitations, would invariably discuss technical conversations with her, and was always amazed at her responses.

*With just a two-year college education, she tends to have a better understanding of subject matters than most second year medical students,* thought Dr. Abramhoff.

"So that will make it easy for the project in Kankakee," contended Sabrina.

"Exactly," answered Abramhoff.

"She, Dr. Dickerson that is, not only identified the correct chemical solution but also was able to localize the type of individuals most likely to be positive."

"It looks like she has done her homework," said an excited Sabrina.

"She just might have paved the way for simplification of the Kankakee Project."

There was a knock on the door.

"I forgot, sir, Dr. Achampi has an appointment for 8:30 a.m.," Sabrina announced.

"I know, bring him in to the conference room. I will meet him there," Abramhoff instructed, as he headed to the bathroom.

Sabrina was still in shock about how loose Dr. Abramhoff had been that morning, especially with his demeanor and his conversations. That was rare for her and she loved every moment of it.

"Come in, Dr. Achampi," beckoned Sabrina, as she opened the door.

"Hi, Sabrina, Dr. Abramhoff is expecting me."

"Yes, he is. He asked that you wait for him in the conference room," said Sabrina, leading Dr. Achampi to the mahogany table and leather-seated conference room.

Dr. Achampi sat at the middle of the large table, admiring the plaques on the wall. *Dr. Abramhoff has amassed a lot of plaques and numerous recognition awards in his lifetime*, thought Achampi. He particularly admired the recently acquired plaque from the governor congratulating Dr. Abramhoff on his achievement in the field of medical advancements. He remembered the meeting with the governor at the Hilton Hotel.

"Good morning, Dr. Abramhoff," said Dr. Achampi, as Dr. Abramhoff walked into the conference room.

"Good morning," answered Dr. Abramhoff. "How was your weekend?"

"Excellent, sir, I traveled to Munster, Indiana, to visit my folks."

"How is your dad? He had what…a mild coronary last week?"

"Yeah, he is doing very well. He is taking his aspirin and beta blocker, and they seem to be helping."

"Glad to hear it."

"How was your trip to Orlando?" said Dr. Achampi, a little uncomfortable talking about his parents.

"It was wonderful. That's why I called you for this meeting. Care for a cup of coffee?" Abramhoff offered.

"Sure."

After both fixed their coffees, they picked up their crystal china cups and saucers and headed to the conference table. Dr. Abramhoff sat at the head.

"We are now in a position to blow this whole project wide open," began Abramhoff.

"We are?" asked a curious Achampi.

"Yes we are," confirmed an excited Abramhoff. "Do you know Dr. Dickerson from San Diego?"

"I have heard of her. Isn't she the one who is also working on the HLA antigen loci?"

"That's her. What do you know of her work?"

"I read an article she authored in the journal a couple of years ago about the veracity of the HLA B loci and the possibility of its association to deviancy."

"That's just the beginning of her experiment."

"It is?"

"She went further than we did. She presented a paper at the conference, and in that report she specifically linked HLA B66 to criminality."

"How did she do that? We have been working on that for almost two years now, and we have not been able to isolate a specific position on the B loci."

"Well," explained Abramhoff, "after her presentations, I was able to have dinner with her. She went into a little bit more detail about her experiment.

"What made the difference," continued Dr. Abramhoff "is in the gel mixture she used to isolate the HLA loci."

"How so?" asked Dr. Achampi.

"Well, she added a 5 percent dextrose solution of ethylene benzoic."

"Isn't that the new untested purification solution for DNA extractions?"

"Yes," answered Abramhoff.

"Why didn't we think of that?"

"Using the new purified solution, she not only did not drop any established HLA B loci, but was able to isolate HLA B66 as the position that identifies criminality." Abramhoff's sense of jealousy was obvious to Achampi.

"No kidding," responded an impressed Achampi.

"What's more, she has already experimented on it."

"How did she do that?"

"She did not go into detail, but she was able to use the help of San Diego Police Department and has shown that the most heinous criminals, like that guy in Hobart, what's his name? Alex Andalusia, are almost all HLA B66 positive."

"Really," said Achampi, still amazed. "That kind of makes our job a little easier, don't you think?"

"That's exactly my thinking," Abramhoff concurred.

"So where do we go from here?" inquired Dr. Achampi.

"I have it all planned out," Abramhoff explained. "We will pursue an executive order or permission signed by the governor. We will then isolate the worst of the worst in the maximum security section of Kankakee Prison. We will probably need a minimum of 200 subjects to make a scientific statement. We may also need heinous cases from our neighboring states; like that same Alexander Andalusia guy from Indiana, whom I can bet my life, will be positive for the HLA B66."

"That nut, oh yap, I bet he is," Achampi concurred.

"I need you, then, to get a list of all inmates at the Kankakee maximum-security prison. Select those with heinous crimes, and then randomly pick about 200 to 500 of them. In reciprocity, we will pay 200 to 500 medical students, and, if possible, residents, for age- and sex-matched cohorts."

"Dr. Dickerson did not randomize her sample I presume?" asked Achampi.

"No, she did not," answered Abramhoff. "That's why her findings are anecdotal. Ours will grace the cover of JAMA."

"I would probably need some extra…," said Achampi.

"Whatever extra money you need," Abramhoff interrupted, seeming to read his mind, "Sabrina will handle the expenses. Also use as many staff members from the research fellowship as you need."

The buzzing of the phone brought a moment of diversion to the conversation.

A few moments later, Sabrina knocked at the door.

"Come in," yelled Abramhoff.

"Dr. Dickerson from San Diego," whispered Sabrina.

"Anything else?" asked Abramhoff looking at Achampi.

"Not that I can think of," answered Achampi.

"Can you then report back to me, say…Thursday or Friday?"

"That would be fine, sir."

Dr. Achampi left through the side conference room door, and Abramhoff went straight to his office and closed the door behind him.

# CHAPTER SEVENTEEN

"Hello, Regina," Abramhoff greeted.

"How are you, David?"

"I'm fine. To what do I owe this call?"

"I was just calling to see whether you have any new leads."

"As a matter of fact, I just finished a conference with my assistant, Dr. Achampi. We are going to conduct a scientific research using your theory."

"How are you going to do that?"

"The governor has already signed on to our project, so we will use his executive decree and conduct a full-scale research with a random comparative population."

"What random comparative population will you use?"

"We will use paid medical students and willing residents, of course."

"That's easy enough," agreed Dickerson.

"I think you probably need to expand your sample population, and match them with students also."

"Yes, I can certainly expand my inmate population, but what population size are you planning to work with?"

"I told my associate to gather data from 200 to 500."

"Oh, that's going to be a difficult number for me. I am only working through our local police department and the San Diego Correction Facility. My highest ranking supporter is the chief of police."

"Well, gather as much as you can, and compare them to the student populations."

"Okay, I will try that," agreed Dickerson.

Expecting to say good-bye, Dr. Dickerson instead asked, "By the way, are you a religious person?"

Taken back a little bit and surprised by the questioning, because nobody had ever asked Dr. Abramhoff of what persuasion he was. In fact, religious conversation hardly came up during any of his academic discussions.

"I am, why?"

"Do you go to church?"

"Often enough," Abramhoff added.

"You should read the Bible more often. I find it educational."

"I will remember that," answered Dr. Abramhoff skeptically.

"Call me as soon as you have something, and I will do the same."

Dr. Abramhoff wondered why she brought religion into the conversation. *What was that all about?*

666

For the next couple of months, there were several telephone conversations between Abramhoff and Dickerson. Dr. Dickerson was able to solicit more help from the warden through the persuasive powers of the San Diego Chief of Police. They were able to add about 200 more hardcore prisoners on death row for testing.

Dr. Abramhoff, for his part, banked over 500 inmates from the states of Illinois, Indiana, and Wisconsin.

"How did you get the medical students to sign informed consent?" asked Abramhoff.

"What I have been telling them here is that we have a new genetic marker that might predict criminal behaviors, and it has not been a major problem. You know what will be the ultimate dilemma, especially when the test results are tabulated—what will happen if and when some of the medical students or residents test positive?" said Dickerson.

"Now that's an intriguing question," Abramhoff agreed. "We can always invoke the privacy act, especially in view of the new HIPPA regulations."

"Always the politician," Dickerson responded. "But seriously, what shall we do with the positives in the comparative population?"

"I really don't know, but they will not be able to know either unless they sue," Abramhoff stated matter-of-factly.

"Let's, for the moment, suppose they do just that."

Sensing a very serious concern in Dickerson's tone of voice, Abramhoff skillfully suggested, "Then I think we need to engage the state attorney general's office early rather than later."

"I think that's a good idea."

# CHAPTER EIGHTEEN

Abramhoff spent the entire evening and into the wee hours of night pouring over and pondering the analytical data given to him from the statistics department of the medical school.

Having convinced himself of the results, he called Dr. Achampi to join him in his office.

It was about 9:17 p.m.

The drive from Lakefront towers, where Achampi rented a one-bedroom apartment condo, to the university was short, but the traffic on Lakeshore Drive did not help matters any. It only added time for Achampi to contemplate the possible scenarios that would have precipitated Abramhoff to make this urgent late-night call. Perhaps the Center for Disease Control and Prevention, the CDC, finally approved the multimillion dollar grants.

But that would come in the mail and everyone would have known about it during the day. Perhaps, Pfizer people must have called late to give Abramhoff a heads up on the approval of their grant request, because if they had disapproved it, Abramhoff most certainly would not have called. That had not been Abramhoff's style. He was too vain to accept defeat, and on top of that, had to broadcast the bad news late in the evening.

Dr. Abramhoff's face looked joyous, sitting in his office flipping over what appeared to be a printed report.

"Good evening, sir," Achampi greeted.

"Hi, Maxwell," responded Abramhoff, calling Dr. Achampi by his first name. "We have good news."

Achampi was already anticipating some kind of good news from Abramhoff.

"This is the preliminary analysis of the data from the statistic department on the numbers collected from Kankakee death row as compared to our medical students and staff residents."

"Oh," said Dr. Achampi, who had anticipated otherwise.

"Here," Abramhoff handed over the entire report to Achampi.

Achampi studied the report intently, and then declared, "That's amazing. 93 percent of the death row inmates we tested were positive, while less than 2 percent of our staff tested positive. According to them, that's nearly 99 percent sensitivity and specificity with a confidence interval of almost 99 percent."

Abramhoff sat there speechless, face glowing.

"That's unbelievable," continued Achampi in amazement.

"Few, if any, scientific testing has yielded such positive findings," Abramhoff agreed.

"That goes to the core proof that HLA B66 is the marker for hardcore criminals," added Achampi.

"Yes, and what else?" urged Abramhoff, ever the instructor.

"Kind of, through the back door, lends credence to the theory of predestination," ventured Dr. Achampi.

"No! I don't subscribe to the theory of the back-door entrance," argued Abramhoff, with his right index finger pointing at the document with vivacity. "This is through the front door.

"This directly is our front door for the basic concept of predestination. Look, it proves that heinous criminals are preprogrammed or destined for their criminality. The question, therefore, is what other preprogrammed behaviors exist on the HLA antigen that have not yet been discovered?

"The way I see it," continued Dr. Abramhoff, "when all the positions are finally discovered on the HLA antigen, we may be able to determine who is destined to succeed in life, and who is destined for failure, and in theory determine who is destined to commit crimes. Heck, we might even be able to determine who is destined to be the president of the United States."

"A little science fiction, don't you think?" said Achampi, calming the conversation to reality, as he sensed Abramhoff's euphoric disposition.

"Yeah it is, but who would have thought in a million years that we would be able to quantify, and in the process determine the link, that connects all criminal elements together?"

"Heinous criminals mostly on death row," corrected Dr. Achampi.

"Yes, for now, but with further testing I am convinced it will eventually be translated to all criminals."

"That will require a lot of testing."

"Yes, but with this result now, you watch."

666

"Our results are simply phenomenal!" proclaimed Abramhoff on an early-morning telephone call to Dickerson.

"Which results?" Dickerson inquired, as she signed a document placed in front of her by her secretary.

"The percentage of positive HLA we discovered on our death row inmates."

"I told you in Orlando about my preliminary findings."

"The statistics are overwhelming," continued Dr. Abramhoff, opening the blinds to peer at the traffic streaming along Lakeshore Drive. "I received the statistical analysis yesterday, and our results were close to 92 percent."

"That actually reconfirmed what I already observed." Dickerson motioned to the secretary to hold off on the second document. "I actually was able to add an extra 472 death row inmates to our data, and needless to say, the analysis remained the same."

"So you think that we are onto something?" Abramhoff could hardly contain himself.

Dickerson smiled because she realized that her research finally had a collaborator.

"Yes, and I believe this is just a beginning." Dickerson motioned to the secretary to give her five more minutes. "So what's next?"

"The news media, don't you think?"

"Why?" Dickerson's smile immediately faded. Repositioning herself on the chair, she suggested, "I thought we could collaborate and publish our findings first, before the media exposure."

"Yes, in a standard debatable study such as a 60 percent positive finding." Abramhoff finally sat down. "But with this magnitude of positive findings, we can do both simultaneously."

"But what would come of it?" asked Dickerson, who had expressed her aversion to the news media previously.

"Two things," Abramhoff sensed the lack of enthusiasm from Dickerson. "One, we will launch a national awareness, and secondly and most important of all, we will be able to garner any amount of money we ask for."

*He might be right, but I hate to politicize this,* Dickerson thought.

"One question that needs answering, however, is what to make of the less than 2 percent positive finding in the student population," she again queried.

"Listen, we will make that question the core of our national agenda, the finding that 1 to 2 percent of the population, who are normal in behavior, yet will ultimately test positive on the HLA," Abramhoff theorized.

"I see where you are going with that. You think that there might be a trigger mechanism on the HLA B66 positive folks."

"Exactly," concurred Abramhoff, right hand clenched in delight that finally Dickerson agreed. "Take the case of that British physician who killed twenty-three of his widowed patients over a span of fifteen years. He was, after all, a perfectly normal and respected doctor in the community until he was caught."

Dickerson wondered about that. There were, after all, other cases just like Abramhoff mentioned. Also her research had suffered immensely because of inadequate funding from the university. National exposure would invariably pump in the necessary money she needed to take her research to the next level. Her conscience, however, still bothered her about labeling individuals' criminal intent, even before they commit any crime.

With more funding and further testing, there might be a way to avert that.

"So what media outlet should we use?" asked Dickerson, finally consenting to the media exposure, even though she had never faced the media before.

"I have always been biased toward the CBS station in Chicago. I know the general manager. I can contact him, and he can give us an exclusive interview, or we can call a general news conference in Chicago or San Diego and invite all the news outlets."

"I prefer the second option but, how do we get all to attend?"

"Don't worry about that, here we have a public relations department that will arrange all that. Believe me, when they beckon, all the news outlets, including the print media, will be there."

tas...

"For pu... ...kerson responded in
asked Abramhoff.

"I have always liked the ... ...uld you prefer?"
Medical Association."

...merican

"That's fair enough."

They finally agreed to have the news conference in Chicago in two weeks, on Wednesday at two p.m. central time, noon pacific time.

Dickerson would fly to Chicago the weekend prior to the news conference. Sabrina would arrange for all her flights, and also a hotel stay at the Hyatt.

Monday and Tuesday would be spent coordinating and going over data from both campuses, for eventual publication, and also in preparation for the press.

Waking up early Saturday mornings had always been difficult for Marion Moheri.

Somehow, in the back of his mind, he realized that he really did not have to get up this early in the morning, especially on Saturdays, but with Mr. Moheri's schedule at the Johnston's Chemicals, his internal alarm always woke him up every 5:30 a.m. This early April Saturday morning was rather pleasant.

A small, bobolink songbird, perched on the birch tree overlooking the bedroom window, was chirping away a tone that sounded like the instrumental version of "Amazing Grace."

Marion lay there on the bed, eyes wide open.

Susan was snoring away at the other end of the bed. Susan Moheri always snored. Closer to dawn, her snoring would degenerate into a deep multi-nasal melody, that once Marion woke up it was practically impossible for him to go back to sleep. Each night, he made every effort to be in bed asleep prior to Susan; otherwise he needed a glass of gin mixed with few drops of tonic water to fall asleep enough not to be disturbed by Susan's early-night monotonous grunts.

Most times Marion had done that, he had invariably woken up the next morning with a slight hangover.

Entering the bathroom fully awake, Marion turned on the lights. He brushed his teeth and gurgled with a mouth rinse. He showered, dressed in his weekend business casual attire, kissed sleeping Susan good-bye, and headed to the office.

Today, he was meeting with Tina Coffee, the assistant research fellow from the cosmetic department. They were collaborating on a new Johnston's product for easy removal of nail polish. The huge chemical plant in Whiting, Indiana, just south of downtown Chicago had been one of the biggest employers of Whiting and the neighboring towns.

"Good morning, Tina," greeted Dr. Moheri as he entered the laboratory. He was surprised to find that Tina had arrived earlier than him.

"Good morning, Professor," Tina responded, calling Moheri by his commonly referred title among the workers.

"Too early for you, huh?" asked Moheri.

"As a matter of fact yes," responded Tina. "I was like… I don't know how you do this time after time."

"I call it my pituitary alarm," said Dr. Moheri. "An internal brain alarm that rings at exactly 5:30 a.m."

"I wish I had one of those, but then again, I didn't graduate sum cum laude from Indiana University."

"It takes years to develop, and sometimes you have to pay a heavy price for that," responded Dr. Moheri without elaborating.

"So what do you think?" asked Tina, sitting down at the corner of the laboratory table that had several reagents, three Bunsen burners, and four computer terminals on it.

"About what?" asked Dr. Moheri smiling, while settling down at the desk overlooking the main laboratory, kitty-corner to where Tina was sitting.

"About the new product, silly," smiled Tina, crossing her legs.

"I think that if we have a better testing method or material to evaluate how effective it will work in humans, we have a shot at it."

"What are you suggesting? You know the last test we did on the rabbit nail nearly took out all the hairs in the poor animal's paws."

"Yes, but after further refinement, the subsequent test on the tongue depressor was flawless."

"Tongue depressors are made of wood...hello?"

"Yes, I know," Moheri shook his head in disbelief. "But there are no indications that what happened to the rabbits would occur in humans. After all, humans, especially women, don't have hairs on their hands or feet for that matter."

"Then, Professor, all we need is like..., human volunteers."

Moheri shook his head, this time in agreement, while Tina bit at her finger nails.

"If I volunteer, what do I get?" Tina teased.

Moheri paused. Ever since Tina was assigned to collaborate with Moheri on this project, she had developed a personal attraction for Moheri, disregarding the snide remarks of the other female employees.

"A cruise to the Caribbean?" responded Dr. Moheri, looking directly at Tina, and making an offer he knew she would not refuse.

"You're kidding?"

"I'm very serious."

"I'm going by myself?"

"I'll go with you," Moheri volunteered.

"You are not…kidding."

"Look, we can accomplish two tasks together—one, a good test for the JRC-23–0018–2008 product, and another, a trip to the Caribbean."

"But…but what if my fingers fall off?"

"I will personally get you the best plastic surgeon in Chicago to either re-attach them or give you prostheses," answered Moheri with a self-confidence he was known for.

"Gee…thanks…prostheses?"

"Seriously, I doubt anything will happen except instant removal of the nail polish."

"Okay," said Tina, taking a deep breath. "Let me paint my nail first with my favorite color, red."

"Oh, I love red nail polish on a woman," complimented Moheri.

Tina's heart skipped a beat. *That's sweet,* she thought, *if only Oliver would be that sensitive.*

Tina was recently engaged to Oliver Edwards, a supervisor at the Luckiest Luck Casino and Resorts. They met during one of Tina's many trips to the casino. Although engaged for a few months, they were already planning for a June wedding, next year. Oliver lacked sensitivity as far as Tina was concerned, but he made up for it in so many other ways.

"I am ready," said Tina, showing her beautiful nails in red.

"You painted all ten fingers?" asked a surprised Dr. Moheri.

"Yes, so that the test will be complete."

"Okay."

Tina immersed all ten fingers into the pink-colored solution. Within ten seconds all the red nail paintings disappeared. Withdrawing her fingers, and under close examination, there was no ill effect seen on any of Tina's fingers.

Drying them with a paper towel, she spread them in the air in a joyful exhilaration.

Simultaneously, they reached for each other in a congratulatory embrace.

Suddenly, within the embrace, their eyes met and their lips locked in a sensual kiss.

Ten to fifteen minutes later, they both sat there momentarily, sweating and breathing heavily. After a few more kisses, while reaching for their clothes, they noticed a broken glass container on the table.

Apparently, neither heard it break, except for the security guard who knocked on the door at that moment.

"Is everything all right, Dr. Moheri?" asked the security guard outside the locked door.

"Yes," screamed Dr. Moheri. "We were just celebrating."

"My," whispered Tina, "isn't that a good one?"

"That was really good, Tina," Moheri commented while clearing his throat.

"I would like to do that again," Tina replied.

"We will get plenty of opportunity on the cruise."

# CHAPTER TWENTY

Driving home that same afternoon, Moheri noticed that the sun was shining brightly over the lagoons of Lake Michigan. There were no clouds in the air. It was unseasonably high, in the low eighties, early April spring.

The lake had a bluish hue viewed from I-90, and there were a number of people fishing along the inlets. A faint, fowl, custard-like smell from the steel mills permeated the air, yet Moheri rolled down the car's front windows to enjoy the April breeze.

Arriving home, Moheri found the house empty. Susan and the kids apparently had gone out shopping. Leaving his briefcase on his office desk, he went upstairs, showered again, and changed into his Saturday afternoon attire of jeans and pullover. He settled in front of the computer in his office, and wondered aloud what to name the new product.

Instant Nail Polish Remover?

Instant Johnston?

Tina Johns?

Immediately his mind reverted back to the sex in the lab. *Not bad*, he thought. Ever since Tina had started working on this project with him, he had imagined what it would be like to have sex with her. But because of his status in the company, he had been very cautious not to be perceived as making the obvious move, for fear of sexual harassment accusation. He did not want to be accused of inappropriate sexual advances. Susan would go ballistic at the news.

In fact, Dr. Moheri had anticipated something this morning, but what he did not calculate was that it would actually happen. Tina took him up on his challenge and…

"Hi, honey." Susan's greeting startled him.

"Hi, guys," responded Moheri.

"How was the office?"

"The office…? Yes, we tested the new nail polish remover, and it worked fantastic," Moheri answered with a smile and a thumbs-up sign.

As Susan pushed opened the door to the kitchen, she skeptically inquired, "How does it work?"

"You just dip your finger in the solution, and *viola*, the whole nail polish disappears in less than five seconds," an excited Marion explained. "Let's assume you apply a nail polish and for whatever reason wants to change to a different color, you could do so in an instant."

"What about the fingers? Some discoloration or…you know, something," Susan asked from the kitchen.

"Nothing happens. It does no harm to the fingers," Moheri exclaimed.

He then rose up, buckled his belt tighter around his rotund waistline, and headed toward the kitchen. The two boys, meanwhile, ran to the living room to finish playing their Nintendo games.

"I am proud of you, honey. What are you gonna call it?" Susan asked, and then laid down the shopping bags on the kitchen countertop.

"That's exactly what I was thinking when you guys came in. Listen to this, and tell me what you think. 'Tina Johns.'"

"Tina Johns, and…?" Susan turned to look at her husband, hands folded across her chest.

"Tina John's Nail Polish Remover," Moheri responded, gesturing with both hands in a lecture-like fashion.

"You gonna sell that name to women?"

"Yes."

"Bad, bad name. Too man-like, cheap, bar-like name and a cheap catch word."

"Okay, okay, okay," Moheri conceded. "What do you suggest?"

"How about 'Instant Nail Polish Remover,' nice, short and simple and will appeal to all women?"

"Instant nail polish remover," Marion reflected, with a frowned forehead.

Pointing with his right index finger, he congratulated, "That's not bad. I like it."

"You are lost without me, aren't you?" Susan asked, strutting her way to the refrigerator to retrieve cold lemonade.

"Yes, honey," Marion answered. "Look, sweetheart, we should probably be announcing the product to the public in two weeks, and then the company plans an official lunch."

"Let me guess, on a cruise ship again?" Susan stopped her drinking and asked like she knew already.

"Of course, that's where we get the most attendance."

Moheri could not help but think of all the women he had lured to these cruises. The conquests, as he called them. So far, since joining the company, he had netted three and counting. This time, Tina would probably travel on Moheri's expense account.

666

*The Sea Princess* was not one of the larger ships on the sea, Moheri could tell.

While docked next to the Royal Caribbean, Brilliance-of-the-sea in San Juan, Puerto Rico, Moheri noticed that the *Sea Princess* ship looked rather small.

*But no matter, all cruises depend on what you make of it,* he concluded.

To Moheri, they were all spectacular, especially the food and the entertainment.

He made sure Tina had a room less than five doors removed from his. Tina certainly was entertaining night after night.

On the third day of the cruise, the female voice announcer broke the silence of the morning, as always, with her routine early morning announcements.

"Attention, ladies and gentlemen, welcome to the Island of the Dominicans. Today's special excursion is to Mount Hibiscus Bay."

Dr. Moheri's most interested spot. He always wanted to visit the Hibiscus Bay.

Hibiscus Bay, a tiny hilltop location on the northeast corner of the island, was made famous by the mysterious pond. According to National Geographic, which Moheri watched on a cable channel a month ago, legend had it that the pond occasionally took a breath. It constantly emitted misty clear fumes, and every ten to fifteen minutes the pond could be seen heaving, just like taking a deep breath. The local government mandated that nobody be allowed within one hundred feet of the pond for protective reasons. Most importantly, local legend believed that a swim in the pond, whether accidental or otherwise, would result in instant, what the locals called, "well-done cooked meat."

A special permission, fees, and security clearance were required by the Dominican government for only a half-liter of the fluid per person. Any bona-fide scientist from countries listed in the Dominicans official government dossiers as safe could obtain the half-liter.

Dr. Moheri, through the state department, was able to procure permission, and he paid the fees for his half-liter. The solutions usually were not handed over to an individual, per se, but rather shipped directly to a verifiable, legitimate, business address.

"That's a creepy place," suggested Tina.

"It actually does breathe, doesn't it?" Moheri asked as the group headed back to the boat.

"Yes." A chorus of simultaneous responses came from other members of the excursion team.

"Luckily, this is at the highest elevation of the island, miles removed from the general population," Moheri observed.

"I am assuming this must be a gaseous fume from some volcanic activities below, but apparently the fumes are not deadly, won't you say?" Tina asked.

"Apparently not, otherwise those attendants that have worked here for years would have all been dead," Moheri laughed.

Before returning to the boat, Moheri visited the American Consulate office on the island, signed all the necessary documents, was photographed, and then was issued a receipt for his half-liter bottle.

Back in Indiana, Moheri could not wait to get to the laboratories. It was, however, not until seven days after the trip that the package actually arrived.

Moheri ran an analysis of the sample solution to determine if previous analyses of the liquid done at other facilities were consistent. His lab only re-confirmed that the fluid indeed contained about 92 percent alpha amino cupric acids, 2 percent fumaric acid, 2 percent trace elements, 3 percent nitrogen, and 1 percent heavy metals, a solution not amenable to either human consumption or contact. He was not surprised. Those were the same percentages shown on the geographic show.

As a research scientist, Dr. Moheri, for the past four years, had been secretly working on a new acid. He wondered if a percentage of this new solution in combination with his formulated acid would result in anything.

After eight weeks of different percentage combinations and concoctions, and a near disaster in the lab, Moheri formulated a new concoction comprising the Dominican fluid, mixed with hydrochloric acid, citric acid, benzoic acid, and diethyl benzyl ammonium sulfate.

The final solution, alpha amino serpenteric acid, he called "Moheric acid." The final mixed percentage of each solution he kept exceptionally confidential. He hid the piece of paper with the information inside the sole of his expensive work shoe that he wore practically at all times. He figured that even if he left the shoe at home, he could not imagine anyone looking under the sole of his shoe for anything.

All ten rats and five rabbits tested, with varying doses of Moheric acid, died in less than thirty minutes with the smallest kill dose of 2.5 mille-equivalent per deciliter. By accident, he discovered that less than half a teaspoon of Moheric acid in a quarter cup of coffee would kill a rabbit in one to two days, depending on the size of the rabbit.

Autopsy of the rabbits showed massive liver necrosis, or decay. Toxicology studies showed evidence of very high concentration of ammonia and hydrogen chloride, chemicals normally found in the liver.

"To put it bluntly," concluded Moheri to himself, "this is a clean death."

# CHAPTER TWENTY-ONE

Ashland Auditorium, traditionally used for larger university lectures, and for the weekly medical school Clinical Pathology Conferences, was packed with reporters. There were cameras mounted at all corners of the room. There were at least fifteen of them on tripod-like stands. The auditorium was standing room only. Media groups, students, many faculty members, and staff supports were in attendance.

Information was sent previously throughout the university about a major medical breakthrough announcement, and everyone was invited to attend. By 1:45 p.m., the auditorium was filled, and further admissions were denied at 1:55 p.m. when the standing room was also filled. The conference started promptly at two p.m.

The president of the university, who was standing on the podium, motioned for attention, and then went ahead and introduced Drs. Abramhoff and Dickerson. Both were seated at the table, in the middle of the stage, with about fifteen microphones between them.

"Thank you all for coming," began Dr. Laposite. "Let me begin by introducing our distinguished Professor Dr.

Abramhoff, who is the Chairman of the Department of Immunology and Oncology."

Applause followed.

"And also, our distinguished guest, all the way from San Diego, California, Dr. Regina Dickerson, Chief of the Department of Hematology-Oncology and Immunology at the University of La Jolla, School of Medicine."

Applause followed.

"Today, the Loop University of Chicago is, and has always been, at the forefront of medical research. The university called this news conference to announce a breakthrough in our joint scientific research with the University of La Jolla. These two prominent individuals have championed an important finding. They also have dedicated a lot of man and woman hours in order to achieve this monumental result. The university is highly indebted to both of them. And without further ado, I present to you Dr. Dickerson."

Another round of applause followed as Dr. Dickerson stepped up to the podium.

When the applause finally died down, she methodically narrated her background and training. Finally, in more general information manner she explained the research concept and their preliminary findings. She then relinquished the podium to Dr. Abramhoff for the conclusion of the presentation.

Dr. Abramhoff, in his egocentric manner, proclaimed that all criminals are medically programmed at birth, and given the right environment, will perpetuate what they were destined to do.

"We have scientific evidence that proves our theory." he concluded.

In a question and answer session that followed, Dr. Dickerson, however, managed to suggest that their finding may have implications far beyond medicine, possibly into the realms of religion, and religious beliefs.

The news conference dominated the evening programs. Many news commentaries wanted to know exactly what religious implications Dr. Dickerson alluded to.

The communications department at the Loop University Medical School received several calls requesting appearances for Dr. Abramhoff and Dr. Dickerson.

Abramhoff arrived home that evening highly pleased. He surmised that the opportunity for a national recognition had finally begun.

Flying back to San Diego the next morning, Dickerson was upset at Abramhoff for suggesting that his laboratory was first on the HLA B66 scene. She cursed softly but decided not to do anything, for the moment. She arrived in San Diego to a hero's welcome. She was mobbed at the airport when her itinerary was leaked to the news media.

Luckily, Pinkett arranged a police escort and a limo for the ride back to the university.

A hastily scheduled meeting of all department heads was held. After the congratulatory remarks, the university president directed that all future funding associated with the HLA research be separated from the rest of the University 101 general finds.

That settled, each department head pledged support for the research, and offered whatever help they could.

Dr. Dickerson appreciated their support and went home satisfied.

"Doc, I am proud of you," congratulated Detective Pinkett on a telephone call that night.

"Thanks, Pinky," responded Dickerson.

"The whole department was talking about your news conference, you know. One thing everyone agreed on is that it would make our job a whole lot easier if we can use your HLA right now," said the detective.

"That's exactly what I am afraid of," replied Dickerson. "Every criminal in the United States now has to be tested and proven positive, then after that start testing the rest of the population to see who tests HLA B66 positive."

"That will be an impossible task, and will require a lot of time, money, energy, and a social upheaval."

"That exactly is my point."

# CHAPTER TWENTY-TWO

While Dickerson was in the shower contemplating her next ventures, the phone rang and rang incessantly. She ignored the ringing, choosing instead to bask in the cool refreshing water.

Shower over; Dickerson finally sat down to eat breakfast, but the phone starting ringing again. The caller ID signaled an unknown name and an unknown number. There were earlier calls from the same unknown caller, but the caller left no messages.

"Hello?"

"Dr. Dickerson?" inquired the caller with a strong foreign accent.

"Yes, how can I help you?" Dickerson asked.

"I am Professor Allahaji Abdullah, and I teach theology at the University of Cairo, here in Egypt. My specialty is in Judean, Islamic, and Christian religions, and I am also an expert in ancient religious history."

"How are you doing, Professor Alla ji…"

"No, Alla-ha-ji," enunciated the professor.

"I am sorry, Professor Alla-ha-ji Abdullah," corrected Dickerson, slowly enunciating the words.

"That's correct." There was a faint chuckle at the other end.

"As I was saying, I saw you on KNN-International, and also some of our local TV discussed your findings," said Abdullah.

"Thank you very much. I hope you find it interesting."

"I was particularly struck when you mentioned the religious implications of your HLA findings."

With Dr. Abdullah's accent, and the long distance connection of the call, Dickerson had her left hand over her left ear to shield out other noises.

"Could you speak a little louder; I can barely hear you," she finally suggested.

"I was saying…," started the professor.

"That's better."

"I was saying that you mentioned the religious implications of your HLA findings."

"Yes?"

"I believe you are on the verge of making a discovery of biblical proportions," continued Abdullah.

"How do you mean?"

"I know that you were thinking of the number 666, the number that stands for the beast, the mark of the devil, and you were wondering how it may relate to your research," postulated the professor.

"As a matter of fact, yes I am," responded Dr. Dickerson, curious as to how this man could deduce her implication that quickly.

"First of all," explained the professor, "instead of the large letter B, use the small letter b, and then you should search any library of ancient Middle Eastern philology and the development of the minuscule. You will be surprised to know that in many of them, but particularly in one, the letter b and the figure 6 often are...are...What am I thinking?" pondered the professor in the middle of his explanation.

"Interchangeable."

"Yes, interrelated, thank you."

"When you do," the professor continued, "you will then understand that you may have discovered the location of the marker 666, the sign of the devil."

That was exactly what Dr. Dickerson had hoped for, a possible link between her scientific research and the book of Revelation.

*There may indeed be a connection between the two after all,* she thought. *If so, let the religious battle of the war of the world begin.*

The phone rang again.

This time, the Pearl K. Hanson Company, the famous talk show host from Chicago, called to request a solo interview with her to discuss further what she meant by the religious implications. She promised to give it a serious thought before accepting. She then promptly notified Dr. Abramhoff who encouraged her to go ahead.

"The more outlet the better," Abramhoff pointed out.

The caller, however, did promise that Ms. Hanson herself would call soon to set up a mutually acceptable time and date of an interview if live appearance was impractical.

# CHAPTER TWENTY-THREE

Oak Ridge Country Club in Schererville, Indiana, earned the reputation of being the place to live. An exclusive gated community for the upper class society of northwest Indiana, it had its own clubhouse, and it sprawled over two towns. In the middle of this 2,000-plus acreage site, a manicured, eighteen-hole, grade-A golf course punctuated the entire estate.

In northwest Indiana and sections of south and southeastern parts of Chicago, the golf course had always been home to the avid golfers. The estate part of the community resided many specialty doctors, specialized dentists, affluent lawyers, bankers, and millionaire business owners.

At 487 Cricket Court, resided a picturesque mansion, about six homes removed from the clubhouse, and close to the third tee golf area, Dr. Lee Kwon Nsi was busy entertaining guests. Congressman James Packard, the special guest of honor, was being showered with praises and donations from the many friends of Dr. Nsi.

Dr. Lee Kwon Nsi, at age fifty-two, had made a name for himself. A handsome, medium built, self-made millionaire, he emigrated from South Korea to the United States with his older brother at age ten.

He had been the most influential cardio-thoracic surgeon among the six area hospitals scattered throughout northwest Indiana. His rise to fame was very rocky, and sometimes even unpleasant, something Dr. Nsi had repeatedly refused to discuss. Dr. Nsi also had a way with women.

"Ladies and gentlemen," shouted Dr. Nsi to the noisy crowd in the huge family room that was designed like a self-contained stage.

"Ladies and gentleman, please," shouted Dr. Nsi a second time as the noise began to die down.

"Today, I am honored to introduce to you my very good friend, the honorable Congressman James Packard," began Dr. Nsi.

A round of very protracted yet polite applause followed.

"Congressman Packard has done so much for northwest Indiana," continued Dr. Nsi after the applause. "He has championed millions of federal dollars for infrastructure developments in northwest Indiana, and we are greatly indebted to him."

Another round of applause initiated by Dr. Nsi followed.

"For that, we are sponsoring a drive to rename Calumet Avenue to Packard Boulevard, in honor of our great congressman, and also in appreciation of the leadership he has shown in the expansion and extension of Calumet Avenue."

Another round of applause followed.

"The congressman's job is not finished yet. Today, he is here in person to tell you about his next major project for our area. Of course, gentlemen, he is going to need your strong support in this endeavor. So, without further ado, I present to you, Congressman Packard."

A thunderous applause followed this time, lasting about sixty seconds that even Congressman Packard was taken back slightly.

"I want to personally thank Dr. Nsi, our premier cardio-thoracic surgeon, his wife, Lynn, and their two children, all here tonight for this wonderful occasion," Congressman Packard began his prepared message after pulling out a piece of paper from his coat jacket.

As the congressman was delivering his speech, Dr. Nsi's eyes roved around the room and noticed Dr. Marion Moheri brooding over a glass of Heineken. He made his way toward the beautifully decorated bar and tapped Dr. Moheri on the shoulder.

"Hello, Doc," responded a startled Moheri.

"Mario!" Dr. Nsi, who preferred to call him Mario, shouted.

"Come with me to the deck," Nsi beckoned, as he motioned Dr. Moheri toward the French doors.

Outside, two golfers were still at the third teeing ground attempting to tee off on this chilly April evening.

"I didn't think you were gonna make it," said Dr. Nsi. "But I'm delighted you did."

"It was hard, but I had to come to give you the good news," Moheri responded.

Moheri and Nsi had become friends while golfing at the country club, and over the years began to share common interest, especially with Moheri's ambitious chemical researches.

Nsi, a gifted golfer, labeled as suave and a womanizer could engage anyone in any conversation and within minutes dominate the discussion.

"I have the final concentration now and I seriously believe that in an enough quantity of…what I called M&M juices, there may be a total obliteration of any human organs," informed Moheri, his head bouncing up and down as his glasses hung on the bridge of his nose.

"You mean…?" responded a wide-eyed Nsi.

"If you dump an organ, say the kidney, in the juice, it disappears in a matter of minutes. In layman's terms, yes, total evaporation."

"Wouldn't you see blood or particles floating in the solutions?" Nsi asked curiously.

"Right now, there is only a slight discoloration, but I believe that in enough, or a higher concentration, that color would probably disappear."

"You mean," persisted an unrelieved Nsi, "you can literally dump someone into that solution, and *puff*?"

"Yes, *puff*," answered Marion, pulling his glasses up slightly with his right middle finger.

"Lee, the congressman is looking for you," a voice said through the opened French doors.

"I am sorry; I will be right there," Nsi apologized to the intruder.

"Enjoy yourself, we'll talk some more," Nsi whispered to Moheri.

Walking through the crowd, clapping at the congressman's remarks, Nsi made his way to the podium.

"Isn't he wonderful?" said Dr. Nsi to more applause.

"I would like to thank everyone again for this wonderful occasion," Nsi remarked. "Please, there is plenty to eat at the dining room, and those of you who would like a picture taken with the congressman, the set-up is at the sun room. Also, don't forget to stop at the office any time. That's the door to your left. Monica is patiently waiting. No amount is too large."

The crowd laughed.

"Monica will have all the information you need."

# CHAPTER TWENTY-FOUR

"I saw you in the newspaper yesterday," smiled Marge Fisher with the same sexy smile she had used in the past to charm Dr. Nsi.

Marge, the former head nurse at four-wing-three, a cardiovascular and surgical step-down unit at Indiana University Hospital in Glen Park, was now the head nurse for the operating room.

"You collected about $100,000 for the congressman, that's phenomenal."

"Yes," responded Nsi, half paying attention while adjusting the surgical cap, which he then tied around his head.

It was 6:30 a.m., and Nsi's patient was prepped for a major quadruple bypass surgery.

Nsi had already talked to the patient, changed into scrubs, and was in the midst of his final preparations. He left the operating room to wait for the anesthesiologist's final induction of the patient.

Standing outside at the hallway that led directly to the employees parking, sipping a cup of coffee, Nsi was accosted by Nurse Fisher.

"That surprised me too," Nsi agreed. "I didn't expect that much donation."

"Dr. Nsi, I know this is the wrong time, but I really need your help," Marge commenced her begging.

"What is it now?" asked an irritated Nsi.

*Marge always picks the wrong time to ask for favors, and most of her requests always revolve around money,* thought Nsi.

"Don't say it like that."

Ms. Marge Fisher, a blond, petite, forty-six-year-old, had been romantically involved with Dr. Nsi for two years. A secret they had shared together. Ms. Fisher was a recently divorced mother of a seventeen-year-old high school girl, who had been in and out of trouble with the law.

Recently arrested and charged with possession and intent to distribute, she was again arrested while she was smoking marijuana with some friends in the high school parking lot. Since this was her fourth major offense, bail was set at $45,000.

Ms. Fisher had arranged for detoxification and counseling for her daughter and was about to sign the agreement when this recent incident happened.

"What actually do you want me to do?" asked Nsi.

"I would like to bail her out so that she can get the help she needs."

"I agree with you, go ahead."

"You know I don't have that kind of money," Fisher replied, fiddling with her fingers.

"What makes you think I do?" Nsi asked, teeth clenched, barely audible.

Gifts that started innocently as lunch money of twenty dollars here and there had moved up to $1,500 for trips.

Six months ago, Nsi, in a desperate move not to leave any traces, paid cash for her new Volkswagen Jetta because the same daughter crashed the only car they used after the divorce.

Ms. Fisher pleaded that she had no other means to commute to work.

"Didn't I just buy you a car…free…six months ago?" Nsi reminded her.

"Yes, and I am still very grateful," replied Fisher as she looked up at Nsi with a teardrop off the left eye.

"So when is this gonna end?" Nsi persisted.

"When is what gonna end?" asked Fisher, wiping away tears.

"What do you mean what…this, this…crazy idea of constantly asking for money?" Nsi grimaced angrily.

"Who was it that said 'if you need anything just let me know'?" Fisher fired back. "Aren't you the one who promised to help me whenever I am in trouble, or have you forgotten what you said at the La Quinta Inn?"

"When did I make such a promise?" inquired Nsi with a disgusted look as he peeped down the hallway to be sure nobody was listening.

"Oh, so you are now playing possum?" Fisher's jaw dropped.

"What on earth does that mean?"

"Look, Nsi, are you gonna help me or not?" Fisher straightened her scrub coat.

"I have to think about that," Nsi replied while walking away.

"Please, don't take long."

"Dr. Nsi, we are ready for you." The anesthesiologist came out of the operating room to inform Nsi. He glanced at Nurse Fisher and was about to ask—

"Thanks, I will be there in a second," Nsi interrupted.

Without saying another word to Ms. Fisher, Nsi headed straight to the sink to scrub and gown for the operation.

Unlike most of his surgeries, complications started soon after the operation. The patient had excessive fluid retention and needed two extra days of intubations. If it weren't for the aggressive, daily vigilance of the anesthesiologist and the chief cardiology resident, the patient would have coded and possibly died.

This was not the kind of outcome associated with Nsi, and he blamed it all on Ms. Fisher. Another complication like this, and another patient might actually die. Ms. Fisher had to be stopped, Nsi convinced himself.

"I heard about Mr. Charles Edward, your patient that nearly died." Four days after the surgery, Marge phoned Nsi.

"I have you to thank for that," Nsi replied, still worried about that surgical complication.

"What did I have to do with it?" Marge smirked.

"More than you know."

"Sorry," Marge smiled, "you are the surgeon, and you take the responsibility."

"The question is how many more bad outcomes are in the wings for me because of you?" shouted Nsi over the phone.

"Listen, let's stop arguing; I have some good news." Marge realized she had never heard Nsi this angry before.

"Hmm…what good news?" asked Nsi as he took an audible deep breath over the phone.

Nsi was hoping that she would finally move to Arizona.

Marge had hinted, at the height of her divorce that she was contemplating moving to Arizona with her daughter just to get away from it all.

"They have lowered her bond to $35,000, but I must pay it in two weeks or else she goes to jail," Marge voiced with a happy tone.

"How did you mange that?"

"I met with Attorney Terrence Lacrosse, from Dyer, and he was instrumental in lowering the bond. I really need this money. I am willing to do anything, including making monthly payments until it's all paid off."

*Why Attorney Lacrosse?* Nsi wondered. *Isn't he that notorious lawyer, who made his career suing doctors and collecting huge sums of money. Is she sending me a message?* Nsi's thoughts began racing. *If I don't comply, will I be next? I didn't do anything but sleep with her and all of the sudden she is demanding huge sums of money. The end result of all this is not gonna be pretty. Last year's case was clearly my fault.*

The family, however, had accepted the death as natural after talking to them extensively. Marge knew the family well and she was also the scrub nurse on the case.

Something had to be done quickly before this whole thing got out hand.

"Okay, I will get back to you in about a week," Nsi finally responded after what appeared to Marge as an unusually long silence.

"Oh, thank you so very much; you will not regret this," Marge rejoiced, patting her right red cheek.

"I didn't say I was gonna give you the money."

"I know, I know, but thank you, anyway."

She hung up, and momentarily Nsi thought he heard a second click just before he hung up.

*Is she taping our conversations?* Nsi wondered.

Driving home that evening through the crowded and construction-laden Indianapolis Boulevard in Schererville, Indiana, Nsi decided that Marge had to be dealt with immediately. Arriving home, he went into his private office, locked the door, and then made a call to Marion.

"How is the M&M juice coming along?" asked Nsi.

"I think it is now at a concentration that even the bones will melt and disappear," Moheri chuckled.

"I guess the next step is a test, don't you think?" Little tiny perspiration appeared on Nsi's forehead.

"Actually, yes, I was planning on using one of our rhesus monkeys as a test animal."

Without hesitation, Nsi suggested, "I may have someone to be used as a test subject."

"Someone…like a person?" a baffled Marion asked.

"Yeah," answered Nsi, letting out a loud heave.

"In that case all I need is an address," Marion chuckled.

Marge was working late. Today, the surgery schedule stretched until almost 8:30 p.m. An emergency quadruple bypass surgery, that took four and half hours, was the last case. After the case was over, and the operating room cleaned out, the operating room nurses and technicians dressed and left for the day.

Marge, instead, opted to work in her office to finish next week's assignments. When Marge finally looked up again, it was 10:30 p.m. She needed to go home and get some sleep. Tomorrow she was scheduled to meet with Attorney Lacrosse at eight o'clock in the morning to go over the terms for her daughter's bail.

Rushing out of the east end exit of the hospital, near the surgical wing, close to the employees' parking places, Marge did not notice the man standing, hidden behind a dark blue sports utility van.

She had made these late-night short trips to her car several times before, and always waved off the security personnel behind the surgical suite waiting room desk, whenever he offered to escort her to her car.

"Are you Marge Fisher?" asked the man dressed appropriately in a business suit, without a tie.

"Yes, can I help you?" answered a startled Marge.

"I was supposed to give you this." He showed Marge a package in his hand.

The pleasure was all over Marge's face as she approached to accept the package that she thought was the moncy from Dr. Nsi.

The blow was so severe; Marge thought she was having a stroke. She did not know where it came from. Within seconds, she was unconscious.

6 6 6

Wild Bobby's Auto Demolition shop, located north off Route 30 in Lynwood, Illinois, was a sprawling area full of old demolished cars, including cars that were recently involved in accidents.

The shop's main building at the southeast corner could not be located by a newcomer, because it was the most wooded section of the entire facility. It housed the repair shop, two upstairs offices, an oven, a car wash area, and a washing room for car engines.

A big casket-like bucket in the middle of the room was clearly visible. Ten gallons of the newly formulated Moheric acid was at the corner of the room. The two assailants fitted Marge's very limp body in the big bucket. Blood was still oozing out of the crevice made by the blunt trauma to her head.

The first five gallons slowly evaporated the skin and most of the fatty tissue. After three more gallons, most of the internal organs were no longer visible, although there were many particulate matters still floating.

When the final two gallons were poured in, the bones melted down like hot wax. After a few minutes, the entire solution appeared dark orange with small scattered flakes. An extra gallon was required for the entire solution to turn colorless but a little thicker than the original solution.

Bobby, the owner, Dr. Moheri, and Dr. Nsi were very impressed. Each one speechlessly smiled. When the spectacle was finally over, they drove off the compound. Bobby left instructions for the security men to lock up.

# CHAPTER TWENTY-FIVE

Two television stations in San Diego were still reeling with the presentations of Dr. David Abramhoff of Chicago and Dr. Regina Dickerson, the San Diego local physician and research scientist. Several attempts were made by different television networks for a joint appearance, all to no avail.

"What do you think of this joint appearance thing?" Dickerson remembered asking.

"Not yet," Abramhoff responded emphatically. "Let them maul over it for a while."

Even Dr. Millons was impressed.

"Good morning, Dr. Dickerson," Millons greeted, as they walked along the hallway leading to the cafeteria.

"What can I do for you now?" retorted Dickerson with a dejected voice.

"Listen, I come in peace," Millons responded, smiling broadly.

"Or in pieces," uttered Dickerson, who had long given up on Millons.

"Listen, please, I am very serious," continued Millons, unperturbed by her attitude, "I would like for you to give me a fresh start. I honestly apologize for all my past sins against you."

"Sins against you!" Dickerson half laughed, half chuckled. "That's a new one for you."

"Sins, transgressions, callousness, call it what you may, I was all that, but I would like forgiveness from you, and I am requesting a chance to work with you on your new project."

"Oh, now you want to work with me; I thought you loved working against me," Dickerson persisted and continued walking uninterrupted.

"Now…now, you know I am the best-qualified physician on campus to assist you and the most likely one to help push this project forward."

"What do you mean? Was I pushing it backwards?" ask Dickerson, still unconvinced, and smarting at the chance to finally put Millons in his place.

"I didn't mean it like that. What I truly meant was that I can be of tremendous assistance to you."

"You look kind of sincere and serious," said Dickerson, as she finally slowed down to notice his sincerity.

"I am that serious," Millons responded with a stern countenance.

Dickerson thought for a while, took a deep breath, stopped in front of the cafeteria door, turned, looked Millons straight in the eye, nodded her head, and said, "Okay, I will give you a response tomorrow."

"That's great…thanks." Millons was overjoyed.

"You're welcome." Dickerson had a broad smile on her face as she walked into the cafeteria.

After lunch, while walking down the hallway toward her office, Dickerson reflected,

*This is the same guy that gave me so much grief in the past, now he wants to work with me.*

Arriving in her office, the department secretary handed Dickerson letters that she wanted her to see immediately. One was marked urgent and personal from the National Institute of Health.

Another was a letter from the PHS Productions, Inc. in Chicago—the Pearl Hanson Show production company.

The National Institute of Health mail was an approval of the grant she re-submitted with Abramhoff. They both would share a $10 million grant for massive testing in San Diego and Chicago. The National Institute of Health instructed both centers to test at least 10,000 inmates. The majority of the test would be hardcore criminals, but allowance was granted for criminals with strange and bizarre crimes.

Picking up the phone in excitement, she called Dr. Abramhoff's office. Sabrina answered the phone.

"Hi, Sabrina, this is Dr. Dickerson, is Dr. Abramhoff in?"

"Good morning, Dr. Dickerson," Sabrina saluted. "No, he is not here. He is teaching a class. Can I have him call you when he gets back? He will be done in about 20 minutes."

"That would be fine. Just have him call my office."

"I will do that," Sabrina reassured.

Dickerson then called the dean of the medical school to notify him of the grant.

"Congratulations," a hoarse voice answered at the other end. "You know the university will support the project 100 percent."

"As long as the project is profitable to the university, of course I will be supported 100 percent," Dickerson commented after hanging up the phone.

Dickerson then went to the laboratory, which was located at the south corner of the building, and called an impromptu meeting of the staff.

"I would like to thank all of you for the support and dedication you have shown to the HLA project," began Dickerson. "Well, your efforts have yielded great results. Today we have been approved for a $10 million grant from the NIH."

An outburst of joy filled the room; some shouted, others clapped their hands, while a few had tears in their eyes.

"We, however, have to combine data, collaborate, and submit a joint report to NIH, with Dr. Abramhoff's people in Chicago," Dickerson concluded.

No matter, the news was a welcome relief for most of the workers who had put in long overtime hours with average compensation, hoping for this day to arrive.

666

Back in the office, the call finally came from Chicago.

"Did you receive the notification?" Dickerson asked.

"Yes, I did," a melodious Abramhoff answered.

"So what's next?"

"Well, here in Chicago, we already have the support of the governor," Abramhoff stated. "He has signed executive order for us to go ahead with the testing, and we already have arranged with the Kankakee facility, and they are ready to go. I think we will need to include a few other facilities here in Illinois to be able to come up with the 10,000 inmates who fit the criteria."

"I know; I might have to do the same thing here in San Diego," suggested Dickerson.

"I strongly believe that you need to involve the governor to be able to get a better result. I think he might be looking forward to meeting with you."

"Politics and politicians are not my cup of tea...even though I don't drink tea," Dickerson chuckled.

"As it stands now, you are heavily involved in politics, and when this whole thing blows wide open, you and I will be front and center of world politics."

"This whole thing is becoming interesting and bizarre," Dickerson resignedly observed.

"Give the governor's office a call, and take it from there."

# CHAPTER TWENTY-SIX

When Dickerson finally called the governor's office in Sacramento, she was surprised to learn that the governor was indeed anticipating her call, just as Abramhoff had predicted. The governor wanted her to come to Sacramento, if at all possible, for a joint public appearance. Dickerson immediately seized on the opportunity and agreed to meet with the governor in two days.

At the cafeteria to grab a noon salad, Dickerson ran into Millons again.

"Hi there, any encouraging news?" inquired Millons.

"Yeah…what is this, you hang around the cafeteria all day long?"

"As a matter of…"

"Never mind, as a real matter of fact, I've decided that you can join the team," Dickerson answered.

Before an excited Millons could even say thank you, Dickerson berated an instruction.

"Any crude remarks, sexually charged comments, or inappropriate behaviors, and you are off the team."

"Trust me, you will see my best behavior," answered Millons, crossing his chest.

As she was about to exit the cafeteria, Dickerson turned, hesitated for a moment, then with a smile on her face asked, "By the way, I am meeting with the governor in two days in Sacramento for a photo-op, would you like to come?"

"Would I like to come? Yes, of course, I would love to come," answered Millons, excited just like a little kid in a candy store.

666

The meeting with Governor Luis N. Nagoya was cordial, brief, and very productive. The governor promised to sign an executive order allowing Dr. Dickerson's team to use the two state facilities in San Diego County, and a couple more if needed in Los Angeles County, to conduct their research.

Pleased with the outcome, Dickerson and Millons returned to San Diego to arrange and plan strategy for their massive testing.

Meanwhile, back in the office early next morning, Dickerson received a call from PHS Productions.

The director of communication and guest appearances for PHS Production was able to finalize the arrangements for Dickerson's appearance.

Ms. Hanson could not come to the phone due to a taping conflict.

"Your appearance will be a live feed," stated the director. "We have…"

"What is a live feed?" interrupted Dickerson innocently.

"What that means is that as Pearl is talking to you and you are responding; it will be seen live on national television so that there is very little room for editing or retakes. We have never interviewed a scientific doctor one-on-one before, so this is kind of new for us."

"I…I think I can handle myself," Dickerson reassured, while inwardly feeling less self-assured.

"We like that confidence in our guests. It helps with the jitters."

"Thanks, but how do I get there?"

"Oh, we'll take care of that, Doc. You are our special guest. We will send you packaged information containing all the details; the tickets, hotel stay, limousine, food, and all incidentals will all be taken care off. All we need is you."

"That's fine by me…oh, by the way, what date are we looking at?"

"June 6, nine a.m., Chicago time."

"June 6, that's weird, but so be it." Dickerson jotted the information down in her calendar.

On the early morning Sunday show that weekend, while Dickerson was getting ready to attend the 10:30 a.m. Mass, she picked up the remote and turned on the weekly "Meet the Press" Sunday hour.

Three panel members happened to be discussing the HLA phenomenon. One was a minister, the other the senator from Tennessee, and the third a political pundit.

"What do you think the national agenda should be if this HLA theory proves true?" asked the moderator to the senator.

"First, let me begin by saying that there has been a significant rise in violent crimes in the United States in the past few years. Secondly, federal dollars are being stretched to the max to accommodate the growing number, and building new prisons is not the answer."

"But what do you think of the HLA finding?" redirected the moderator.

"The government has appropriated $10 million for further studies of the HLA. I hate to speculate, but if the HLA findings are true beyond reasonable doubt, a congressional hearing will be needed to draft a national response."

"Abramhoff might be right after all," observed Dr. Dickerson aloud before turning off the television.

666

Two days prior to flying to Chicago, Dickerson received a call from Abramhoff.

"How are you coming along with your numbers?" asked Abramhoff, his voice a little raspy. "Did you meet with the governor yet?"

"Yes, we met with the governor, all right," responded Dickerson, trying to narrow down what clothes to wear to the show. "He was very charming and welcoming. We had a photo shoot with him, and that was all over the newspapers in California."

"I am glad. You keep referring to 'we;' do you have an assistant now?"

"Yes, Dr. Peter Millons. He is a gene specialist and has a good statistical background. He used to be very envious of the project, but now he is a strong ally."

"The meeting you had with the governor—how was that?" Abramhoff sneezed.

"God bless you. He promised to sign an executive order allowing us to use facilities in San Diego County and, if needed, a couple more in LA County."

"So how is it going?"

"We have been busy. I believe currently we are approaching 82 percent completion," responded Dickerson, wondering why Abramhoff sounded rushed, with all that cold. "How are you coming along with the project and your cold?"

"Don't worry, this is just allergy, but Governor Milton has already committed dollars prior to the National Institute of Health grant," responded Abramhoff, gloating. "We also have been working hard at our two facilities. We added two more centers in the interim, one in Springfield, Illinois, the other in East St. Louis. I believe we can finish the initial analysis in the upcoming week."

"Next week will be tight for me," responded Dickerson, feeling a little thwarted, "but I think we can manage."

This was the first time Dickerson had felt a competitive atmosphere between herself and Dr. Abramhoff and for now, it appeared that Abramhoff had a slight edge. Attempting to neutralize that edge, Dickerson countered, "We have what I called 'a periodic statistical analysis' as we progress, that way, our final cumulative data will be much easier to calculate."

"That's interesting!" Abramhoff responded with a subdued voice. "What numbers are you getting?"

"The preliminary results are matching what we saw previously." Dickerson felt vindicated.

"That's what you expected, right?"

"Yes," Dickerson concurred. "And by the way, I will be in Chicago in two days for a live Pearl show. I will call you when I get to Chicago."

"Congratulations," was all Abramhoff could say, while wondering aloud why the Pearl people did not call him, and he was in Chicago.

# CHAPTER TWENTY-SEVEN

Studio B was very chaotic the morning of the interview. People were moving rapidly in and out of various hastily constructed offices.

Dickerson had never been in a television studio before.

The trip to Chicago, the hotel, and the limousine ride to PHS Studios were all peaceful, but inside Studio B, there was chaos.

She was ushered to her makeup room and after a few nervous introductions, Pearl finally walked into the room.

A very imposing person, as everyone in the room acknowledged her presence upon entering. She was much nicer than what Dickerson had read from gossip tabloids.

Pearl introduced herself, and then made flattering comments about Dickerson's non-traditional doctorial attire. Pearl and Dickerson huddled to the corner office to go over the cues.

The live show, taped in a huge auditorium-like theater, had the audience seated in a semicircle arrangement. The stage had more lights than anything Dickerson had seen before.

Finally...; lights, camera, action. Dickerson could hear the applause from the audience while standing behind the curtain.

She could hear Pearl saying, "Today we have a first..., a special guest. She has not been interviewed, one on one, in front of the camera before, and we have not had a medical scientist on our show before, so ladies and gentlemen, be nice to her."

There was laughter from the audience.

"Without going further, I give you Dr. Regina Dickerson," concluded Pearl, clapping, while she watched Dickerson enter the center stage. Then, another round of applause followed when she finally reached the center stage, standing in front of a lounge chair positioned for her.

Slight beads of sweat could be seen on Dickerson's forehead. When everybody finally settled down, Dickerson became a little calmer.

"Please, sit down," motioned Pearl, as the clapping died down.

"We all watched your news conference with Dr. Abramhoff here in Chicago," Pearl opened the dialogue, "and being a Christian myself, we were all in awe at the possibilities you insinuated, but I would first like for you to give us a little bit of background about yourself and your motivations for this project."

Dickerson wasted no time talking about herself and her motivations. That said, Pearl finally stated the real reason for Dickerson's invitation.

"At the press conference, you seemed to suggest that there may be a religious connection or implication to the HLA findings. Well, is there?" asked Pearl, who first looked at Dickerson, then let out a little cough and then looked at the audience.

"Yes, there is a definite connection," answered Dickerson, who first looked at Pearl then turned to look at the sea of faces.

"What exactly do you mean, and how exactly did you arrive at that connection?"

"What I meant is that I've had a very strong religious upbringing myself, and from the recent biblical studies that I have undertaken at Creighton University's Department of Ancient Scriptures, I strongly believe that there is a connection."

"Creighton University…isn't that the Jesuit University in Omaha, Nebraska?" Pearl elaborated with a meticulous gesture at the audience.

"Yes, that's the one," answered Dickerson, shifting her position on the chair.

"So the Creighton University research you did helped you to make the connection." Pearl clasped her hand in front of her in anxious anticipation.

"I will assume here that we are all familiar with the number 666 from the book of Revelation?" Dickerson, with little sweat beads on her forehead, looked at Pearl for a gesture of support.

"Yes, and I know we Christians are all aware of its connotation to the devil," Pearl again elaborated, while nodding her head at the audience.

"Well, the night after the press conference, I received a call from a theology professor in Cairo, Egypt."

"Cairo, Egypt? That's kind of far, isn't it? Did you happen to know this professor from a previous meeting?" Pearl looked at Dickerson with some admiration.

"Not really; he unwittingly volunteered his services to me."

"What did the good professor say, then?" asked Pearl, crossing her legs and leaning slightly forward.

"He asked me to substitute the small letter b in the HLA B66 for the capital letter B and then research the ancient use of the small letter b, and to focus my research in ancient philology and the Aramaic languages."

"That's original. Well, did you?" asked Pearl, leaning a little closer.

"As a matter of fact I did, and that was done in conjunction with the extensive search at Creighton University library." Dickerson finally settled down and appeared ready to lecture.

"What did you find?" Pearl continued to look directly at Dickerson, not bothering to include the audience this time.

"It so happened that in a small community of Beer-La-hai-roi, near Kadesh, located in ancient Canaan, the modern letter b, which was never used in their language, was represented by the number 6 in their Aramaic alphabet. For example, Abner is written as A6ner, also Ibrahim as I6rahim. The same community was also known as the community of people who can see."

"Who can see...? Who...? What can they see?" Pearl appeared puzzled.

"In ancient times, according to the Old Testament, folks believed that anybody who saw God died immediately. Therefore, whenever God manifests His presence, you must prostrate yourself and dare not open your eyes, lest you die. But the people of Beer-La hai-roi, however, were known to have seen the Almighty and lived."

"That's a very long time ago in history. How did that translate to the twenty-first century?" asked Pearl, looking half perplexed.

"I'm glad you asked, because in modern Russia, for example, in terms of the writing of the figure 6 it has a transliteration for the letter b."

"Pardon my obvious curiosity, transliteration? What's that?" Pearl asked, acutely aware of the awkward silence among the audience and the crew members.

"That's the changing into corresponding characters of another alphabet or language, which was done over the years in history," explained Dickerson.

"But how did that tie to your HLA findings, if I may ask?" Pearl queried.

"In the book of Revelation, according to the Catholic version of the New American Bible, Chapter 13 verse 18, if you read carefully what it said, I quote: 'Wisdom is needed here, one who understands can calculate the number of the beast, for it is a number that stands for a person,' end of quote." Dickerson lectured while gesturing with the right index finger.

"Yeah, I think I have read that before," Pearl replied, shaking her head as if unsure whether she did or did not.

"I interpret it to mean that with some wisdom, and eyes opened, in other words, with a little understanding, one can find the way to calculate that number."

"Don't tell me that you have figured out a way to calculate that number?" asked Pearl with her mouth slightly ajar.

"I certainly did." Dickerson smiled with a sense of assurance. "Look, realizing that the modern Bible is mostly a Greek-to-English translation, and some letters may be absent in some languages, you can intuitively transpose the letter b with the number 6."

The silence in the studio was such that you could hear a pin drop.

Dickerson continued, "If that is too simplistic then, the next question is why the HLA antigen is located on chromosome six, at position 66? Is that another 666 calculation or explanation?"

A speechless Pearl spread her hands and shook her head in disbelief.

"Now, let's do some other calculations; are you ready?"

"Be my guest."

"There are three sixes in 666. Six divided by three equals two. B is the second letter of the alphabet. By inference, therefore, b transliterates to 6. These are some of the calculations the Good Book wants us to do. The HLA B66 therefore, based on all the evidence, is the location of 666, the stamped image."

With mouth wide open in obvious astonishment, Pearl responded, "You are shi…you nearly made me say a bad word on television."

Huge laughter erupted from a previously mute, yet attentive, audience.

"The implication, the way I see it," continued Dickerson, "is that, in the book of Revelation, the beast's number is marked in the person who is a descendant or a chosen disciple of the beast. That marking is in the histo-compatible antigen located at position B66. Therefore, with good wisdom, understanding, and appropriate calculations that position actually corresponds to 666."

A silent hush fell again on the audience.

Even Ms. Hanson, with her mouth half open, could not believe what she was hearing.

"Dr. Dickerson, I admire you immensely," one of the audience members stated during a brief question period. "My question is; what do we do now?"

"You know, this is going to be a very controversial issue," said Ms. Hanson, trying to extrapolate on the question.

"Listen, over the centuries, every God's manifestation has always been controversial," Dickerson responded with a sense of religious authority.

"But why were you chosen?" Ms. Hanson mused.

"That, I really don't know," answered Dickerson.

"How…what am I trying to say…how plausible is this?"

"The correct question actually should be: what if? And why is the revelation being manifested to us now?" stated Dickerson.

"And with that, we will be right back," concluded Pearl, looking directly at camera number three.

# CHAPTER TWENTY-EIGHT

That evening, Abramhoff called Dickerson at the hotel. "You sure made a Revelation believer out of me, but most importantly, you have added a real sense of urgency to the project."

"That's a very interesting observation, thanks," Dickerson replied.

Back in San Diego, Professor Abdullah called from Cairo.

"Congratulations, we saw you on the KNN evening report. They were talking about your television appearance with that famous woman," said Professor Abdullah.

"Pearl Hanson," Dickerson smiled.

"Yes…yes, now let's hope you can use it the way God intended it to be used."

"*Enshalla,*" Dickerson responded in her limited Egyptian research, not sure whether Professor Abdullah could understand what she was saying, especially with her American accent.

"God's willing," translated Professor Abdullah, as he smiled.

He promised to keep in touch.

# CHAPTER TWENTY-NINE

It was television's most watched show in United States history. The medical and scientific communities were sharply divided on Dickerson's personal interpretations of the HLA B66 findings.

An elderly Catholic priest, who supposedly performed a successful exorcism in St. Louis, Missouri, in 1952, was on national television offering his services to anyone found HLA B66 positive.

"Doc, you have caused a major-league chaos, you know that, don't you?" suggested Pinkett on the telephone.

"What do you mean, I caused a major chaos?" Dickerson chuckled.

"You are all over the darn channels, and now you have all these nut balls on TV pretending to know everything."

"Pinky, you know everybody is entitled to their opinion. I just explained mine in the simplest way I could."

"Doc, I don't call that simple. That's as complex as it gets. Now, we don't know whether we are coming or going."

"I think we are going forward, that is, with our project, officer Pinkett."

"Speaking of the project how is that coming along?"

"Well, we've completed our initial analysis of 10,002 inmates in San Diego and LA, thanks to Dr. Millons."

"Wait a minute…Dr. Millons…? Isn't he that creep who loves to give you a hard time?"

"Yeah, that's him. But guess what?"

"What?"

"He is my assistant now, and he is working his tail off on the project, probably to show me how sincere he is."

"I won't touch that man with a ten foot pole, mark my words."

"We are in the medical science profession. This is not the precinct."

"I guess you are. Anyway, what were you saying, something about initial analysis?"

"Yes, our initial analysis showed an almost 94 percent positive HLA on the mass murderers, grotesque killers, and also the psychopathic killers, especially those who exhibited no remorse about their crime."

"Darn, you know there are a lot of those in our criminal system now."

"Even among those that kill in attempted robbery, carjacking, or drug dealings, a high percentage of them, 62 percent, were positive for HLA," Dickerson continued.

"With such high percentage it makes it difficult not to label all criminals B66."

"There are far more normal people than these criminals, in case you missed the boat," reminded Dickerson.

"Thank God for that."

At the University of La Jolla, a phone bank was set up at the department of immunology for the deluge of calls that came for Dr. Dickerson. Even her home phone was recently changed to a security-cleared unlisted number. Her department-issued cellular phone number remained the same, however.

The *Washington Post* reported that most letters sent to members of Congress had been in support of Dr. Dickerson, and many of those mails were calling for nationwide testing for HLA B66. The United States Senate in response scheduled several behind-closed-doors committee meetings in an effort to provide a measured response.

"I have completed my analysis with great help from Dr. Millons," Dickerson answered in a phone call from Abramhoff. "We have some incredible results."

"I heard. How many inmates did you study?" asked Abramhoff.

"We analyzed about 5,002. I bet you had doubled that number?" Dickerson inquired.

"Between all the facilities we nearly topped 6,000, I think. I have to check to be exact." Abramhoff sounded upbeat.

"That's great. That's more than the National Institute of Health required for publications."

"Speaking of publications, which journal should we assign to publish this report?"

"Personally, I have nothing against *JAMA*," answered Dickerson, citing her favorite journal.

"But, don't you think since this is about human behavior, the *Journal of Behavioral Science* should get the nod?"

"The problem with that is subscription. The low subscription rate may not fare well for it."

"I know. How about the *Journal of Science,* they have a neutral board, and it has an international appeal."

"That's fair, the *Journal of Science* it is," Dickerson relented.

"Have you heard that we might be called to a Senate hearing?"

"No…not really…why?" asked a bewildered Dr. Dickerson, wondering how Abramhoff acquainted himself with all this political stuff.

"Just keep it to yourself for now. It may happen in the next few days or weeks."

# CHAPTER THIRTY

New York City's precinct fifty-seven Investigative Detective Edward Tom Pellagrini's personal habits revolved around reading ghouls, goblins, and ghosts novels—"triple G," he called them. Left to him alone, he would like to rename the precinct the "G-Precinct."

He took great pleasure in taking on cases that were the most bizarre. For example, his last case involved an odd ritualistic scene where real human body parts covered with blood-tinged bird feathers surrounded by coral beads were found in Central Park in early June. He successfully and single-handedly solved that case.

"A clan of Nigerian immigrants who believe in human sacrifice must have performed such a ritual," theorized Detective Pellagrini, "as an initiation for membership to the most powerful and notorious Nigerian gang operating in New York City."

Prior to the resolution of the case, nobody knew such a gang existed. Detective Pellagrini researched and befriended many Nigerians, and called on a Nigerian historian at Cornell University for help. He pieced together all the information that eventually aided in the arrest and conviction of all the participants of the crime, even though he was unable to infiltrate the gang itself.

He personally believed that some, but not all, mystery writers have some occult knowledge of the crimes they write about. He sometimes contacted these mystery writers for either an analysis or insight into some of his complicated cases. Such a case involved a Mr. James "Dean" Bellshaw.

Mr. Bellshaw, an avowed HIV-positive homosexual, was on trial in Manhattan third District Court, Criminal Division for the rape and murder of seven young runaway boys who had been missing and were last seen around Times Square.

Each of the victims had been brutalized. Their bodies were found at various hidden locations around Central Park near the aqueducts, where they could have been easily dumped from an overpass.

It was Detective Pellagrini, the strict vegetarian, who set the trap that eventually led to the capture of James Bellshaw. He methodically studied the modus operandi of the assailant.

"Look, let us follow his crimes objectively," began an eloquent Pellagrini.

"Jim, we have been following this crime now for six months," Detective Stubbs, his partner, reminded him.

"But we have never looked closely at the pattern," insisted Pellagrini.

"I don't see a pattern," Stubbs responded, looking around at the others in the station's small meeting room.

A bald-headed young man in his late thirties, Stubbs more or less followed Pellagrini sheepishly. He sometimes had an idea, only to be critically and analytically refuted by Pellagrini, an exercise that both took no personal offense at.

"Me neither; I don't see any pattern," Sergeant Maria Chintzy, who had followed the case with Pellagrini and Stubbs, chimed in.

"Okay guys, pay attention." Pellagrini picked up a chalk, walked over to the board on the west corner of the detail room, and began to illustrate.

A slim, fifty-something-year-old gentleman, he hardly ever wore a suit, believing that suits actually masked one's true identity. Often considered too analytical by the rest of the group, he seldom got invited out to drink with the boys.

"The first body's time of death was analyzed to be approximately eight p.m., the second body, twelve midnight, the third body, three a.m., and the fourth, four a.m., on different days."

"Then there was a three- to four-week delay."

"Three and a half," Detective Stubbs interrupted in jest.

"Smarty," retorted Pellagrini. "Four weeks, then it began again, first at nine p.m., then one a.m., then three a.m., again different days..."

"I am lost," Chintzy interrupted, looking totally confused.

"Just bear with me for a second," begged Pellagrini. "Look at the intervals between them and the days separating each discovery. We have four, three, and one, intervals in both the time and the days. Those corresponded to eight p.m., twelve a.m., three a.m., and four a.m. That also corresponded to the number of days apart.

"Then he started again, four weeks later, and had five and two intervals, again corresponding to nine p.m., two a.m., and four a.m. time and days apart."

"What the heck does all that mean, professor?" hissed Detective Stubbs in exasperation.

"What does it all mean, gentlemen and lady," illustrated Pellagrini, posing like a college professor, "I think this guy is trying to give us his address."

"You are crazy," blurted out Stubbs. "Why would he give us his address, so we can go and catch him? Just send us a note and we will be done with it."

"Maybe he wants us to catch him in a bizarre kind of way, who knows," answered Pellagrini. "A cry for help, just plain crazy or demonically possessed."

"Let him go jump into the Hudson River; that will solve our entire problem," suggested Chintzy. "Or better yet, just drop us a note like I suggested."

"Not these psychos," professed Pellagrini.

"So you think he lives at 43152…what?" Chintzy asked, finally appearing to follow Pellagrini's logical thinking.

"It is not 43152…what." Pellagrini was anxious to reveal his thoughts. "I think it is number four hundred and thirty one, on 52$^{nd}$ Street. Notice the four-week interval between four hundred and thirty one and fifty second."

"Far out, Detective, that is funky. I would never have thought of that," said Chintzy, nodding her head in admiration.

"So what do we do now? Arrest everyone living in the building on suspicion of murder?" asked Stubbs.

"No," answered Pellagrini. "I don't think he's finished yet. I believe his next move is for the apartment number. It's been two weeks now and no bodies have been found. However, we are not going to wait for him. I suggest we set a trap for him."

"How do we do that?" asked Stubbs, showing objection. "The last trap we tried nearly cost a life."

"We need to start canvassing the building this time, taking nightly pictures of all suspicious characters, follow them randomly to various locations in the city and see where that leads us."

"That will need a lot of man power, you know what I mean," said Stubbs.

"And maybe woman-power too," corrected Chintzy.

"Well excuse me," Stubbs rolled his eyes in resignation.

"I will have a meeting with the chief tomorrow, and I need everyone's support," pleaded Pellagrini.

"You got mine," Stubbs and Chintzy said almost simultaneously.

Detective Pellagrini was able to convince the chief of his plan. The plan was approved, and within two days twelve officers were assigned to the project.

After four days of active daily surveillance, Mr. James Bellshaw was subsequently picked up. He was followed twice to Central Park. On each occasion, he stopped at the north-end drive near the pond, came out, surveyed a particular area, then drove back home. Each occurrence happened late in the evening.

A thorough search of his two-bedroom apartment revealed videos and sexual materials of older men with young boys in various sexual acts. Also a bracelet and an ear piece that were discovered eventually matched those of victims six and seven. He was charged with their murder pending further investigations of the other victims.

In court, Mr. Bellshaw, after initially pledging innocent to the charges, eventually changed his plea to guilty on the grounds of demonic possession.

He claimed that his descendants were from Salem, Massachusetts, and that he was possessed by his great, great grandniece, a theory found ridiculous by the court but not by Pellagrini.

"What do you mean, that's possible?" asked the chief when the gang returned to the precinct.

"I read somewhere that—" began Pellagrini.

"Here we go again," two voices muttered, interrupting Pellagrini's explanation.

"Hey, let the man speak," cautioned the chief, eyeballing everyone. "After all, he is the one that solved this case, not you. Go ahead."

"As I was saying, before I was rudely interrupted," continued Pellagrini, shaking his head in fun disbelief, "there was this bizarre ritual among the witches in Massachusetts in the seventeenth century after the famous Sarah Good and Rebecca Nurse trials.

"The story was that, whenever a witch got burned on a stake, the other witches, after bribing the municipal office holders, were allowed to scavenge the remains of the dead witch.

"These remains were then used in the making of a secret potion. Those secret potions were revered because when taken in daily drops, they acted as protection against conviction of witchcraft and being burned on the stake.

"If, however, a witch who happened to drink the potion was caught and burned, the spirit of that witch would automatically be transferred to the next of kin in that family."

"Incredible, and unbelievable, but what does that got to do with this case?" Detective Schumann, another detective recently assigned to the case, asked.

"Well," continued Pellagrini, "after these spirits passed on from person to person they became restless and through some…occultation transformation…took on bizarre behaviors like Mr. Bellshaw."

"Occultation, hey, I think you made that one up. Can you spell and explain that in English, please?" mused Detective Stubbs.

"You are not gonna understand, even if I explain it ten times," said Pellagrini.

"Try me," Stubbs insisted.

"Please spare us," interjected the chief. "Are you implying that if we execute this guy, it is possible that his spirit will enter into one of his relatives' bodies, and another killing spree will start all over again?" asked the chief.

"According to the annals of witchcraft…yes," answered Pellagrini.

"I never heard of such annals," Chintzy stated.

"That's because you don't read enough," challenged Schumann.

"Yeah, I do, once in a while," continued Chintzy. "Check this out, I read about these two homosexuals who rented a truck and were randomly killing people at gas stations using a high-powered rifle. They must have mowed down eight people before they were finally caught. The strange thing was when he sent that note to the police chief saying, 'I am the beast; you and your children are not safe.'"

"Creepy, but listen to this," said Stubbs. "There was this bizarre case in either Chicago or Milwaukee of this man who molested and killed a dozen young boys and buried them all in his basement. I forgot how he was caught."

"I think that was in Chicago," said Pellagrini.

"Speaking of Chicago, I remember this one vividly, that creep who seduced young boys brought them to his house, killed them, then cooked and ate them," Chintzy stated, nodding her head in anticipated approval.

"She remembered that one vividly," mocked Stubbs.

Before an angry Chintzy had a chance to say what was on her mind about Stubbs, Pellagrini interrupted, "I don't think he cooked the whole person all at once, but rather cut him up piece by piece, stored him somewhere, then later cooked him."

"I don't think homosexuals commit all the gruesome crimes," said Schumann. "Take the case of the husband

and wife that needed babies so badly that they searched three states, found three pregnant women and proceeded to cut out the babies off from each womb. Mind you, no anesthesia, and no gloves."

"I remember…that was gross," agreed Pellagrini.

The conversations suddenly degenerated into who could recount the most gruesome crime.

"Oh let me tell you this one, I read…I said *read*," Chintzy shook her head at Stubbs, "about this case from Los Angeles, where they were finding dead bodies with different parts missing. Some were Latinos, two black, two Asians, one Caucasian, and one American Indian. They finally arrested the psycho killer, and in his stinky basement floor, they found the missing different parts sown together. When they questioned him, he claimed that he was about to create the perfect race."

"Now, is that twisted or what?" commented Officer Martha Henry in her usual loud voice as she walked in and overheard the conversation.

"Here goes the tattooed lady," said Schumann, who had made it known he disapproved of her.

The guys whistled in support of Schumann.

"You know, fellows, two wrongs do not make a right, but two dumb dudes always make a doo-doo…," retorted a cavalier Officer Henry, who is always quick with a response.

There was a burst of laughter in the room, including Pellagrini who winked an eye at Officer Henry as if to say, "Nice comeback."

"By the way, Schumann, do you have something against tattoos?" asked Officer Henry, spreading her hands and exposing the tattoo on her chest. "Or is it because you wish to have one?"

Officer Henry, an abrasive policewoman, was recently assigned to the precinct. She had caused such a stir in the precinct, where most officers were conservatives in their attire.

Officer Henry, however, wore slacks and shirts with belly sometimes exposed. She sported a beautiful butterfly tattoo on her left chest, sitting right on top of her upper breast area. She also had a tattoo of her dead brother's name on her back.

Being slightly well-endowed, a point she made obvious by her clothes, she would often get comments like, "Oh, that's a beautiful butterfly." To which she would always respond, "Wouldn't you like to have one?"

"No, I don't break laws," Schumann answered when asked the same question.

After a moment of intense stares from all, Henry spoke up.

"What the dickens are you talking about?" asked Henry, frowning, while everyone else looked at Schumann.

"There are no laws against tattoos," joined the chief.

"In the Bible there is," continued Schumann.

"I didn't know you read the Bible. You surprise me all the time," said a baffled Pellagrini. "But which law in the Bible are you talking about?"

"The law of 1928," answered Schumann without hesitation.

"What…?" echoed at least four voices in the room.

"Leviticus, the Book of Laws, chapter 19 verse 28, better known as the law of 1928, and it said, and I quote, 'You shall not lacerate your bodies for the dead and do not tattoo yourselves, I am the Lord.' I call that the law of 1928."

There was a momentary silence, and a look of awe on everyone's face.

"You fascinate me," Pellagrini responded. "I will check that out."

"That's a bunch of crap," said Officer Henry finally. "People have been tattooing themselves since antiquity."

"Now, that's an educated woman," said Stubbs, who could not resist.

"Yes, and I think you better reco-nize." Officer Henry nodded while showing her familiarity with the street slang, by dropping the "g" in "recognize."

There was some hissing and muttering in the room.

"Ladies and gentlemen," interrupted the chief. "Let's not lose track of the issue at hand, and that is to congratulate Jim on a job well done."

Everybody applauded.

"Way to go, Jim," blurted out Stubbs.

"Don't forget next Thursday's banquet at the Sheraton in Manhattan in honor of our illustrious detective. The governor and the mayor will be there with all the precinct chiefs. I want you guys and gals to behave yourself," the chief finally instructed.

"Don't we always?" asked Chintzy.

"Yeah, yeah, just remember, Jim will be an honoree," concluded the chief.

After the Chief left, "Hey, you, where is the law against gays?" Stubbs asked, not wanting to let go.

"I am glad you asked," answered Schumann. "That will be the law of 1822."

"What are you, a preacher or a detective?" Henry asked.

"Fellows, read the Book of Laws, Leviticus that is, so you know how to act," advised Schumann.

"So now you are the only one who knows how to act, just because you read this Leviticus book?" asked Officer Henry, looking at Schumann with disgust.

"Stop hating, Officer Henry, just spread the love," retorted Schumann, letting Officer Henry know that he, too, was street smart.

# CHAPTER THIRTY-ONE

The Senate hearing started without any significant snag. The hall room was packed with reporters. Dickerson wondered why they crammed all these people into such a small chamber.

Of the sixteen senators scheduled to attend, only one was in his chair at ten a.m. when the hearing was supposed to have started. By 10:20 a.m., however, all the senators were seated. The chairman, Senator Seymour Adams (a democrat from Georgia) called the meeting to order.

Senator Adams was the chairman of the Senate sub-committee on Domestic Affairs. He started by thanking Drs. Abramhoff and Dickerson for attending, and then went on to say how the Senate and the nation had been spellbound by the HLA findings.

He cautioned the Senate members to restrict their questions and follow-up comments to the scientific findings at hand, so that an appropriate bill could be promulgated from this discussion if need be.

"In conclusion," cautioned Senator Adams, "this is an issue that crosses party lines, because American lives may be at stake here. I will entertain questions from the panel after the doctors have read their prepared statements."

After the brief statements where both doctors essentially introduced themselves, Senator Adams opened the floor for discussion, "Senator Burton, please."

"Thank you, Mr. Chairman. Could either one of you explain to the panel what an HLA is and how it came to be related to criminals?" asked Senator Burton from Indiana.

Abramhoff responded by giving his usual standard answer of what HLA was, how they were related to diseases, and how this relationship was extrapolated further into human behaviors.

"How specific were the data that linked HLA to criminals?" the senator persisted.

Abramhoff responded on how he started looking at the link between HLA and predestined behaviors.

Dickerson's discovery, on the other hand, was by accident, involving a criminal in San Diego who was so bizarre she thought that he had a genetic abnormality, only to discover that he was HLA B66 positive.

"We found a marker on the HLA B loci that has not been identified elsewhere and further tests bore us out," concluded Dickerson.

"Speaking of the testing," asked Senator Christine Samples of Maine, "what specific tests are we talking about? How do you administer these tests, and how accurate are they?"

"The testing is done through a blood drawn sample," answered Dickerson. "After centrifugation or spinning, to separate the plasma from the blood, we then analyze the blood extract called the white blood cells. We locate the HLA band and identify the locus. The process is standard worldwide, and it is the same process of identification that HLA has been linked to multiple diseases, such as diabetes and multiple sclerosis. As for the accuracy, Dr. Abramhoff and I have run case-controlled studies and age-matched analysis using standard statistics. These were used to make our final analysis. The specificity and sensitivity of our testing are about 92 percent. That is superior accuracy."

"I understand that you have concluded your National Institute of Health funded studies," asked Senator Reuben of Washington State. "Can you share with us your conclusions, or better yet, what are your final analyses?"

"We have pooled our studies together," answered Abramhoff. "We analyzed exactly 10,977 convicted hard-core criminals in the San Diego and Los Angeles counties of California, and the Joliet, Kankakee, and East St. Louis counties of Illinois. Of these criminals, especially the mass murders and those we classified as psychopathic killers, there was almost a 92 percent concordance between them and HLA B66. Even among inmates who committed murders in the act of a criminal intent, such as stealing, carjacking, or bank robberies, there is still almost a 70 percent positive HLA B66 finding. There is no doubt that HLA B66 may predetermine the heinous criminality of certain individuals."

A brief reflective moment permeated the room. Some of the senators began chatting among themselves. The chairman immediately requested order.

"I have a question, Mr. Chairman," Senator Ridge of Texas requested.

"Yes Senator."

"What are the unknowns here? Specifically..., what I am trying to say is, what exactly don't we know about HLA B66?" asked the senator.

"If your question is what else we do not know about these people...," began Abramhoff.

"Yes, I am, in a sense," interjected Senator Ridge. "I am looking for that unknown variable."

"The only thing we do not know at this point is the trigger mechanism," answered Abramhoff. "By trigger mechanism, I mean that these individuals have this HLA assigned or expressed to them at birth. They are not inherited. Expressions can be dormant for a while, but what actual reaction that turns on the switch for them, to unleash behaviors that have been assigned to them, is what we do not know at the moment."

"In other words," asked Senator Adams, "you are telling us that you can pick anybody from the street, test him or her for HLA B66, and if he or she tests positive, that person has already been marked or assigned, and when the switch is turned on, whenever that is, there goes the heinous behavior."

"Precisely, Senator," added a delighted Dr. Dickerson. "And since we do not know where the switch is, or who turns it on, or when it is going to be turned on, we may have millions of loose cannons running around our streets."

"Mister Chairman," shouted Senator Hewlett of Tennessee, requesting attention. "I understand that we are supposed to keep our discussions purely scientific, but I cannot help but ask Dr. Dickerson to comment on her overt interpretation of the HLA B66 findings and its relationship to the number 666 in the Bible."

Muffled discussions were heard among the senators whether to allow Dr. Dickerson to answer or not. Finally, by a majority vote she was allowed to make one comment only.

"I did a lot of research concerning the number 666 in the book of Revelation. I also studied ancient languages and alphabetic writings, with some assistance from a professor in the Middle East, and found that the alphabet B in the lower-case resembles, in fact matches, the figure or number six in an old Aramaic language. To make a long story short, I, personally—and Dr. Abramhoff does not agree with me on this—believe that the number in the book of Revelations is located at the HLA B66 that we are discussing. The question we need to ask ourselves, if there is any doubt, is why this HLA B66 is only found in individuals with devilish intentions?"

"What do you think, Dr. Abramhoff?" asked Senator Hewlett.

"As Dr. Dickerson has said, this is a very personal belief which I do not share at this moment. Without more tests and follow-ups, it will be difficult to make any other conclusion, except the fact that HLA B66 predetermines certain behaviors."

"Thank you all, ladies and gentlemen, for attending the Senate subcommittee hearing on HLA B66. Because of time constraints, we have to conclude this hearing. The Senate members will go into executive session for further discussions. Again, thank you one and all," Senator Adams concluded.

# CHAPTER THIRTY-TWO

The morning after the hearing, the *Washington Post*, quoting an unnamed source, reported that at the executive session that followed the Senate hearing, there was a heated debate about the religious implications of HLA B66 and its bearing on the number 666.

In the end, it was finally recommended to authorize a national testing of incarcerated criminals. The tests were to be limited for now, only to individuals who committed murder, mayhem, psychotic, and heinous crimes.

A selection committee from the Senate, in collaboration with the FBI and the Center for Disease Control and Preventions, selected several prominent regional research institutions for the initial testing.

The nerve centers, however, would remain with Dr. Abramhoff in Chicago, and Dr. Dickerson in San Diego. Their mandate was to test selected inmates in the United States who fit the strict criteria set by the United States Senate.

Drs. Abramhoff and Dickerson were to report back to the Senate at the conclusion of the testing, and based on the result, the Congress of the United States would reconvene and vote on subsequent actions.

The Canadian government, according to the Associated Press, requested and obtained permission to add the University of Toronto in Toronto, Ontario, and McGill University in Montreal, Quebec, as additional test centers to collaborate with the United States government on this venture.

Detective Edward Jim Pellagrini of the New York City Police Department, who gained national fame when he solved the Central Park serial killer, was lobbied heavily by the governor of New York to be the federal watchdog in case of interstate turf battles.

"What do you think of Pellagrini?" asked Dickerson to Abramhoff

"From what I read, I think he is a bizarre individual," Abramhoff responded.

"He is going to need a West Coast assistant, and I will personally nominate Detective Pinkett for the job."

"That's your detective from San Diego, right?"

"That's my girl," Dickerson agreed with glee.

"This is all looking even better."

# CHAPTER THIRTY-THREE

Baptist General Hospital at the corner of Broadway and Interstate 30 in Merrillville, Indiana, boasted a newly renovated and vastly decorated doctors' lounge with a new high-definition plasma television.

Every day at noon, freshly catered lunch attracted a vast majority of the surgeons and a good number of the primary care doctors and specialists to the lounge. Occasions like these were usually the times to discuss various issues and express opinions, among the doctors.

The cable news network was discussing the centers chosen for the HLA testing and were interviewing administrative personnel at the various centers.

"Hi, Nsi, how did the case go this morning?" asked Dr. Mahatma Gupta, the cardiologist, who performed the angiography on Mrs. Elaine Worjorhowski.

"Excellent, the bypass went well, took a little longer than I expected. The mammary artery was a little difficult to harvest."

"She pulled through, yes?"

"Oh, yeah, she is in the recovery room, and her vitals are great."

As if on cue, both men turned to watch the program on television.

"What do you make of that nonsense?" ask Dr. Gupta.

"I think that's a whole bunch of hogwash."

"You don't think those doctors are up to something?"

"They are up to something all right. It's called lining their pockets with money."

"I guess you don't believe in the HLA theory either."

"How can these doctors make us believe that an HLA testing, which is experimental at best, can predict who is a criminal?"

"But won't the testing bear them out?"

"I bet you my bottom dollar they cooked and forged some of those numbers only to get federal dollars."

"I don't know," joined Dr. Obum Linton, a gynecologist, "these are two independent, highly respected physicians and researchers. I would not dismiss them casually."

"You know, and I know, that statistics can be manipulated to obtain the results we want by carefully eliminating the ones we don't want," Nsi explained.

"But they were able to convince the Senate of the United States to fund $150 million for a national testing program," Dr. Nathaniel Weitzman, the endocrinologist, who hardly ever expressed an opinion, noted.

By now, the entire staff at the doctors' lounge had voiced one opinion or the other about the discussion.

Dr. Nsi knew, deep in his heart, that some of these doctors were just jealous of his success, and he also knew that some were blaming him for the disappearance of Nurse Fisher, even though her body had not been found.

Many doctors knew of the liaison between him and Ms. Fisher and also between him and the two previous nurses at Munster who died mysterious deaths. He logically surmised that some of his colleagues had indirectly voiced the opinion that he was involved in their tragedies.

Another prominent cardio-thoracic surgeon, Dr. Emeka Nwazobia, from Nigeria, had quietly confided to friends that Dr. Nsi was not telling all he knew.

"I tell you what; I will challenge them to do a testing of all Americans, and I will be the first to volunteer," said Nsi, as all eyes turned to him.

"They do want to test all Americans," Dr. Weitzman hinted.

"I know, but they should just do it, to prove how bogus the test is," said Nsi.

"I can't stand that man," Nwazobia whispered to Linton as Nsi continued to converse with Dr. Weitzman.

"Who are you talking about?" Linton asked.

"Dr. Eat…you know what; or D.E.S. for short," Nwazobia again whispered.

"Why do you insist on calling him that name? That's terrible," asked Dr. Linton, almost with an identical whisper.

"Because that's exactly what his full name translates in the Ibo language of Nigeria."

"You mean Lee Kwon Nsi is in Ibo language also? He is after all Korean."

"It's actually an Ibo word. Lee Kwon Nsi in Ibo language literally means, eat…you know what."

"I think you are making that up, just because you don't like the man."

"I am very serious. Go ask Dr. Bernadette Acheta, the internist. She is also Ibo."

"That's really strange."

6 6 6

The popular northwest, *Indiana Times* headlines read:

> "Local doctor volunteered for the HLA B66 testing."

The story also dominated other northwest Indiana and Chicago land newspapers. Rumors abounded, but the overriding question among local residents was, "Why would a real popular doctor volunteer for HLA B66 testing?" "What was he trying to prove?"

To Dr. Nsi it was quite clear. If he tested negative, it would prove to his critics, especially Dr. Nwazobia and others that he was not the monster they thought he was. If he tested positive, it would validate his claim that the tests were bogus.

*Why would a successful physician like me with no criminal record or any traffic violation test positive?* he reasoned.

"You shouldn't do this," urged Moheri, calling from his Whiting, Indiana office as soon as he learned of Nsi's intention.

"Why shouldn't I?"

"I don't know, but I am leery of this whole thing, a little spooky, don't you think?" said Moheri.

"Relax, Mario. I have a plan to discredit this whole testing nonsense."

"What if you test positive?"

"That's it, then."

"What do you mean?"

"I will be famous, because that will make me the leader of the opposition."

"I really don't have a clue what you are talking about."

"In due time you will see, but I would not worry about anything if I were you."

"Okay, just be careful."

"Trust me, I will."

"What we need to focus on now is to start looking for vendors for the M&M juice, especially after that successful testing," urged Moheri.

"That's what I am talking about. With the fame that I will gain if I test positive, I will be able to find vendors for our M&M juice amongst others who may be as angry as I am."

*Why is Doc advertising the fact that he may test positive?* Moheri queried. *That's scary.*

Even though Abramhoff tried to dissuade Nsi from testing, he signed the no litigation agreement and a waiver of the non disclosure rules and scheduled his testing.

About five days later. "You tested positive," Abramhoff called Nsi to inform him personally of the test result.

"There must be a mistake," said Nsi, expressing no emotions, neither shock, nor anger.

"No, there was not. We tested it several times just to be sure, and then sent a sample to Dr. Dickerson in San Diego. All the tests were positive," informed Abramhoff.

"What does that tell you, Dr. Abramhoff? What does it tell you? Personally, it tells me that something is wrong with your HLA B66 theory. How can a physician like me test positive?"

"Frankly, Dr. Nsi, I am as surprised as you are," responded Abramhoff, sensing the challenge. "What we do know is that the test is very accurate, and it correlates well. You might be one of those rare findings that invariably show up in every test."

"Dr. Abramhoff, thank you anyway, but personally, I think this whole thing is a farce."

"I don't think so, Dr. Nsi."

"We will see," concluded Nsi.

When Abramhoff hung up with Nsi, he called Dickerson immediately.

"You will not believe this."

"Believe what?" ask Dr. Dickerson.

"That John Doe specimen we sent you that came back positive."

"Yeah, I remember, what about it?"

"It actually belongs to a famous cardio-thoracic surgeon in northwest Indiana."

"You don't say."

"And guess what?"

"What?"

"I just got off the phone with him."

"What did he have to say?"

"Well, he wasn't too pleased to say the least. He called our findings a farce, and it sounded like he is about to do something with it."

"What can he do, because actually, he needs to be watched or closely examined for any past criminal activity or behaviors, cardio-thoracic surgeon or not."

"This is a prominent surgeon. His reputation travels all the way to Chicago and beyond."

"So? Does that give him immunity from criminal behaviors?"

"Not really, but he is one of our own."

"That technically will argue in favor of the objectivity of the test, when it goes national."

"I agree. Anyway how is the national testing coming along?" asked Abramhoff, wanting to change the subject *tout-de-suite.*

"Mr. Pellagrini and Ms. Pinkett are hitting it off well. They have almost finished the organizational process with the centers. All are now computerized, phone banks are all set up, and I think they will be ready to go in a week or so."

"Thanks, and take care, and I will be talking to you." Abramhoff hung up the phone, sat down on his desk, and whispered aloud, "This is getting more complicated than I thought."

666

In a special television news brief report, all five Chicago television stations announced that a local northwest

Indiana physician, who volunteered to be tested for the HLA B66, was found positive.

The next morning, reporters crowded the Indiana University Medical Hospital Administration Building front entrance, where Dr. Nsi had agreed to make a brief statement. After a noisy forty-five-minute wait, Dr. Nsi appeared. He only read a brief statement and took no questions.

"Ladies and gentleman, it is true that I tested positive for HLA B66, a test that is absolute nonsense, manufactured by reputable scientists, with a questionable agenda. This is pure science fiction, but the sad part of the whole thing is that they have succeeded in obtaining federal government funding. I am a cardio-thoracic surgeon. I have transgressed no laws, not even a speeding ticket. I have no intentions of leaving my lucrative medical profession for a life of crime. To that end, I will dedicate my energy and resources in launching a national campaign against this nonsense called HLA B66. We are developing a Web site, www.antiHLAB66.com, **and** I urge everyone to visit the Web site in a few days for more information. Thank you very much."

Pellagrini and Pinkett's national testing program launch occurred two days after Dr. Nsi's television appearance. Both detectives were in daily consultations, and had gotten medical logistical support from Dr. Abramhoff and Dr. Dickerson. A total of about 2 to 2.5 million inmates were slated to be tested.

To obtain an age-matched normal population, monetary incentives and strict confidentiality were promised.

There were long lines of volunteers at all the centers. Two weeks into the recruitment process all the blood samples has been collected from about 2.2 million inmates and approximately 2.3 million volunteers.

Chicago and San Diego were designated as national centers for statistical analysis but with final review at the National Institute of Health and Public Safety. It would take about seven to ten days for the official results to be made public.

Meanwhile, Dr. Nsi took to the airwaves, denouncing the testing and urging for total boycott of the test centers. Ten days after all the blood tests were accounted for, the National Institute of Health and Public Safety scheduled a noon news conference to announce the findings.

Drs. Abramhoff and Dickerson, and Detectives Pellagrini and Pinkett, were all scheduled to be in attendance, with a question and answer session to follow. The director of the National Institute of Health started the news conference by acknowledging the heroic efforts of Drs. Abramhoff and Dickerson.

"Let's also not forget the gallant work done by Detectives Pellagrini and Pinkett who gathered all the information with very short notice."

Applause followed.

"After multiple reviews and several statistical analyses using different methodology," continued the director, "the results showed that among the hardcore criminals, the psychopathic killers, and the mass murderers, designated by the Senate, there are indeed positive results to the tone of 92 percent.

"There is no doubt," concluded the director, "that the HLA B66 does indeed correlate well with these crimes.

"The other interesting findings," the director said reluctantly, "is that about 2.68 percent of the matched population classified as "average Joe" and "average Jill" also tested positive for the HLA B66.

"We will now entertain questions," he finally concluded.

"Who are those 2.68 percent?" asked a reporter.

"Because of strict confidentiality, and HIPPA regulations, we are unable to comment on that."

"But why don't we have them all arrested if the correlation is true?" asked another reporter.

"Because we don't even know who they are, and besides, they have committed no crimes."

"Dr. Abramhoff, you subscribe to the predestination theory. Are these 2.68 percent people predestined, therefore, to committed heinous crimes?"

"Strictly following my theory of predestination, you may conclude that they are predestined for that."

"So would you therefore classify them as criminals-to-be?"

"Even with predestination, individuals have been known to miss obvious opportunities," answered Abramhoff.

"Dr. Dickerson!" shouted another reporter.

"Yes," Dickerson answered, as she moved to the microphone.

"Your theological research showed HLA B66 translated to the number 666, the mark of the devil. Are these

2.68 percent individuals who tested positive translating into the devil's advocates?"

"Based on the interpretation of which I eluded before, you might say that."

"They, therefore, possessed the stamped image according to the book of Revelation, if your theory is followed."

"Theoretically, you may conclude that." Dickerson showed a rare smile. "Realize that the theory is based on my personal interpretation aided by religious education. If you therefore look at it purely on religious grounds, yes, you would conclude that they have the stamped image and are therefore followers of the beast."

"Detective Pellagrini, you are quite versed in bizarre behaviors, demonic possessions, witchcraft, and the occult, why would you not arrest these cases given to you on a silver plate?"

"Like the doctor said, sir, they have committed no crimes," answered Pellagrini.

"So are you gonna wait for them to kill two, three, ten, or fifty people before you arrest them?" asked a female reporter.

"The United States of America's laws are clear, ma'am," answered Pellagrini. "You cannot arrest or persecute or even prosecute an individual for a crime he or she did not commit."

"But we have proof now that they are going to commit a crime someday."

"Sir," answered Pellagrini in exasperation, "we are law enforcement officers, not law enactment officers."

# CHAPTER THIRTY-FOUR

Channel Five, a Chicago television station, somehow managed to arrange an interview with Dr. Nsi in his office in Munster, Indiana.

"What do you make of those positive HLA findings?" began the reporter.

"First of all, what's your name again?" asked Nsi.

"Warren," answered the reporter.

"Let me say this, Warren, the only disease that has shown greater than 90 percent association with HLA is Ankylosing Spondylitis, a chronic back condition seen mostly in middle-aged men. Now, do you want me to believe that murderers are diseased?" Nsi questioned. "Some authorities have made that association, yes, I grant you, but without any scientific proof."

"Okay, let's for the moment assume that they are," pursued the reporter. "Maybe someday, somebody might manufacture a medication or come up with an operation to cure this disease."

"Not all diseases have cures," answered Nsi abruptly.

"Yes, but they can be curbed or controlled."

"Well, locking them up in prisons can be labeled as that curb or control, wouldn't you say?" questioned the reporter, flipping through his notes, "Just like we did in the early days of tuberculosis."

"Fine," Nsi showed signs of infuriation as he stroked the right side of his hair. "But where do we come off telling the public that these criminals are devil's descendants?"

"You are talking about Dr. Dickerson's assertion that HLA B66 is in fact the number 666 in the Bible," verified the reporter.

"Yes," Nsi answered with a sarcastic laugh, "coming from someone who calls herself a scientist, Dr. Dickerson should be ashamed of herself."

"Why?" asked the reporter, eyes wide open.

Nsi leaned forward and eyeballed the reporter. "For one thing, that's total hocus-pocus…one plus one does not equal ten. Do you believe that?"

"You have to realize that the Bible sometimes is hard to interpret, and she did her best to shed some light on this phenomenon," answered the reporter, nodding his head.

"Well, I have my own religion and beliefs, but science speaks a universal language."

"Are you so repulsed by this because you tested positive?" ventured the reporter, avoiding eye contact while writing on his note pad.

"Would you not be, especially when they claim that HLA B66 predestines behaviors?"

Looking directly at Nsi, the reporter cautiously asked, "Are you absolutely sure you have not committed any crime in your life?"

"What are you getting at, Mister?" responded Nsi with obvious irritation.

"I mean, if the premise is true, and you tested positive...I am still at loss for an explanation."

"That's because the premise is not true," Nsi answered, almost shouting.

"I guess we have to wait for more scientific evidence," suggested the reporter, as Nsi attempted to rise from his chair.

"My sentiments exactly," firmed Nsi and then concluded the interview.

Meanwhile, Nsi's Web site, so far had garnered close to 1 million visits. The Web site management issued a call for a massive demonstration at the test sites and a national demonstration in Washington, D.C., in two months.

Within days of the positing, small scattered demonstrators could be seen at various test centers carrying signs that read:

"HLA B66 is a label."

"Stop HLA B66."

Counter demonstrations soon followed with signs saying:

"What are you afraid of?"

"Are you an abhorrent closet criminal?"

666

An estimated quarter of a million demonstrators gathered on the steps of the United States capitol.

Marching down Pennsylvania Avenue, they crossed over to Constitution Avenue, en route to the Washington Monument, where a stage had been set up for the speakers to address the crowd. There were a few unknown speakers, but everyone was waiting for Dr. Nsi.

He did assume the coveted title of the leader of the anti-HLA B66 movement. A few movie stars also addressed the crowd, urging them to resist the HLA B66 testing. Finally, Dr. Nsi took the stage, to the delight of the audience.

"My fellow Americans," began Dr. Nsi with no trace of Korean accent, "today, we are witnessing the beginning of a national persecution campaign unparalleled in American history."

There was a light applause.

"If we let these people succeed, thousands, maybe millions, of innocent Americans will be labeled as criminals, and worst of all, they will be called sons and daughters of the devil."

There was a lot of booing and hissing from the audience.

"Our task, therefore, is to make sure that these perpetrators do not succeed. How do we do that?

"Simple, I want you to contact every congressman and senator in your state and urge them to withdraw the funding for the HLA project and, most importantly, to stop all testing."

666

When Dr. Nsi returned from Washington, he was greeted by a phone call from Bobby Auto Parts owner, Bob Wizard.

"Hey there, Doc," said Bob.

"Hi, Bobby," Nsi coughed, clearing his scratchy throat. Nsi had developed a slight intermittent cough since his return from Washington, D.C. "What's up?"

"The…'em IRS and the state police were just here."

"The IRS! What do they want with you?"

"Well, actually, they were looking at the records of some cars we've demolished for parts."

"That's all?" Nsi breathed a sigh of relief.

"They claim that some of those vehicles were declared stolen." Bobby's voice quivered a little at the other end.

"Bobby, are you in a stolen car business?" asked a surprised Nsi. "I thought your business was up and up."

"How do you think we make all those profits? Sometimes, we commission cars."

"By commission I assume steal, but what does that have to do with me?"

"They also took a lot of records from the file cabinets, Doc. I don't know exactly all that they took, but they went through the entire file cabinets."

"How long ago did this happen?" Nsi's voice changed.

"About two weeks ago."

"What! Why didn't you tell me before?"

"I couldn't reach you, with you on TV…in Washington, and all." Bobby sounded frantic.

"Calm down, Bobby. Have you heard anything since?"

"No, I haven't heard anything yet."

"Well, let's hope it's nothing but the case of simple car thefts," reassured Nsi.

The phone rang again soon after Nsi hung up from Bob.

"Hey, Doc!" greeted Marion.

"Hi, Marion," answered a dejected Nsi.

"What's the matter?"

"I just hung up with Bobby," said Nsi, grimacing. "He was telling me that the IRS and state police raided his establishment."

"Yeah, I know."

"You know?" inquired Nsi with a sense of betrayal. "Bobby called you?"

"I just told you he did. He called me right after the raid, some two weeks ago. I was interviewed by the FBI and state attorney general's office." Marion somehow sounded nonchalant about the whole affair.

"Wait!" Suddenly Nsi became suspicious. "Call me back on my cell. You have the number?"

"Yes I do, why?" asked a surprised Moheri.

"Just do it," commanded Nsi.

"Yes, sir," answered Moheri, as he bowed and then proceeded to call Nsi on his cell phone.

"So, what do they want?" inquired Nsi.

"Look, they started asking about my relation with Bobby, and I told them that he is a good friend, and sometimes we go golfing together."

"Yes, go on."

"Then they wanted to know if Bobby has demolished any cars for me and if I had given him any cars to be demolished."

"Yes, yes…well, have you?"

"Calm down, of course I told them no," continued Moheri with a frown on his face. "Then they wanted to know what relationship I have with you."

"What...? What relationship with me?" Nsi asked, taking a deep breath.

"Yes," answered Moheri, "and I didn't know where that came from."

"But what did you tell them?"

"I told them that, yeah, I know you, and that we've played golf together at Oak Ridge Country Club."

"That's it?"

"No, that's not it. I remember they also asked what business relationship I have with you, and I told them none."

"You know there are some doctors here who do not like me, and they will stop at nothing to get at me," rationalized Nsi. "They are fishing...yes, they are fishing. I am sure that if they come up with nothing from the raid at Bobby's, they have no case."

Moheri shook his head in disbelief, and then said, "Didn't I tell you to lay low from that national and television stuff? But no, you must do it, so you said."

"Don't worry, Marion," reassured Nsi with another throat clearing. "I can take care of myself and the group."

Moheri did not fully understand what Nsi meant by the group. He had that puzzled look on his face as he hung up the phone.

# CHAPTER THIRTY-FIVE

At the doctors' lounge at Baptist General Hospital early next morning, Dr. Nsi ran into Dr. Nwazobia. He could not resist an attempt to query Nwazobia whether he was the one that talked to the FBI.

"Hi, Naxobia," said Dr. Nsi.

Dr. Nwazobia always took offense whenever his name was mispronounced, and he was usually quick to correct the enunciation of "Nwa" rather than "Na."

"Nwa…zo…bia, Dr. Nsi," greeted Nwazobia.

"Nwaxobia, I am sorry," Nsi apologized. "I just wanna ask…I'm planning on taking off in two weeks for a week-long conference in San Francisco, and I was wondering if you can cover me for that period."

*Why?* Nwazobia wondered. *This guy never asked me to cover him before, and I know he knows that I don't like him.*

"Sure," replied Dr. Nwazobia, instead, "just send me a list of your hospital patients before you leave. Do you want me to cover your emergency room calls also?"

"Yes, you can, if it is no trouble," Nsi replied with a measured smile on his face.

"No problem." Nwazobia smiled back.

Nsi turned and headed toward medical records. After two steps, he turned back again to Nwazobia.

"Oh, by the way," Nsi's voice barely audible, "has anybody talked to you recently about me?"

"Excuse me…no…about what?" asked a puzzled Nwazobia as he turned around to face Nsi again.

"About anything," Nsi answered, waving his hands in desperation.

"Not really," replied Nwazobia, frowning.

"If they do, would you let me know?"

"Sure will."

*What's D.E.S. up to now?* Nwazobia wondered, as he entered the doctors' lounge.

*One of these days he is going to find himself in real hot water.*

Two weeks after the conversation with Dr. Nwazobia, and twenty-four hours prior to Dr. Nsi's departure to San Francisco, there was a knock at the front door, followed by the Big Ben sound of the doorbell.

It was 4:30 in the morning. Hardly anyone in this neighborhood got disturbed this early. Nsi could not understand who…unless either Bob or Marion…*no, they know not to come to the house like this…*

The door bell rang again.

"I am coming!" shouted Nsi as he approached the door.

"Can I help you?" asked Dr. Nsi, peeping through the thick glassy part of his exquisite front door.

"This is the FBI. Can we come in?" said a man at the other side of the door with his badge flashing.

"What is this about?" asked Nsi, half shouting trying not to wake up anyone else.

"Can we come in and discuss this inside, sir?"

"What is it, honey?" asked the wife, Lynn, coming down the stairs.

"The FBI is here and I…I don't know what they want," Nsi answered, voice quivering.

"Well, let them in then, so we can see what they want," answered Lynn innocently.

Opening the door, three men entered the house.

Unknown to Nsi, his son also was standing at the top of the stairs peeking at the scene.

"Could you have your son go back to his room?" demanded the officer.

"What is this about?" asked Lynn, frightened.

"Please, ma'am," requested the agent.

"Come on…go back to your room, Jason, we'll be there in a second."

Jason went back to his room and closed the door behind him.

"Doctor and Mrs. Nsi, I am agent Henry Scott; this is agent Watkins," said the lead agent pointing to the second man, both dressed in dark suits.

"This is police officer Eric Palmer," continued the man who called himself Scott, as he pointed to a uniformed officer.

Both men bowed politely.

"What is this about?" asked Lynn frantically.

"I have a warrant for the arrest of your husband, Dr. Nsi," said Agent Scott. "We would like for you, Doc, to get dressed and come with us to the station."

All three men and Lynn looked at Dr. Nsi for a response.

"Don't I have the right to know what I have done?" asked Dr. Nsi, showing very little emotion.

"Sir, you need to come with us so that we can sort all this out at the station."

Dr. Nsi went back to the bedroom, and came back in less than ten minutes dressed in business casual attire with a blue jacket and a gray flannel pant.

"Could you turn around please, sir?" requested agent Scott.

Grudgingly, Dr. Nsi turned around, and he was handcuffed.

"Is this all necessary? My husband is a much-respected physician and our attorney and others will hear about this," Lynn threatened as her husband was led out.

Leading Dr. Nsi outside to a waiting blue Ford sports utility vehicle, Officer Scott escorted Nsi to the passenger side of the backseat and guided him into the vehicle.

Lynn, dressed in her nightgown covered with a white robe, watched frightfully as the car drove off.

666

The charges against Dr. Nsi were overwhelming.

Officer Watkins and the Lake County Prosecutor read the charges against him.

Apparently, ever since the disappearance of Nurse Fisher, the state attorney general's office, in collaboration with the FBI, the Munster Police Department, and the Lake County Sheriff's Department had set up a wire tap of Dr. Nsi's home, office, and cellular phones. These were shown to Nsi.

Also an initial search of Nurse Fisher's home found some incrementing evidence, but not enough to convict. The tapes found at Bobby's auto shop, after careful analysis at the Federal Bureau of Investigation's crime laboratory in Chicago, however, clearly identified Dr. Nsi.

All evidence was catalogued and cross-checked to be sure no mistakes were made. Dr. Nsi, they realized, was a prominent individual.

He sat speechless throughout the entire presentation.

Published reports were quick to report the arrest, and they also quoted the arrest of Dr. Moheri, a senior research scientist at Johnston Chemicals in Whiting, Indiana, and Bob Wizard of Wild Bobby Auto Shop of Lynwood, Illinois. All were charged with murder, conspiracy to commit murder, concealment, and possession of a deadly illegal chemical.

In Nsi's case, the murders of two other nurses in Munster, Indiana, were added to the charges. Bail was set at $5 million for Dr. Nsi and $2 million for the rest.

Since Nsi had been tested and found positive for HLA B66, Governor Milton of Illinois issued an executive order to test Moheri and Bobby Wizard for HLA B66.

Surprisingly, Moheri tested positive, while Bobby Wizard did not.

# CHAPTER THIRTY-SIX

Dr. Lee Kwon Nsi's trial at the Federal Court Building in South Bend, Indiana, became a national event. The leader of the opposition, the head of the anti-HLA B66 movement, who himself had tested positive, on trial for multiple murders. A respected physician, who had used his power and influence to gain fame and even volunteering for the HLA test, a man who after testing positive declared his innocence.

The evidence directly linking Nsi with the two murders in Munster, Indiana, was circumstantial at best, but Moheri did agree to testify, and also to cooperate with federal investigations in exchange for a leaner sentence.

Some of the phone conversations between Dr. Nsi and the perpetrators were presented in court and played on national television. The most incriminating and damaging evidence was the video recording of the death of Nurse Marjorie Fisher. Unknown to Moheri and Nsi, wild Bobby had been video recording all the happenings at his remote repair shop.

Dr. Nsi, however, pleaded innocent to all charges, alleging that the phone conversations, the videos and all, were doctored and engineered by the crocked federal authorities that were all in support of the HLA B66.

Moheri was also found guilty of the murder of Tina Coffee. He was charged with unlawful manufacturing and distribution of a lethal substance, intimidation, and concealment of a dangerous material. He was sentenced to life imprisonment without parole.

"Has the jury reached a verdict?" asked the judge after handing the piece of paper back to the bailiff.

"Yes, your honor," responded the lead juror.

"What is your verdict?" asked the Judge.

There was absolute silence in the courtroom.

"On the count of murder in the first degree, we, the jury, found the defendant…guilty."

"On the count of conspiracy to commit murder, we, the jury, found the defendant…guilty."

"On the count of aiding and abetting in the murder of Nurse Fisher, we, the jury, found the defendant…guilty."

Five other related charges against Dr. Nsi were presented, and he was found guilty on all counts. Dr. Nsi was sentenced to death by lethal injection and was immediately placed on death row.

The entire trial of Dr. Nsi and final conviction became a rallying cry around the nation for universal testing.

Many on national television who had previously been sympathetic to Dr. Nsi's pronouncement that HLA B66 was nothing but "hocus pocus" began reassessing their views.

Dickerson's theory, on the connection between B66 and 666, became the cornerstone of many discussions on television. The United States Senate and Congress had steadfastly refused to debate mandatory testing of all Americans.

On NBC Sunday news story, *Meet the Press,* the major topic was about Dr. Nsi and Dr. Moheri's HLA-positive tests.

Senate majority leader, Samantha Rodgers, a Democrat from North Carolina, opened the argument, "Let's look at this for one second. The essence of mandatory testing is to be able to do something with those that test positive. What do you propose we do with the HLA B66 positive Americans?"

"Senator Burns, what do you think?" The moderator smiled at Mr. Burns.

Senator Wendell Burns, a Republican from Utah, the ranking Republican on the Homeland Security Committee, leaned forward, smiled, and responded, "Look, it does at least gives us a road map to where we are going with this."

Senator Burns, tapping his right index finger on the table to elaborate every word, continued, "What I am trying to say is this…once these folks are identified, we can monitor them closely for any signs of deviant behavior. Just as we have been successful at monitoring terror suspects, we can apply the same mechanism here. You know the old saying, an ounce of prevention is better than a pound of cure."

"How would you feel," retorted Senator Rodgers with an angry look on her face, "if your son, daughter, brother, or sister tested HLA B66 positive, and the government of the United States tagged him or her like a dog to be followed in case he or she deviates, as my honorable friend suggested?"

Sensing her anger, Burns quickly intervened, "I am not advocating that we tag people like dogs. We have mechanisms in place, which I am not at liberty to elaborate here, whereby we can follow individuals and monitor their behaviors without obstructing their daily lives."

"What then should we do with the rest of the world?" asked Senator Rodgers with a faint collegial smile on her face. "Or are we so arrogant to think that only Americans are HLA B66 positive?"

"The way I see it, let's take care of American first," responded Senator Burns, again pointing with his right index finger, "and let the other governments borrow whatever technology they want and test their citizens, and implement whatever law they see fit."

"Some of your Senate colleagues are advocating an asylum-like city," interrupted the moderator, searching for words, "to house all HLA B66 Americans, sort of like an open prison. What do you think of that, Senator Burns?"

"I really don't believe we need to go that far," chuckled Senator Burns, "because that in itself would be cruel and unnecessary punishment for somebody who has committed no crime yet."

"Senator Rodgers?" asked the moderator, looking for a rebuttal.

Clasping her hands in a plea-like fashion, Senator Rodgers responded, "That goes to the core of what I am trying to illustrate. Here we are in the twenty-first century, and we are back to the days of the Spanish Inquisition of 1478 all over again, except this time science has become the judge and jury."

With the non-ending debate raging on the airwaves, President Steve McClellan, Republican from Baton Rouge, Louisiana, called an emergency meeting of the National Security Advisors, the Central Intelligence Agency director, director of the Federal Bureau of Investigation, and the cabinet heads, to a weekend meeting at Camp David.

Leaked reports stated that the consensus among the directors was for mandatory national testing, but given the legal challenges posed by such a move, and the fact the United States Supreme Court, by a five-to-four margin, clearly indicated their opposition to any national testing, the president, who personally opposed national testing, and his crisis cabinet were left wondering what to do.

A proposal by a national security advisor was finally agreed upon. It called for the creation of a national investigative and clearing-house agency to be headed by Detectives Pellagrini and Pinkett. Their task was to investigate all new bizarre violent crimes and other unnatural crimes, at their discretion. A legal cover for the detectives would involve labeling their mission as part of an ongoing criminal investigation. The HLA B66 results would be kept secret, until all the evidences were collected and the suspects charged. For one thing, they envisioned that at least it would accelerate the trial process and save the nation millions of dollars in lengthy court proceedings.

The project, code named the "3 P's," for Pellagrini-Pinkett Project, was coined in recognition of the detectives' work so far. All the police departments in the nation were alerted and made aware of the new agency and the need for unfettered collaboration.

The new agency would work in collaboration with the Federal Bureau of Investigation while at the same time maintaining its independence.

# CHAPTER THIRTY-SEVEN

Within days of the creation of the 3 P's, calls were pouring in from all across the nation.

"We have a new case in Florida," announced an excited Pellagrini looking at the new office computer monitor.

"What is it?" asked Pinkett, peeking at her own new 19-inch flat screen computer monitor.

"Sun City, Florida, police just alerted us of a strange case," stated Pellagrini. "A husband and wife are being held in Sun City for allegedly torturing their five adopted children."

"What bizarre stuff did they do?" asked Pinkett, off-loading a box full of personal stuff.

"Apparently they used electric shock to punish the kids."

"That's horrible." Pinkett paused for a moment and turned to look at Pellagrini on the computer.

"That's not all. Two kids had all their toenails pulled off with pliers."

"Ouch...that hurts." Pinkett sat on the couch, and then clenched her fingers.

"A sixteen-year-old was so starved that he only weighed seventy pounds," continued Pellagrini, "and listen to this, a twelve-year-old who tried to run away had all the digits on her feet smashed with a hammer."

"Lord, have mercy," Pinkett declared, shaking her head. "We definitely need their blood."

"That came across like we are a bunch of vampires," Pinkett joked, realizing what she had just said, then laughed out aloud.

"Look at it this way," suggested Pellagrini, joining in the laugh, "we are the good vampires, if there is any such thing."

666

Two agents were dispatched to Sun City, Florida, to collect blood samples from the suspects. The tests would be performed at an undisclosed National Institute of Health laboratory in Bethesda, Maryland. The lab's analytical teams were under the supervision of Abramhoff and Dickerson.

"One is just coming in now," reported Detective Pinkett, gently manipulating the computer mouse.

"From where?" asked Detective Pellagrini, peering over Pinkett's screen.

"Ann Arbor, Michigan," both detectives read out off the computer.

"Look at that…two kids, both twelve years old, riding their bicycle, disappeared in a wooded area near their home. A two-day search found the two bodies in the woods," continued Pinkett. "Apparently one of the girl's fathers has been arrested, and he already confessed."

"Look!" Pellagrini pointed at the screen. "The man's daughter was beaten and stabbed twenty-two times. That's gross. She was also stabbed in both eyes and ears. The friend was also beaten and stabbed eleven times for—get this—interfering."

"Triple six," came out of their mouths simultaneously.

666

Several days later, a report came from the overseas wire service that the Italian government had arrested two couples who were accused of killing eight people in a satanic ritual in the outskirts of Milan.

The Italian government, wishing to become part of the HLA B66 testing countries, contacted the United States government immediately. Following an inter-governmental negotiations, and upon mutual agreement of both countries, two agents from the project team were dispatched to Milan on a phlebotomy mission.

"Definitely triple sixes," concluded Pellagrini and Pinkett.

The involvement of the Italian government posed a new dilemma for the team.

Already, Spain, France, Portugal, Mexico, Thailand, Brazil, Nigeria, and South Africa had requested to become part of the HLA B666 project. As a result of these requests, all the State Department's recommendations for entering into the project were presented to the president and were approved.

A universal precautionary procedure would be instituted for all blood samples collected, no matter from what country they came; that would eliminate cross-contaminations or transmissions of any viral, bacterial, or parasitical diseases.

"Look…another triple six," said Pinkett with some excitement.

"From where?" ask a cautious Pellagrini.

"This one from Minnesota," answered Pinkett, shaking her head. "An eighteen-year-old Native American living in a reservation first shot both parents to death, then went on a shooting rampage, killing eleven people, wounding twenty, then turned the gun on himself and blew his brains to pieces."

"We have somebody to collect samples, yeah?" asked Pellagrini.

"Already sent," Pinkett winked at him.

"Did you hear about the one from Missouri?" Pellagrini calmly asked.

"What town in Missouri?"

"A small religious town called Mountain View, Missouri," answered Pellagrini, like he had been there before.

"They must have a lot of mountains over there," suggested Pinkett with a jovial tone.

"I don't think so. There's nothing there but flat lands."

"So why did they name a town in the plains Mountain View?" asked a curious Pinkett.

"Beats the heck out of me," answered Pellagrini, scratching his forehead.

"Heck?" asked Pinkett with a strange look on her face. "I thought you didn't swear."

"Oh, sometimes I use a lot of that to replace the actual curse words, especially while I am speaking in front of a lady." Pellagrini smiled.

"Gee, thanks." Pinkett blushed.

"Anyway, this killer bound, tortured, and murdered up to ten women over a period of about twenty years."

"Why did it take twenty years to apprehend him?" asked Pinkett, opening the medium-sized refrigerator at the east corner of the hastily arranged office to retrieve a bottle of water.

"Because, he was never a suspect," explained Pellagrini, dusting off the love seat. "He was a regular church attendee, community leader, and a white-collar employee."

"One of those, no-way-not-him type persons," volunteered Pinkett while she sipped at the bottled water.

"That's an intelligent analogy," congratulated Pellagrini, who then picked up the morning paper at the end table.

"Intelligent? You are just scratching the surface of my intellect."

"I see, I see, says the blind man, to the deaf wife, while the mute child agrees," Pellagrini replied.

"You're full of jokes."

"That's nothing…you haven't seen the depths of my jokes."

"Okay, tell me one good joke," requested Pinkett, as she sat on the stool facing Pellagrini.

"Well, how do you like your jokes, clean or dirty?" asked Pellagrini, putting the newspaper down.

"I don't know you that well, so do a clean one." Pinkett smiled.

"Okay, this one is very clean by New York standards," stated Pellagrini, balancing himself in the middle of the love seat.

"Two Reverend Sisters were being chased by a rapist as they were returning home along a desolate road to the convent. Reaching the fork on the road, they decided to split; in that case, if the rapist chased after one of them, the other one at least will make it safely to the convent and call for help. Sister Jenny arrived first at the convent without incident and a few minutes later, Sister York arrived panting, dressed all rumpled at the bottom.

"'What happened?' asked Sister Jenny.

"'Oh, he came after me all right,' answered Sister York, catching her breath.

"'And what happened?' urged Sister Jenny in haste.

"'I ran faster, he ran faster. Finally I stopped, and he stopped. I pulled up my dress, he pulled down his pants.'

"With both hands over her mouth, Sister Jenny uttered, 'Oh no, what…what…'

"With ease and calm, Sister York answered, 'A nun with her dress pulled up runs a lot faster than a man with his pants down.'"

Pointing at Pellagrini in a friendly gesture, Pinkett laughed for a while then said, "That was good…that was good, that definitely came from New York."

# CHAPTER THIRTY-EIGHT

The Vatican had been exceptionally silent since the news about HLA B66 and its association with criminality, pre-destination, and its allusion to the number 666.

Since Dr. Dickerson's pronouncements, there were massive influxes of attendance, especially those of the Catholic faith. Most worshipers' prayers, according to an AP news poll, showed a great majority of them praying that they, or their family members, not be afflicted with HLA B66. At St. Peter's Basilica in Rome, Italy, there was an unusual throng of people wanting to see or hear the Pope speak.

Such was the case on Easter weekend as throngs of worshipers filled St. Peter's Square in an unprecedented number. At the midnight Mass commemorating Easter Virgil, the Vatican police and the Swiss guards had to turn huge crowds back for fear of overcrowding.

The homily given by the Pontiff was done in four languages, English, French, Italian, and Spanish. After wishing the worshipers a happy Easter and urging his followers to remember the reasons for Christ coming on earth, the resurrection into a new life, the Pontiff for the first time addressed the issue of HLA B66.

He cautioned against what he termed the rush to irrational judgment. He noted that all scientific discoveries had to withstand the test of time. Therefore, according to the Pope, time was needed before conclusions would be subsequently accepted as part of human history.

He posed a question to those whom he described as being in haste for judgment, the same question a United States senator posed one month before on national television.

"The question one should always ask himself or herself is this: What if my relative, sister, brother, or father tests positive, with no evidence of a sinful past or present, would you judge him or her any differently, or should we explore other alternatives?"

He concluded the homily by urging caution.

666

"What other alternatives are there if one tests positive for HLA B66?" People asked on the radio and television phone calls. "Is there a magic solution or pill that can cure them of their stamped image?" "Are chromosome transplants a remote possibility?"

A new debate dominated the HLA B66 issue. Since the disease, if one could call it that, had been identified, what can be the cure? Others argued that this phenomenon was not a disease, but that of predestination in an already-chosen person.

Some proposed an immediate solution, stating that this was like identification, a stamped image, a marker for the followers of the beast, and there was only one cure: that of extermination, relationship or not.

One of the supporters of the last theory was Dickerson herself, who in a very rare telephone interview to KSD station in San Diego expressed that, "The Good Book clearly stated that the stamped image was given by the beast."

"By the stamped image you're implying the number 666," asked the famous radio station talk-show host, Stan the Man.

"Yes, I mean 666," Dickerson replied emphatically, "and as I have stated, B66 and 666 may be considered one and the same if we think wisely, and follow proper calculations."

"What do you think about those who said that your theory holds no water?"

"They say the same thing about mystical apparitions and miracles," Dickerson lectured. "I will bet you that if one of the famous prophets came down to earth and performed miracles, there would be those who would call that a fake."

"Maybe," Stan feigned a laugh. "So help me to understand what it is that you are suggesting we do with the HLA B66s, or triple sixes, as the 3 P's calls them."

"My question back to you is this," Dickerson retorted. "What will you do if you are looking at the devil in the face and you have the mechanism in place to do something?"

"Being a quasi-Christian, and I am definitely convinced of what it is I am looking at," stammered Stan, "obviously my inclination would be to destroy it."

"That exactly is the rational thinking I was hoping for," said Dr. Dickerson joyfully.

"But, by what means should we destroy it?" persisted Stan. "I guess what I am getting at is the new debate raging on, and that is, what is the best mechanism for the destruction of the so-called followers...a total annihilation? Or redemptive cures...kind of like exorcism?"

"I don't think exorcism is the answer, because these people are not possessed, but rather are the engraved followers and disciples. There are no supernatural powers here."

"So then, you are in support of complete destruction or annihilation?" asked the seasoned reporter.

"To tell you the truth, I really don't know, because on one hand, the Bible teaches that, 'Thou shall not kill,' but it did not spell out who we should or should not kill. It simply stated 'Thou shall not kill.' This is the dilemma that's waiting for an annunciation."

"That's deep."

Next day, on the early morning shows, the television networks were showing a live feed from Sweden. They interrupted their regular programming to broadcast a news conference by a certain Dr. Stefan Andersen.

Dr. Andersen, a Harvard-educated genetics doctor of the University Of Gothenburg School Of Medicine, had just finished his analysis of all the hardcore criminals in Gothenburg. The undisclosed study commissioned by the Swedish government had been ongoing ever since the news broke about HLA B66 in the United States.

"Good evening," Dr. Andersen greeted in English laden with a heavy Swedish accent. "The HLA B66 experiment was commissioned by the Swedish government working in collaboration with the University of Gothenburg. We were able to analyze all our 932 hardcore criminals in the Gothenburg province.

"We defined hardcore criminals as those who had committed serial killings, multiple murders, crimes that defy imaginations, unspeakable abhorrent acts, and cult killers. I cannot go into detailed description of all their crimes. A copy of their crimes can be obtained with permission of the government.

"Anyway, we analyzed all blood samples using the same chromatographic analysis obtained with the permission of the United States government. After careful testing and retesting we were able to find 89.5 percent positive correlations between these criminals and HLA B66. It is still a very high correlation, but not as high as that of Drs. Abramhoff and Dickerson."

"Any questions?" concluded Dr. Andersen.

"*Monsieur,*" began a French reporter, "do you have an explanation as to why you were able to correlate only 89.5 percent, while the United States had almost 93 percent correlations?"

"I would not classify 89.5 percent as *only,*" stated Dr. Andersen. "Eighty-nine and a half, by any statistical analysis, is still a very high number. As to why that number differs from that of the United States, I can only infer that it might be in the selection process."

"What do you mean by that, *monsieur?* I thought you were more selective than they were," retorted the reporter with a follow-up question.

"No, actually the United States people were more selective than we were," Dr. Andersen stated. "We had to practically empty our long-term jail population, but in the United States, they only tested a very small fraction of their prison population."

"What do you make of the high correlations between these criminals and HLA B66?" asked a reporter from Stockholm.

"It's like any discovery in science," answered Dr. Andersen, "there is a high incidence of HLA B66 among hardcore criminals. Presently, I am not at liberty to make any further interpretations."

"I guess what I am trying to ask is," continued the reporter, "do you think that HLA B66 is a sign of predestination for criminal action, as Dr. Abramhoff stated, or are you of the opinion that HLA B66 is synonymous with 666?"

"Looking at it purely scientifically, you would agree that HLA B66 does indeed tend toward criminal behaviors," Dr. Andersen pointed out. "Looking at it religiously, one cannot help but wonder why these HLA B66 individuals have these devilish minds."

"Based on your studies, would you suggest a mass screening on behalf of the Swedish government?" a local reporter asked.

"There are more qualified government officials than I am to make that determination," Dr. Andersen answered calmly.

"Have you had any communications with either Dr. Abramhoff or Dr. Dickerson?" asked a British reporter.

"As a matter of fact, I have," answered Dr. Andersen. "At the initial phase of the study, they were instrumental in the logistics of the set up."

666

After Dr. Andersen's interview, the United Nations International Science Committee had a three-day emergency meeting on HLA B66.

A communiqué, issued after the meeting, stated that a joint international study had been agreed to by Britain, America, Singapore, Italy, Canada, and Sweden. It would be labeled "the BASICS Study."

The United States and the rest of the countries were to select teams of doctors, who were research-oriented and familiar with, or had experience in, HLA typing. They would all agree to share information on a regular basis.

Each country was required to finish the selection process in three weeks, and the first meeting of the scientists would be scheduled at the United Nations Headquarters in New York City for a get-together session of the scientists.

# CHAPTER THIRTY-NINE

Sabrina Marley buzzed Abramhoff's line through the intercom.

"Yes?" answered Abramhoff, disconnecting the ear piece to the Dictaphone.

"It's Dr. Dickerson calling, sir."

"Put her through," answered Abramhoff.

After pushing down the third blinking line, "Hi, Regina," Abramhoff greeted.

"Hi, David," Dickerson answered, realizing that this was one of those rare occasions she got called by her first name again.

"Did you have a chance to watch Dr. Andersen's news conference?"

"Yes, I did." Dickerson sounded elated. "What did you think?"

"I think that if they had not emptied their prison cells, like he said, their result would have been the same as ours," Abramhoff surmised.

"If he was more focused and or more selective, you mean?"

"The surprising thing, however, is that he did get a very high correlation."

"Which argues, then, that the HLA finding is not an American phenomenon only?" answered Dickerson as she sneezed.

"Bless you," Abramhoff offered.

"Thanks; and thank God for HLA universality, because I recently read that America is being referred to as the harlot, Babylon," answered Dickerson, borrowing a passage from the Bible.

"Where did that come from?" asked a puzzled Abramhoff.

"I guess you didn't read the book of Revelation after all?"

"No not at all."

"That's nothing," Dickerson chuckled. "On a more serious note, have you heard about the St. Louis, Missouri, project?"

"Yes I did, peripherally. What was that all about?" asked a baffled Abramhoff.

"Do you know Dr. Alexander Hill, of the old Deaconess Hospital?"

"Yes, isn't he the one that discovered the allogenic transplantations theory?" Abramhoff's forehead wrinkled in thought.

"That's him," congratulated Dickerson. "It appears that he has been conducting his own HLA B66 investigations with a generous donation from the Anheuser-Busch Foundations."

"I wonder what his findings will be," said Abramhoff, letting off a loud grunt.

"Are you okay?"

"Just stretching, go ahead."

"Well, he is supposed to have a news conference next week," Dickerson conferred.

"It's beginning to look like that's the quickest way to get on television," suggested Abramhoff with a sense of envy.

"What seems to be?" asked an innocent Dickerson.

"Conduct an HLA B66 study," Abramhoff responded emphatically.

"What do you think about the BASICS Study proposed by the United Nations?" Dickerson asked, sidestepping Abramhoff's remark.

"Why?"

"I am just a little skeptical."

"When you conduct international studies like that, egos get in the way, and turfs emerge from nowhere," answered the politically-suave Abramhoff. "It goes without saying that they have to assign some leadership role here."

"Let's hope that's the case," Dickerson answered, knowing in the back of her mind that Abramhoff desperately wanted that position. "Have you been contacted about that?"

"No, but the governor informed me that the State Department is attempting to set up diplomatic status for the doctors in general before informing them," Abramhoff responded, hoping Dickerson would let him take that leadership role.

"What's this I hear about California and HLA testing?" Abramhoff asked, quickly trying to change the subject.

"I strongly believe that the governor is poised to announce statewide HLA testing," Dickerson volunteered with great reluctance.

"Wow, you guys are ahead of everyone else on this issue. I have to notify Governor Milton about this."

"Don't quote me please, because the information I have is still unofficial," pleaded Dickerson.

"One second, please," requested Abramhoff.

In the background, Sabrina's voice could be heard, "Dr. Achampi is here sir, to see you."

"Tell him I will join him soon in the conference room," Abramhoff instructed.

"I can call you back later," suggested Dickerson.

"Oh no, that's okay. You were saying something about the California initiative." Abramhoff's curiosity reached a zenith. "This much I know, if California goes ahead with mandatory testing, the news will dwarf the BASICS project."

"You think they'll probably ask us to join the American team, for that project?" asked Dickerson, moving away from the California discussions.

"I would certainty suspect so," answered Abramhoff with great authority.

Dr. Achampi was sitting at the middle of the rectangle oak desk when Abramhoff entered.

"I just got off the phone with Dr. Dickerson," stated Dr. Abramhoff, as he sat down at the opposite end of the desk facing Achampi.

"Oh! What did she say?" asked Achampi, pulling his chair forward.

"She was just telling me that California may become the first state to order mandatory testing for HLA B66."

"No way," answered Achampi in frank astonishment. "The way I understand it, the federal government refused mandatory testing, and that's why they set up the Pellagrini-Pinkett Project."

"I know, I know," answered Abramhoff, who then got up and went to the door to ask Sabrina for two coffees.

"Water for me, please," interrupted Achampi.

As soon as Sabrina left, Abramhoff continued, "She said that right now the governor and the state attorney general are crafting the legal language to protect the state of California."

"Can they do that?" asked Achampi, stroking his freshly shaved face.

"California has been known to do whatever they want, and then when the initiative becomes popular, it spreads to the rest of the states," answered Abramhoff, who appeared lost in thought.

"Are you planning to call Milt, to see if Illinois will follow suit?" asked Achampi, seeming to sense what Abramhoff was thinking.

"Yes…yes, I will, but before that, have you heard about the BASICS project?" asked Abramhoff, directing his attention back to Achampi.

"Yes, I read about it in the *Hammond Times* of Indiana, when I went to visit my dad over the weekend," answered Dr. Achampi.

"I seriously believe that we are going to spearhead that project," Abramhoff confided.

"Did the governor…?"

"No, I have not talked to the governor, yet," answered Abramhoff, not letting Dr. Achampi finish his question. "I just finished discussing it with Dr. Dickerson."

"What did she say?"

"I think she is taking a pass," answered Dr. Abramhoff. "I am convinced that the governor of California is about to tap her for their mandatory testing."

"That will be a daunting task for her."

"She told me that she now has an assistant, a certain Dr. Millons."

"So how do we organize this world study?" Achampi asked, convinced that Abramhoff would lead the project.

"First we should insist that all blood samples be processed only in two places to avoid inter-continental errors," Abramhoff answered, already assuming the role.

"That's fair."

"Then we should insist that all data analyses be done here in Chicago."

"Why?" queried Achampi.

"Because, let's say they agree to that, then the bulk of the funding for the project comes to Chicago," theorized Abramhoff.

"That's interesting."

"Secondly," continued Abramhoff, looking like a man on a mission, "Chicago then becomes the staging ground for all major news conferences to follow."

*Such ego,* thought Achampi.

666

Not wanting to wait any longer, Abramhoff called the governor.

"Hi, Milt, I hate to disturb you at this critical legislative moment."

"Oh, don't worry about it…those knuckleheads are out of their mind if they think I am going to sign a deficit budget," fumed the governor.

"I was just wondering," started Dr. Abramhoff, who did not want to go off on a tangent, "if you have heard anything about the BASICS project."

"About the…who project?" asked the governor, seemingly lost.

"You know, the proposed international HLA B66 project," reminded Abramhoff.

"Oh yes, the State Department called me early about two days ago to inform me that they have accepted our request to make Chicago the nerve center of the project, only if London and some bio-something research complex in Singapore were also added."

A huge sense of relief dawned on Abramhoff's face. He wanted to break out in a spontaneous dance, but with the governor on the other end, he decided to compose himself.

"That's the new billion-dollar research facility complex. I know exactly which one you are talking about in Singapore."

"Must be, they did not give me all the specifics, but I went ahead and accepted. I hope that's okay."

"Yeah…oh, yes, that's okay." Abramhoff's joy finally exploded. "Can they also arrange for the statistical analyses and the news conferences to be conducted here in Chicago?"

"Doc…Doc," responded the governor, sensing Abramhoff's enthusiasm. "I'll see what I can do when I talk to them again."

"Thanks a million, Mr. Governor."

"Don't mention it."

# CHAPTER FORTY

"This is the wrong time to be looking for a landing strip," observed Semonjene, shaking his head.

"This is the perfect time," Aryan answered in disgust. He then turned to Semonjene and smiled.

Aryan was getting tired of Semonjene's complaints.

"What do you mean, perfect? It is 10:45 at night; soon it will be midnight. The mosquitoes are eating me alive. There is no freaking moon to tell us where we are going. How do you even know where you are going anyway?" Semonjene persisted.

Aryan Broughton and Semonjene Raloux had been looking for an abandoned airstrip. Aryan was contacted by the Micaela drug cartel from Colombia to investigate an airstrip they were planning to use for their midnight drops for the Louisiana regional supplies center.

The cartel figured out that the drug market in New Orleans and the surrounding states had gotten so lucrative that faster deliveries were needed to meet the market demand. A downloaded satellite search through Google at the Micaela computer room in Barranquilla, Colombia, located what appeared to be an airstrip in Louisiana.

Mr. Aryan Broughton, the local coordinator for Micaela Business International, was immediately contacted. He researched old archived local town papers and found that about seventy-five years ago, there had been a landing strip that substituted for a small airport, where rich merchants lived on what used to be a beautiful terrain. Now an abandoned community, it had been swallowed up by Baton Rouge and New Orleans.

"I used to be a Green Beret, and missions like this are my specialty," Aryan boasted.

"But, does it have to be in the middle of the darn night?" asked Semonjene.

"Yes it does, on specific instructions from Micaela," answered Aryan.

"You know, since you are good at this, you could have come by yourself, that way you don't have me to cause you any darn problems."

"Semo, you curse too much! To be in the professional world, you have to learn how not to curse all the time," suggested Aryan.

"Listen, soldier boy, I am not a professional world person. I like what I am doing, and it pays me good, even though it may be…"

"Be quiet," whispered Aryan suddenly, "and stand perfectly still."

Semo, as he preferred to be called, stood perfectly still, and then hit himself on the neck to ward off insects.

"Did you hear that?" Aryan whispered.

"Hear what?" Semo, looking around sheepishly, whispered back.

"That," whispered Aryan again. "It sounded like a girl trying to scream."

"I don't hear a thing," whispered Semo.

"Your gun is fully loaded, right?"

"Yes, last time I checked,"

"Make sure it is in a place you can reach easily."

"Okay."

"Put your left index finger in my back pocket and follow me closely. If I stop, you stop; if I move, you move, and by all means, do not bump into me, got that?"

"Yes, sir," answered Semo sarcastically, in a louder voice.

"Shut up," snapped Aryan, still whispering. "Let's go."

Semonjene took a deep breath and quietly followed Aryan. After a short distance of cat-like walking, a building silhouette could be seen in the distance. Then after about half a block or more, a two-storied tower finally appeared, and there were faint lights coming from the inside.

*This place is miles from civilization,* thought Aryan. *Who knew about this place? Some other cartel may have beaten us to the punch.*

Approaching cautiously, Aryan turned to Semonjene and said, "Don't touch anything. Don't cough. Don't even take a deep breath, just follow behind me. Where I step, you step. You don't want them to know we are here. If they do, we're dead."

Semo wanted to whisper something back, but because of the fear of death, which he had always harbored, he did not utter a word.

Aryan was able to discern three cars parked in what looked like the front of the building. He moved Semo quickly to the window where the light was coming from. Two visible cracks could be seen from the wooden planks used to seal off a window. The building looked old, dilapidated, and uninhabited, yet there were at least three people inside. Aryan heard muffled conversations coming from the inside of the building.

Aryan motioned to Semo to peek through the crack at the upper end. There were three men in the room moving around, looking for something. A very frightened young girl had what looked like a handkerchief stuffed in her mouth. She was still trying to say something but only a moaning sound could be heard from her. She was about sixteen or seventeen years old, a little chubby. Her hands were tied behind her as she sat on the floor, shaking, in the far corner of the room.

One of the men in blue jeans with a New Orleans Saints T-shirt on, rough salt-and-pepper beard, unlocked a door and went into another room and dragged out an old mattress. The second man was standing over the girl, apparently to prevent any attempt to escape. He was a bigger, bulkier man than the first guy, a little older, in his fifties, clean-shaven, wearing jeans with a navy blue shirt.

The first guy reappeared from the other room with what looked like a bed cover and spread it over the mattress. A third guy appeared from the shadow. He was a short, stocky man also in his late fifties, wearing a ruffled, light gray suit. He was clean-shaven with a sinister look on his face. He had small saddle nose deformity, a cigarette in his right hand.

He took a puff of the cigarette and threw the rest on the floor and extinguished what was left with his right foot.

"You ready, guys?" he asked with a faint British accent. "You all know the routine. I go first, then today Jewel is second, then you, okay?"

"If you say so, Boss," answered the fellow referred to as "you."

Jewel and the third man untied the struggling teenager and dragged her to the bed with her legs kicking, while the man in suit and tie, attempted to control the flailing limbs.

The poor girl's hands were tied to two steel pipes at the corner of the makeshift bed. Next, the legs were spread apart and tied to an old mahogany table legs at the south end of the mattress. The one called Jewel then pulled out a huge hunting knife and systematically cut off all her clothes.

The man in the suit climbed on the bed, kneeled between her spread legs, and unzipped his pants. Her moans were deafening and disheartening. Finished, Jewel went next, then the third guy. The young girl was so exhausted after Jewel's performance that she hardly uttered a moan with the third person.

"Okay, let's sacrifice, and head out of here," said the man referred to as "Boss."

"Next Friday, can I go first?" the third guy asked with a deep Southern accent.

"You know the rules; I go first, then you two take turns," answered the boss with an unflinching face.

"Can we get a pretty one then?" asked Jewel with his deep baritone voice.

"Our suppliers already have one coming from Arkansas," answered the boss.

"Yeah, my cousin lives in Arkansas, Fort Smith," said the third guy.

"Yes…yes, let's finish this and go," said the boss.

They rolled the girl over in a prone position, after unhinging her, then moved her forward with her whole head and neck hanging over the edge of the bed.

She was again tied down in that position. Mr. Boss-man took out a small book from his coat pocket, read out loud some unintelligible words in a prayer-like fashion for what appeared to be eternity. Then, putting the book away, he picked up a small ice container off the floor. He took his coat off, rolled up his sleeves, and revealed a hairless arm.

The third man pulled the girl's head flexed backwards, revealing her neck. Jewel again pulled the hunting knife. With the precision of a butcher, he slit her neck wide open. Blood was pouring out and the Boss-man was collecting all that he could.

Upon seeing the throat slit, Semonjene made an attempt to sit down with his right hand covering his mouth to muffle his gasp. The three men looked up immediately.

"Did you hear something?" asked Jewel.

"I thought I did, but you know there are plenty of rabbits here," answered the third guy.

By now, the blood had dwindled to a trickle. Mr. Boss-man put the ice bucket closer to collect the last drop. He then opened an outer door and whistled.

"Did you guys hear anything out there?" he asked whoever was in the outer chamber.

"Nothing, sir," a man's response was heard.

"We done," said the boss. "Let's get ready to get out of here."

He came back to the room and helped Jewel and the third guy clean up. They tied the corpse in a fetal position, picked up the body and the blood collected, and returned the mattress.

Jewel cleaned the floor and turned off the kerosene lantern. Within minutes, five men emerged from the building, dumped the body in the trunk of one of the cars, and drove off.

"Why didn't you do something?" asked Semo in resignation. "You are the darn Green Beret, aren't you?"

"Do something like what?" asked Aryan, looking at Semo in disbelief.

"Go in there and shoot them. At least we could have saved the girl," suggested Semo.

"Did you see the other two guys that were watching the front?" answered Aryan. "Those guys have Uzi subma-chine guns."

For a moment, neither man said anything, except to contemplate on what just happened.

"I think these guys are devil worshipers," suggested Aryan. "Did you see how they slit her throat and collected her blood after that freak…that scary guy they called Boss said some mumbo-jumbo prayers?"

"They raped her," Semo blurted out. "How can these guys have sex with a young girl, one right after the other?"

"They are not amateurs; I can tell you that," observed Aryan. "They have done this before several times and so far have gotten away with it."

"What are you planning to do?"

"I don't know, but we should do something."

"We should do something?" asked a bewildered Semo. "Remember, soldier boy…we are drug dealers scouting for a secret airfield for illegal transportation of drugs…hello?"

"We should do something," insisted Aryan.

"Let's get rolling out of here."

666

"There is no way on earth we will ever use that airstrip," said Mr. Micaela when told about the incident. "Those people have desecrated the place," he shouted while crossing himself.

"So what do we do now?" asked Aryan, who had called Mr. Micaela for suggestions or what to do after the gruesome discovery.

"We will find another location," suggested Mr. Micaela.

"I mean, what do we do about those guys in the house? Should we report them to the police? Because I think they are planning to do the same thing next Friday. The ceremony might be a routine Friday satanic church ritual for them…," Aryan was about to go on and on.

"Okay, okay, shut up; let me think," answered Micaela, as was customary with him.

There were some background conversations, and Aryan knew that they were scheming up something.

"Okay, this is what you do," answered Micaela, "you call us here, and then we will connect you to the Baton Rouge Police Department. You don't give them your name. Tell them you want to report a crime, you describe what you saw, tell them to go check the locations out if they want to, and let them know about what they planned for, next Friday."

"But if they ask what I was doing there…?" Aryan asked.

"Tell them you went camping or fishing or rabbit hunting; I don't know, make up something," answered Micaela. "All I know is that they will not be able to trace the call."

666

The arrest of John Bradford Fleming and four accomplices at the scene of the crime was sensational in Baton Rouge and New Orleans. The state attorney general, the FBI, and the Pellagrini-Pinkett Project were immediately notified. Massive quad-state investigations resulted in the uncovering of bizarre satanic cult rituals where young, so-called virgins from across Louisiana, Arkansas, Mississippi, Alabama, and as far out as Texas were abducted and brought to the airstrip house.

"Tell me, Mr. Fleming," asked the state lead prosecutor when the case finally went to trial, "what made you, or better yet, what prompted you to the juju cult?"

"Objection," Fleming's assistant attorney shouted for the countless time.

"Overruled," the judge ruled without a hesitant thought. "Answer the question, Mr. Fleming," the judge ordered.

A sinister smile shone on Mr. Fleming's face.

"I presume you are a Christian?" asked Mr. Fleming, looking directly at the prosecutor.

"Answer the question, Mr. Fleming, what prompted you to join the juju cult?" the prosecutor asked again sternly.

"I am sorry to say, but it is like me asking you what prompted you to be a Christian," answered Mr. Fleming.

"I trust by your answer that you do not believe in God," asked the prosecutor, as he strolled toward the jury team seated at the right corner of the courtroom.

"Your honor, what's the relevance?" interrupted Mr. Fleming's attorney, as he stood up where he was seated at the left-corner defense table, facing the judge.

"Your honor, this particular belief is the central core of this whole trial," the prosecutor explained.

"Go ahead, Mr. Fleming," instructed the judge.

"All I can tell you is this, Mr. Attorney—there is an old Nigerian wise tale in Pidgin English that says, 'God dai, na'im be poor man's juju.' Translated, it means 'poor people believe in God because they cannot afford juju,'" proclaimed Mr. Fleming to a shocked jury.

Along with seven accomplices, Mr. Fleming was found guilty in the murder of three missing teenagers from Louisiana, Alabama, and Mississippi. Forensic evidence was still underway for another twelve, possibly twenty other missing teenagers in the five-state area with possible link to Mr. Fleming's business operations.

# CHAPTER FORTY-ONE

Dickerson finally received a call from Sacramento, California. Governor Nagoya's executive secretary called to see if Dickerson had some time to discuss key critical issues with the governor. Dickerson's secretary responded, "One moment please."

"The governor's office wants to know if you have time to discuss some critical issues with the governor," she asked Dickerson.

"Yes," responded Dickerson immediately.

"Good morning, Governor," responded Dickerson, a little apprehensive.

"How busy are you next week, Tuesday about two p.m.?" asked the governor, straight to the point.

"Let me see," answered Dickerson, opening her Tungsten III palm pilot cover, pulling out the pointer, and scrolling through to Tuesday.

"I have noon grand rounds that usually last one hour, maximum ninety minutes, so two p.m. is okay with me." Dickerson figured that no matter what, she would keep this appointment.

"I will be in San Diego at the Seaport Village near the Hilton Hotel. We have scheduled at two p.m. news conference," informed the governor.

"I will be there before two p.m., that's if you want me to be there," Dickerson reasoned.

"Good, then let me update you on what we are planning," continued the governor.

"Yes, sir." Dickerson, not accustomed to calling any man "sir," ever since she had stopped calling her dad "sir" at age fourteen, sounded strange saying that. She had always equated the word "sir" with being somewhat subservient, and subjugated a position to place herself into. She had always been first, or at the top, in all her classes, and everyone else looked up to her. She had adamantly refused to use that word throughout high school, college, and medical school. Her formal greetings were usually Mr. So-and-so or Dr. So-and-so. Yet, here she was, using the word for the first time since age fourteen, not sure exactly why she did. Maybe she was just excited.

"We have had several meetings and consultations with the attorney general's office and the state's legal team over mandatory testing," began the governor. "After researching the laws, we feel that the state is within its legal jurisdiction to order mandatory testing of its citizens.

"But before I proceed further," the governor interrupted himself, "how do you feel about mandatory testing?"

"I support it 100 percent, sir, but the question I have, and it is the same question I have been asked over and over again, is what to do with all the HLA B66 positive fellows?"

"That's also was the question that posed the most challenge for us," answered the governor.

"How did you all resolve that?"

"What we have decided to do is to collect the data, including the DNA of all citizens, but we will have separate files for the HLA B66 positive people," explained the governor. "We will have this information stored in the computer, the same way we have all social security information and driver's license information stored in the computer. If a crime is committed, the crime scene investigation team findings will be first tested against all our DNAs and HLA B66 for any match. If there is a match, then that individual will be questioned extensively. If any connection is made, then so be it. If the suspect's alibi is airtight, then the individual is subjected to surveillance monitoring while the investigation continues. At least, we do have a suspect."

There was silence on the other end after the governor finished.

"Are you still there, Doc?" inquired the governor.

"Yes…yes I am," answered Dickerson. "One thought though. If that be the case, then the HLA B66 positives are all suspects prior to any investigation."

"You can look at it that way," said the governor, taking a little time to formulate a response, "but with a positive match, at least we have a lead. Besides, you and Dr. Abramhoff proved that the HLA B66 individuals are destined or programmed by a stamped image to commit crime. What triggers them, according to you, we do not know, but at least we are trying, or going to try, to do something."

"You've got a point there," answered Dickerson. "What do you want me to do?"

"We need to set up test centers in all the hospitals and clinics, the same way the state collects statistics on all HIV and syphilis cases, for example," explained the governor. "For the remote areas, we have multiple state medical mobile units to go to these communities and accomplish the same mission. Of course, these mobile units will be accompanied by state police officers, just in case of any organized resistance or violence."

"What about those who refuse to test?" Dickerson asked, playing the devil's advocate.

"We will easily track them down. The legislatures are currently working on a bill that will deny or forfeit driver's license, welfare checks, social security checks, identification, taxes, and so on, if you have not been tested for HLA B66 within a certain period of time."

"That's very intrusive, wouldn't you say?"

"Unfortunately, that's the era we are in right now."

"So where do I come in?"

"You will assume the title of the state medical director for the mandatory HLA B66 program."

"Is it a paid position?" asked Dr. Dickerson in jest.

"As a matter of fact, it is," answered the governor seriously. "You will be responsible for centralizing the data there in San Diego, reporting on the statistical findings, and answering all relevant medical questions about the HLA B66."

"I am honored," responded an elated Dickerson.

"Is that a yes?" inquired the governor.

"Yes."

"Then I will see you next Tuesday at two p.m., at the Seaport Village. My advance team will contact you for logistics."

666

A mild-mannered California sun was shining throughout San Diego on Tuesday. A sense of calm appeared to have descended over San Diego. The day before, it had been cloudy and had drizzled virtually all day long, finally ceasing at about 6:30 p.m. There were no clouds in the air on Tuesday. At the San Diego bay, overlooking the Seaport Village, on toward the hanging bridge, it looked like a picturesque twenty-first century fishing village.

*The governor's advance team could not have picked a better setting,* thought Dickerson.

"Why doesn't the state quarantine all HLA B66 positive individuals?" asked the *San Diego Union* editorial reporter after the announcement by the governor that the state would institute mandatory testing beginning the first Monday in August.

At the opening of the news conference, Dickerson was introduced as the state medical director for the HLA B66 project coordinating the state findings and reporting directly to the governor.

"There is no reason to quarantine someone who is free of communicable diseases, and poses no health threat to the state," responded the governor.

"But, they will become criminals at some point in time, and that may then pose a health threat," insisted the reporter.

"We have put in place a mechanism to deal with that scenario," answered the governor and abruptly pointed to another question.

"Aren't you violating people's rights?" asked the *Los Angeles Times* reporter.

"We are not violating anybody's rights. The state has the right to require HLA B66 testing same way we require yearly TB testing for all its citizens."

"How can the state, with clear conscience, let a person roam around, knowing full well that one day, that person will commit a heinous crime? That is scary, don't you think?" asked another reporter.

The governor deliberated for a second, and then slowly responded, "In the United States of America, we follow the law. The law as it stands now does not give us the power to arrest and detain an individual based on a test that shows that one day a crime will be committed. That statute requires an act of Congress. But to answer your question, the reason the state is instituting the mandatory testing is to be able to identify the HLA B66 positives, and in the process at least know who they are."

"Will the rest of the people in the state at least know who they are?" insisted the reporter.

"Unfortunately not," answered the governor with a faint smile on his face. "We do not want vigilantes, or some sort of witch hunting against anybody."

"Dr. Dickerson, I heard that the folks in Boston are working on a possible medical cure for HLA B66. Any truth to that?" asked another reporter to Dickerson, who was standing behind the governor with the rest of the local officials.

The governor stepped sideways, making room for Dickerson to stand at the podium.

"I have not heard or read of any substantiated medical cure for HLA B66. HLA B66 is a chromosomal marking," Dickerson responded with a furrowed forehead while attempting to identify the reporter that asked the question. "You cannot take a pill for a HLA B66 cure, as you call it. This or any other markings require careful gene manipulations."

"What is chromosomal?"

"That's a very long lecture," answered a smiling Dickerson at the reporter. "But, basically, chromosomes are unique structures in the cell nucleus where nearly all human information is encoded and stored."

666

"Congratulations," said Abramhoff, calling Dickerson hours after the nationally televised California news conference.

"Well, thank you. I did well, didn't I?" inquired Dickerson, feeling self-assured.

"So what do I call you now, the California medical director?" asked Abramhoff jokingly.

"I don't know whether that's an official title yet," Dickerson cautioned.

"Is that a paid position?"

"Yes, it is."

"If I may be bold to ask, what's the pay?"

"You know, they have not told me yet, and that's the truth. The governor assured me that it is a paid position when I jokingly asked him the same question."

"Dr. Achampi thinks the task might be daunting for you, but I have every confidence you can do it."

"Thanks for that vote of confidence. I think we can handle it here. The state will most probably assume the pay of all my technical and logistical support. I believe by that, they mean the salary of my entire staff."

"That's great."

"Before I forget—the BASICS Study, how is it coming along?" asked Dickerson, letting out a mild-mannered cough to deflect attention from aggrandizing.

"Oh, we almost finished with all the preparations," Abramhoff finally gloated. "Chicago has been chosen as the central hub for the story. We, however, have to share the spotlight with London, Singapore, and Brazil."

"Why include Singapore?"

"Why not, since they have that billion-dollar research complex?" Abramhoff responded with envy.

"Oh, yes, I know," Dickerson empathized.

Within weeks, the Illinois House passed legislation, becoming the second state to require mandatory testing. The bill was to go the governor. That was followed almost simultaneously by Texas, Pennsylvania, Florida, Alabama, North Dakota, Wyoming, Georgia, and North Carolina.

Illinois, as expected, picked Abramhoff as their chief medical officer, while the rest of the states, on a recommendation from Dickerson, chose their respective state health commissioners as coordinators.

# CHAPTER FORTY-TWO

Barbra Bent Brigham and Women's Hospital of Boston, Massachusetts, the oldest teaching hospital of Harvard Medical School, located on Huntington Avenue along the T-line, had attracted pioneers in medical research and therapeutic innovations.

Dr. Dominic St. John, chairman, department of hematology oncology, who specialized in newer and innovative therapies for leukemia, was one of those researchers. An intelligent and highly educated professor, he prided himself on being neatly dressed at all times. The trendier the fashion in men's suits, the more likely it would be found on Dr. St. John's body, at any given time.

His laboratory coats had a beautifully monogrammed name on the left chest area. He spoke fluent French and English with such simplicity that one would think he was a French citizen, educated in Europe, even though he was born in Cambridge, Massachusetts, and educated at Harvard. A soft-spoken gentleman when he lectured, he had a temper that was memorable throughout the hospital.

Dr. St. John had been working on acute lymphoblast leukemia, a very difficult blood cancer, especially in children, that was not easily curable, unlike most of the other blood cancers. Recently, one of Dr. St. John's patients, a seventeen-year-old girl, Ramona, with lymphoblast leukemia, suffered from recurrent anemia. She had required multiple blood transfusions for the anemia.

"How is Ramona recovering?" asked Doc. St. John, as he was commonly known.

"Not so good," replied the senior oncology fellow as they led the oncology team along the hallway of the seventh floor oncology ward toward the nursing station. "You know she also has early Crohn's colitis, and that makes her transfusion difficult. She continues to lose blood through her bowels…"

"I already know," interrupted Doc. St. John. "Just tell me something, how many transfusions has she gotten from this hospital?"

Fumbling for words, the fellow finally responded, "I truly don't know."

He realized immediately that he should have checked the old records last night before this morning's rounds.

"Seventeen," Doc. St. John answered his own question. "What's her HLA status?"

"She was positive," answered the nurse when she sensed hesitation by the fellow and the residents as they gathered at the nursing station.

"What percent of Crohn's patients with leukemia are HLA positive?" asked Doc. St. John, looking at the group as he adjusted his glasses.

"About 65 percent," blurted out the ever loquacious senior resident.

"Don't ever give me that 'about'…response again," instructed Doc. St. John, slamming the chart on the desk as he looked intently at the resident.

"75 percent," rescued the oncology fellow.

"Good," responded an unflinching Doc. St. John, and he nodded his head. "So, what's the story with Ramona?"

"Ramona, after her last transfusion, which was her eighteenth, had the HLA test redrawn," the senior resident started the morning report.

"And the result was…," berated Doc St. John at the resident.

"It is now negative," answered the subdued resident.

"So, what do you think happened?" asked Doc. St. John, looking around for some intelligent answer.

"I think the multiple chemotherapy treatments must have altered some genetic sequence of her chromosome," answered the resident.

"That's a possibility," concurred Doc. St. John without appearing upset, "but you must realize that most of those alterations are for nonsense coding that invariably results in new cancer."

Dr. Arvin Rupert, an attending physician at the department, who happened to be at the nursing station seeing a patient, became involved in the discussion. He published extensively on genetic mutations.

"What I think," interjected Dr. Rupert, "is that we have to look closely at the multiple chemotherapies, yes, coupled with the blood transfusions that she has received. I wondered whether they have in some way altered or replaced specific loci on her chromosome."

The residents and the fellow cleared a path between Doc. St. John, who was standing near the patients' charts, and Dr. Rupert, who was still sitting on the station desk, his patient chart still opened in front of him.

"That's in line with the current theory," concurred Doc. St. John, grinning at Dr. Rupert. "Basically, we have to explore whether allo-immunization theory is applicable here, or whether in some way she has become unresponsive or immune to the Crohn's disease antigen through allo-immunization of the HLA…"

"I love when he talks technical like that," whispered the first-year resident to the fourth-year medical student standing next to him. "He sounds so Harvard."

"Did you understand what he just said?" whispered the fourth-year student back.

"A little," answered the first-year resident. "Allo-immunization is kinda like when you become immune to your own antigen."

"Specifically," continued Doc. St. John, "she has become immune to the effects of the allogenic antigen, therefore on testing for the HLA, there are no more reactions; since the receptor sites are now immune to Human Leukocyte Antigen on B27."

*Is Doc. St. John trying to suggest that by mere chemotherapy and blood transfusions you can virtually eliminate coded signals in the body?* thought the oncology fellow. *I don't think so.*

Meanwhile, at West Virginia Commonwealth University (WVCU) Medical School in Charleston, West Virginia, Dr. Eugene T. Norfolk, a senior research fellow at the department of pediatric oncology, who had been researching cure rates for childhood leukemia, observed a significant cure rate for a select group of children whose blood cancer, no matter what stage they were diagnosed at, was essentially cured with high dose of the cancer drug, cytarabine, diluted with normal saline.

The purified water for the normal saline (pure water mixed with an appropriate percentage of salt), came from the Peak Hole Mountains at the eastern corner of West Virginia between the big Allegheny and the Back Creek Mountain near the little town of Minnehaha Springs. Peak Hole is the steepest corner between Allegheny and Black Creek. The origin of the water had forever been a legendary mystery, but it ran down through the steepest corner of the mountain, into an unreachable gully, to the foot of the mountain.

At approximately one hundred feet below sea level, pure water continuously gushed out a small funnel-sized indent, in a cave created by the mountains. The spring water, initially discovered and analyzed by the geology department at WVCU, was made the exclusive property of the university. Many alleged cures had been attributed to this water. The university often distributed the water to many religious organizations and churches for baptism and also for the formalization of holy water. The university had vehemently refused to commercialize the water, fearing that it may lose whatever value, and/or power, it possessed.

Dr. Norfolk treated a lot of patients with these Peak Hole water solutions and documented fascinating results, especially in young patients with leukemia and lymphomas.

666

"Shirley," shouted Dickerson across the open door to the outer office, "who is Dr. Norfolk?"

"I don't know," answered the secretary. "He said he would like to talk to you about a possible cure he has discovered for HLA B66."

"A cure, you said!" asked Dickerson with such a surprised tone.

"That's what he said," Shirley answered, repeatedly blinking her eyes nervously.

"What does he mean...cure?" asked Dickerson, stepping out of her office to be sure Ms. Shirley had the right information.

"I guess that's what he wants to discuss with you."

"That's weird," said Dickerson.

Dickerson reflected for a moment, took a few steps back toward her office, then turned back to Ms. Shirley and said, "Get me Dr. Abramhoff first, on another line, and keep Dr. Norfolk or hold for a little bit."

"Yes, Doctor."

"Hi, David," greeted Dickerson, picking up Abramhoff's line first, "do you know a Dr. Norfolk from West Virginia Commonwealth University?"

"No. I have never heard of him, why?" Abramhoff sounded inquisitive.

"Well, he is on the other line. He wants to talk to me about a cure for HLA B66."

"Cure...like in, take an antibiotic and strep throat is cured?" Abramhoff asked with a little chuckle in his voice.

"I don't know, I haven't talked to him yet; he is still on the line," Dickerson replied. "I mean...let's hear him out and see what he has to say. I was thinking maybe we can have a three-way conversation, so that you can also hear it firsthand."

"Oh, yes, I would be delighted."

"Okay, hold on for one second."

"This is Dr. Dickerson, Dr. Norfolk?"

"Yes Ma...m, I..."

"Before you start," interrupted Dickerson, "I have Dr. Abramhoff also on the line, and I was having a conversation with him when you called. How can we help you?"

"That's lovely, good morning to you both," greeted Dr. Norfolk.

"Good morning," answered Abramhoff, making his presence known.

"I'm Dr. Eugene Norfolk, as I was saying. I'm the senior research fellow with the pediatric oncology here at WVCU. I know about the HLA B66 and both of your findings and interpretations. I just want to ask if any of you know about Peak Hole Mountains in West Virginia."

"No not me." Dickerson went first.

"Me, neither," echoed Abramhoff.

"Oh, it's a beautiful mountain nestled between the great Allegheny and Back Creek. At Peak Hole, there's this water that runs down the steep end of the mountain. It collects at the basin inside a cave. The university has exclusive rights to this water. I am surprised y'all haven't heard of it, because folks around here believe the water has healing powers."

"Wasn't that supposed to be at Hot Springs, Arkansas?" Abramhoff quipped.

"Apparently Peak Hole also, but from what I have heard so far, I believe you are insinuating that this water can cure the HLA B66?" asked Dickerson abruptly.

"Well, let me tell y'all what we did," answered Dr. Norfolk, eager to enlighten. "In my studies, we exclusively use Peak Hole water for our mixture with dextrose in normal saline solutions. These are the only solutions allowed for mixing chemotherapy agents for our acute leukemia patients, and we have a much higher rate of complete remission than any studies I have seen in the literature."

"How does that tie in with the HLA?" Abramhoff again jumped in.

"Well," answered Norfolk with a smile, "two of our patients had childhood rheumatoid arthritis, and they both tested positive for the rheumatoid factor antigen and the HLA B27. After four cycles of chemo, they went into complete remission for the cancer and the rheumatoid factor. Most interestingly, when we retested them for HLA B27, it was no longer there."

"This is getting interesting," Abramhoff was quick to add. "So you are suggesting that in some way we can also make HLA B66...vanish."

"I don't know, because our patients are cancer patients treated with chemo agents mixed in Peak Hole water. Is it the chemo? Is it the water...?" queried Dr. Norfolk. "Our conclusion, however, is that it has to be the water only, because we have treated these types of patients for years and there has never been any documented complete cancer cure, and there has never been any HLA interference previously."

"So let me understand you, and try to make some sense as to where you are going with this," started Dickerson. "You would like us to give this water, intravenously of course, and see if it wipes out HLA B66."

"That's one way of doing it," answered Dr. Norfolk. "We can also try it with blood transfusions, as Dr. St. John in Boston is suggesting, or try it with chemo…kinda like a three-arm study."

"How are you planning to design this study?" asked Abramhoff.

"That's why I am calling for help. All we need, I think, is probably about ten to twenty HLA B66 positive people, in each arm, then follow the three arms and see where they go."

"When do you suggest calling it off, if nothing happens?" asked Dickerson.

"I think six months will be sufficient. What do you think?" smiled Dr. Norfolk.

"I don't know," Abramhoff responded with a strong doubt in his voice, "I can see giving the water only, for six months, but to give someone chemo or a transfusion when it's clearly not indicated, that's a whole different issue."

"Can you at least give it a thought, and then let me know?" begged Dr. Norfolk.

There was silence at both ends of the phone and then, "I guess that will be okay," Dickerson interrupted.

"I have no problem with that," Abramhoff concurred.

"What do you think?" asked Dr. Dickerson after Dr. Norfolk hung up.

"I don't know. I have strong reservations about the outcome. How do they know it wasn't the cancer cells themselves that obliterated some regions on the B locus?"

"I think they are reacting to the nuances of this water, and its supposed wondrous deeds," surmised Dickerson.

"I know, but there are just too many variables here for legitimizing the association between the water and the supposed obliteration of HLA B27," Abramhoff suggested.

"You know what I think?" Dickerson interrupted. "I can foresee doing only a two-arm study here, if at all—one for the water only, and the other for the HLA B66 positives who happen to be either anemic and require frequent transfusions like the hemophiliacs, or sickle cell patients, and certain cancer patients."

"If it is the water we are after, let's just do the water for three months and see what happens," countered Abramhoff.

"You know what? Let's just sleep on that and converse later."

"Okay."

# CHAPTER FORTY-THREE

"How are you doing?" asked Dickerson, answering a phone call from Detective Pinkett.

Dickerson was surprised to hear from her friend. Ever since she relocated to Washington, D.C., to co-spearhead the Pellagrini-Pinkett Project, there had been little communication between them, except for occasional information exchange phone calls, and there had been little time between them to talk and gossip.

"I am fine. We're very busy here in D.C.," answered the detective. "The constant daily phone calls around here are tasking. Hours of investigative work, dispatching field agents to collect the triple six samples."

"Triple six?" exclaimed Dickerson. "You guys are so cavalier, about that number."

"Why shouldn't we?" responded Detective Pinkett. "If your theory is correct, and so far it appears to be, these people should be treated like the scum they are."

"I guess you've got a point there," answered Dickerson, a little subdued.

"What's the problem?" asked Pinkett, detecting a little resignation on Dickerson's voice. "You sound somewhat down or something."

"Oh, nothing," answered the doctor. "There are just too many little things happening around here."

"Like what?"

"Like…like running the state mandatory testing program…like running the university's Heme-Onc lab…like…"

"Hey…hey, what's a Heme-Onc lab?" Pinkett asked.

"Hematology-Oncology, that's my department," Dickerson made a hissing sound like Pinkett should have known that.

"I didn't know what that meant," retorted Pinkett, "and don't be giving me that hissing sound. You really don't feel well, do you?"

"I am fine." Dickerson was emphatic.

"Again I ask, what's the problem?" Pinkett persisted.

"Well, if you must know," Dickerson took a deep breath, "the federal government is taking us to court."

"Uncle Sam is taking you guys to court…for what, dereliction of duty?" Pinkett laughed.

"No, silly, they claim that the state of California violated federal statute by imposing mandatory testing on United States citizens."

"What kind of crap is that?" asked the detective, sounding angry.

"I don't understand that one either. I thought states had rights to test their population of certain conditions, if they chose to," pondered Dickerson. "Just like the alcohol breath test, not all states have the alcohol breath test. Even the test itself varies from state to state."

"And that's absolutely true," agreed the detective. "That's why you guys should fight this all the way to the Supreme Court if necessary, because I see the courts as where the final decision is gonna come from anyway."

"You may be right on that one. The governor is already preparing the defense team."

"What about the testing? It continues while the case is being argued in court, doesn't it?"

"No."

"No! And why not?"

"The federal government had an injunction against us to cease and desist until the resolution of the case."

"That's ridiculous. I thought we were all on the same page on the issue. Why is mandatory testing an obstacle to them folks on Capitol Hill?"

"I believe the order came directly from the president. He directed the attorney general to file a suit against California."

"You guys should fight this."

"We intend to."

"I wish you luck."

"Thanks."

"Take care of yourself, seriously."

"Don't I always?"

Dr. Dickerson wondered out loud why Pinkett should ask her to be careful. *Does she know something I don't know?* Dickerson asked herself. Dismissing it as nothing, she headed toward the ladies' room.

# CHAPTER FORTY-FOUR

At the Ronald Regan Federal Court Building at the corner of 10<sup>th</sup> Avenue and L Street in downtown San Diego, Federal Judge Alberto Finney was presiding over the case of the United States Government versus the State of California.

The federal solicitor in his opening statement noted, "First of all, your honor, the state of California went ahead on its own and ordered a mandatory testing program without consultations." He was waving a pencil in the air, at about an eye level, as if to write home his point as he argued his case.

"Mind you," he continued to argue, "the state did not even bother to notify the CDC and NIH before undertaking such a colossal task that may supposedly have both national and international implications. This is something the federal government should be deciding, not the state government."

The California state attorney general responded, arguing that the state has every right to test the citizens of California in matters of health and civility of its citizens.

Witnesses were called to the stand to argue for the federal government.

In rebuttal, the state of California had the state health commissioner, and the Pinkett-Pellagrini Project directors testify. Dickerson was also called to the witness stand.

With leading questions from the California attorney general, she meticulously, and with such ease, explained the HLA B66 findings, their implications, and she also shared the latest statistics from the Pellagrini-Pinkett Project. Avoiding her own personal interpretation of the HLA B66, she maintained that the state had the right to monitor the citizens who may have been HLA B66 positive.

At the conclusion of the day-long testimony, Judge Finney thanked the participants for their enlightenment and promised to render an opinion in less than a week. After that, Dickerson called it a day and went home to retire early.

Driving on Highway 5, after grabbing a quick bite from the cafeteria, Dickerson thought about the entire proceeding. She had been to court before, usually as a defendant consultant involved in malpractice cases. The lawyers would always attempt to have her commit to the fact that another accused physician did not follow standard medical practice.

She would always refuse to be pigeonholed into making such a pronouncement; instead she would always only defend the medical recorded facts of the case. Here, she found herself defending the state of California.

What a jump, from testifying about patients who thought that they had been wrongfully treated, to defending one of the most powerful states in the Union.

The road was slippery wet. It had been raining all day. The rain was coming down heavily. Dickerson could barely see less than a mile in front of her. *And they say it never rains in southern California. What a farce*, she thought. Dickerson had the windshield wipers on full cycle.

Even though she could hardly see more than half a mile in front of her, other cars were zooming by like she was crawling instead of driving. From the rearview mirror she noticed two strange lights behind her. *These new cars with their strange lights*, she thought.

"But why is this driver not moving over to the fast lanes?" she asked aloud.

Dickerson decided that she was not going to drive any faster, not on this awful rainy night, on the account of some lunatic. Suddenly the car moved to the left middle lane.

"Thank God," muttered Dickerson.

The car approached, and became parallel with her Mercedes 320E. She looked to see who the heck the driver was. She could hardly discern the face because of the rain, but it appeared the driver was trying to say something to her.

Dickerson could not help but entertain some wild thoughts; could this be abduction, sexual assault, carjacking, but most frightfully, homicide? She decided that at the next exit she would get off and head to the police station.

All of the sudden, her passenger side glass window became the man's face. A face in his late sixties, clean-shaven, handsome, but somehow looked like a Persian cat. The face, however, was reassuring, as Dickerson was visibly shaking all over, sweating, and heart racing. She was frightened out of her mind.

"*No me preocupo. Me preocupo sobre lo que está detrás de usted.*"

*Why is this Anglo-Saxon, distinguished, cat-like man speaking to me in fluent Spanish?* Dickerson wondered.

Dickerson's Spanish may not be perfect, but she understood clearly that the face on the glass was not the problem, but the driver behind was either dangerous, a bad driver, or someone she needed to be wary about.

She looked at the rearview mirror only to see two headlights that looked just like the one driven by the face on the passenger side window. The lights were far behind her. Turning to see or ask who the maniac was apparently speeding toward her, she realized that the face in the window and the car itself were no longer apparent. The car behind her was closing in quickly. She definitely did not seem to be making progress at all.

Exit 243A, one mile ahead, the sign read.

*Thank God,* Dickerson prayed.

"Oh no," Dickerson shouted, "this idiot is about to ram me off the road before I can reach the exit."

Looking to be sure there were no cars around in case of an accident, she wondered why the guardrails on the opposite side of the road looked like picket fences. She decided to speed up a little. Suddenly, she could clearly hear an old Michael Jackson song, blasting from the approaching vehicle. It was loud enough even with all her Mercedes windows rolled up.

*Do you wanna be startin' something?*
*You gotta be startin' something.*
*Do you wanna be startin' something?*
*You gotta be startin' something.*
*It's hard to get over, yeah, yeah.*
*Too low to get under, yeah, yeah.*
*You stuck in the middle, yeah, yeah.*
*The pain is thunder, yeah, yeah.*

She decided to quickly take the approaching exit in order to get off the highway, which suddenly appeared almost deserted, except for the maniac racing toward her. As she took a sharp turn toward the exit, she felt a loud thud that shook her whole being.

Her car immediately spun out of control, hit the guardrail, sailed over the ramp, and was slowly descending head-on onto the road about twenty feet below the expressway. For an instant, her whole life flashed in front of her. Next thing she knew, the car somehow landed on the Bay water some distance from Enchanted Island.

*How did the water…I thought…the road…?* Dickerson's mind was racing.

But with no apparent injuries, Dickerson somehow was still driving the car at normal speed, but on the water.

The Spanish-speaking, cat-faced man was sitting on the trunk of the car, paddling.

Just then the phone rang.

Dickerson woke up from a vivid nightmare, shaking. She removed the comforter and discovered that she was soaked in sweat.

Her breathing, still rapid, began to slow down some. She checked her pulse, and discovered that her heart was still racing.

The phone rang again for the fourth time. She finally picked it up.

"Hello?" Dickerson answered with an absent-minded voice.

"Hello, Doc." It was Pinkett. "Sorry to wake you up so early. I was unable to sleep, thinking about what I said to you, to be careful."

"What time is it?"

"3:33 a.m. Sorry again to wake you up."

"Why are you calling this early? Is everything okay?" asked the worried doctor.

"You sound like you just ran a marathon," observed Pinkett.

"I just woke up from a nightmare," Dickerson panted.

"Well, I am glad I called then. Tell me about it."

"When...? Right now?" Dickerson wondered.

After settling down a little, "I was about to die or drown in my car. I was in an accident...I was rammed off the road, and I crashed. But I didn't crash. I landed on the water...that was so weird, oh, that was so frightful."

"Where did this happen?" asked a concerned Pinkett.

"It was one of those dreams that appear so real, I am still shaking."

"Calm down and tell me exactly what happened."

"I was driving home on Interstate 5 north of the airport when this car drove close to me and this handsome man—"

"You and handsome men," interrupted Pinkett.

"Do you mind?" responded Dickerson.

"Sorry, I'm sorry."

"This handsome man's face appeared on my passenger's glass window, or the glass turned into his face, I don't know which. In any case, he spoke in Spanish and warned me to be careful of the car behind me." Dickerson paused to catch her breath.

"As I turned to look at the car in the rearview mirror, the handsome man's face and his car were gone, and this fool behind me ran me off the road. As I was just about to crash head-on, the road below turned into water, and Mr. Handsome was sitting on the hood paddling the car. Then the phone rang. For some reason, it appears that the crash was taking forever to happen."

"That was really strange."

"You aren't kidding," responded Dickerson.

"I usually have dreams, weird yes, but not as clear or as near fatalistic as this one," comforted Pinkett. "But listen, I think I need to tell you something."

"Tell me what?" Dickerson appeared fully awake.

"I think that there are evil people out there, and some of them may be out to do you harm."

"Do me harm, why? I haven't offended or transgressed anybody."

"Oh, yes, you have."

"How…? What did I do?"

"You developed the mechanism to expose them," Detective Pinkett explained. "They don't like it, and they may go to extremes to stop you."

"How do you know that?"

"Get some sleep. Let me call you in about four hours," Pinkett suggested.

"I'm awake now, we might as well…," Dickerson wanted to continue.

"No, I insist; please get some sleep," Pinkett demanded.

At exactly 7:55 a.m., the phone rang. It was Pinkett.

"As I was trying to explain to you earlier, we have been watching some suspects closely, some we have bugged. As a matter of fact we have the GEE System focused on one…"

"I told you earlier to continue. I haven't slept a wink since your first call, but wait a minute, what's this GEE System?"

"That's G-double-E."

"I figured that one out already."

"It stands for global eye and ear system. It is a device that we can attach to anything or anybody, for instance, your body, then through satellite navigation we can virtually see and hear you twenty-four seven."

"Like the G.P.S. system in my car."

"Just like that, but more advanced. Actually, we can see you in full detail; even down to the baguette design of the ring on your finger, in Technicolor, no less. Added to that, we can hear, very clearly, everything you say. Sometimes we can hear what you whisper to yourself."

"Yeah, but you probably can only do all that if I am outside, right?" questioned the scientist.

"Wrong, so long as the device is attached to you, we can pick up everything, even if you are in one of the tunnels in London."

"Wow!" gasped Dickerson. "How does it work?"

"The way they explained it to me is that the device creates an invisible cloud or shield around you all the time. It then bounces off millions of tiny microscopic radon on the cloud. The radons are then reflected back to the device. The device then acts like a radio micrometer and transmits back all the information to the satellite brain, which then interprets them as pictures and sounds.

"This device is so good that if, for example, somebody is close to you and the two of you are having a conversation, we can easily see the other individual and also hear what he or she is saying to you. Neat, isn't it?"

"I think you like all that technical stuff, don't you?" Dickerson commented.

"I am having a great time here. This technical stuff, you call it, turns me on."

"At least something turns you on," Dickerson replied in jest, trying to get back at her. "But seriously, where is all this information leading, because you keep referring to you—you, meaning me."

"You are one of the smartest people I have ever met."

"Well, thank you." Dickerson smiled.

"This is what we know so far," began Detective Pinkett on a more serious note. "There is this notorious, well-organized, well-financed gang leader, who has eluded capture for years. He is believed to be in San Diego, even as we speak. I don't know what the implication might be, but to be on the safe side, we would like to protect you by offering you this GEES device. What do you think?"

"You seriously believe that I am a target, don't you?"

"I don't think you are the actual target, but I do believe, and Pellagrini agrees with me, that if they silence you they can retard the HLA B66 movement, especially when it comes to the triple six."

"You think they are out to kill me?" a frightened Dickerson asked again.

"Probably not," reassured Pinkett, "but whatever it is they are planning, we ought to be ready for them."

"So, you are using me as bait."

"No and three times…no. I just want to protect you."

"Thank you, Pinky, you are so sweet." Dickerson sensed deep sincerity in Pinkett's voice, and she was touched. "You do care about me, don't you?"

"More than you know."

After a pause, when nothing else was said, Dickerson finally broke the silence.

"Okay, bring it on. I'll wear it."

"I will be in San Diego in two days to talk to the San Diego Police Department." Pinkett had reverted into a tactical mode. "We will install a monitor in their stations, and I will supervise the attachment of the device."

666

Two days later, at 10:10 a.m., Judge Finney rendered an opinion and ruled in favor of the state of California.

# CHAPTER FORTY-FIVE

Dr. Abramhoff walked into the office, mad at something. Sabrina could always tell when Abramhoff was upset or mad because his facial expression and demeanor would drastically change. He would stride, almost like a galloping horse, and Sabrina could practically hear him breathing. Next, he might look for a poor victim to vent his anger on.

Sabrina, for long, had been that poor victim, during her first two years working for Abramhoff, but with Abramhoff's newfound respect for Sabrina, the next logical victims were the residents.

Ever since the BASICS project had started, tension and aggravation had multiplied. Sabrina, not one to complain, worked harder on this project than anything else previously.

*The constant phone calls from London, Singapore, and Montreal are enough for a second assistant in this office,* she thought.

As if the meetings in New York two weeks ago were not nerve-racking enough, Abramhoff dealt with physicians and researchers he had never met.

*Individuals whose philosophical approaches are totally different from mine,* he surmised.

"Very frustrating," Abramhoff uttered several times.

Even with all that, the BASICS project started on time and data was arriving to Chicago from the different countries. Sabrina often helped Abramhoff let off some steam by a method she knew that worked all the time. She would quickly fetch a cup of hot Ovaltine chocolate with one teaspoon of French vanilla cream.

"Chocolate, sir," Sabrina offered.

"Yeah, thanks," answered Abramhoff.

Taking a sip of the hot chocolate, Abramhoff calmed down, then said, "Thank you, Sabrina, please get me Dr. Achampi."

Sabrina could tell he was calming down already.

"Right away, sir," she answered.

When Dr. Achampi arrived, Abramhoff went at it right away.

"What is wrong with Dr. Richard Kirkland?" he asked.

"Dr. Kirkland, the British team leader for the HLA B66 project?" Achampi wanted to be sure.

"Yes," Abramhoff almost shouted. "He has his differences with both the Italian and the Brazilian doctors. He accused them of sending incorrectly labeled specimen to London for initial analysis prior to transportation to the United States and also not following protocol. They, in turn, have called me to complain about him and his militaristic tactics."

"My goodness!" exclaimed Achampi, still standing.

"Please sit down," requested Abramhoff, motioning to the chair.

"Thanks."

"I just received a call from Dr. Chuang."

"The Singapore guy, isn't he?"

"Yes," answered Abramhoff, raising his eyebrows. "He is threatening to go at it alone if Dr. Kirkland and his staff do not stop hounding them about deadlines."

"You need to have a talk with Dr. Kirkland," Achampi suggested.

"I thought Chicago was the nerve center for this project, not London? All directives actually should come from Chicago," Abramhoff stated, reassuring himself. "I was just wondering; is it just that this British doctor does not know when to stop?"

"Should I get him on the line?" Achampi offered.

"What time is it?"

"9:23."

"It's late in London...it is 3:23 p.m. over there. I hope he is still in the office."

"Sabrina," Abramhoff called over the intercom.

"Yes, sir," Sabrina answered.

"Can you get me Dr. Kirkland in London?" Abramhoff requested.

"Right away, sir," Sabrina answered with some frustration.

Dr. Kirkland, a former military medical officer before joining the staff at the Queen Elizabeth Hospital in London, made punctuality and on-time delivery the centerpiece of his project. He had little patience for not getting things done on time, a theme he reiterated to Abramhoff initially in New York City, and on several subsequent phone conversations.

Abramhoff for his part, being a more suave politician and more diplomatic, preferred gentle persuasions, especially when it comes to cultures that he was not very familiar with.

"I understand what you are saying, Dr. Kirkland, but for the success of the project we need not antagonize our database," argued Abramhoff.

"I have never been a politician in my life, and for the life of me, I cannot understand why chaps cannot deliver what they promised."

"That's why the state of the world is what it is right now, but we have to work with it."

"That's not my cup of tea." Dr. Kirkland was emphatic.

"That's why I am suggesting, from now on, let me handle these little nuances. Any other problems you have over there, let me know and I will find ways to resolve them."

Hanging up the phone, Abramhoff winked an eye at Achampi who sat and listened to the entire conversation.

"Tough individual," observed Achampi.

"He tries to be," answered Abramhoff.

"In any event, how are the data looking?"

"So far so good," answered Abramhoff, breathing a sigh of relief. "The numbers coming in have less than 5 percent deviation from our statistical mean, and that, my friend, argues for a very high correlation."

"So technically this is a worldwide phenomenon isn't it?" Achampi's surprise was clearly evident.

"I didn't doubt it for one bit," answered Dr. Abramhoff.

666

After the ten a.m. lecture at the hospital residential lecture hall, Abramhoff returned to the office intending to call Singapore and Brazil. Just as he walked into the office, the phone rang.

"Dr. Dickerson," announced Sabrina.

"I will take it," answered Abramhoff.

"How are things in San Diego?" asked Abramhoff, happy that this was not an international call.

"Right now things are a little rough."

"You are not the only one."

"What happened?"

"No, you go first," encouraged Abramhoff.

"The law enforcement here thinks that I might be in some sort of danger."

"What...? What happened?" gasped Dr. Abramhoff.

"Well, they think that some criminal element or elements are out to stop me."

"What do they mean...out to stop you?"

"That's the problem," answered Dickerson. "They don't know. Is my life in danger? They would not answer. So they are going to hook me up with a GEES device to monitor my activities."

"What's a GES device?"

"No, G-double-E-S device," corrected Dickerson. "I was corrected also. It's a global satellite eye and ear device that will see me in Technicolor and hear me crystal clear, even if I am hiding in a cave."

"That's exactly what they need to place on all the HLA B66 positives, not you."

"That's probably what it is being developed for, but for me, for now, it is supposed to be a protective gear."

"Make sure they don't mistake you for an HLA B66," Abramhoff joked.

"Oh no," laughed Dickerson, "I have my own private detective monitoring my every move."

"Is it Pinkett?"

"Yeah, Pinkett." Dickerson gazed upwards. "It is that obvious?"

"Oh, I know, both of you are good friends," Abramhoff responded, sitting down on the high-arched leather chair, "but who is this criminal element supposed to be?"

"I just don't know," answered Dickerson. "All I know is that he recently arrived here from New York where he has eluded authorities for years."

"That's so spooky."

"Speaking of spooky, I had a strange dream the other night that some car ran me off the road. I was about to crash when the phone rang and woke me up from my sleep."

"Is that a coincidence or what?" observed Abramhoff.

"That, in a nutshell, is what's happening here. How about your end?"

"Well," answered Dr. Abramhoff, taking a deep breath, "we had a small international crisis, that I hope resolved itself."

"What happened?" asked Dickerson.

"Dr. Kirkland, the British side, wants everything done by the clock, not realizing that patience is needed, especially when it comes to international studies."

"He must not have realized that when it comes to international studies, deadlines are the most missed."

"No, he does not know that."

"What is this I hear about a religious gathering in Rome to discuss the HLA B66?" asked Dickerson.

"I don't know," shrugged Abramhoff. "That's more or less down your alley."

"More or less is correct," agreed Dickerson. "Yes, the Pontiff called a meeting of the Cardinals, and I heard that all of them are attending. Some Jewish, Muslim, and other Christian denominational leaders were also invited to attend."

# CHAPTER FORTY-SIX

Two weeks later, the BASICS results were made public. In a televised news conference, it became apparent that the HLA B66 finding was indeed a worldwide phenomenon. The correlation between real hardcore criminals, heinous crime committers, mass murderers, and bizarre unnatural cult-followers and HLA B66 had been proven beyond any reasonable doubt.

Abramhoff and Dickerson were pronounced pioneers in this field and were cited several times in the report as having discovered something very unique.

Disagreement, however, still festered over the connotation that HLA B66 was somehow related to the number 666 in the book of Revelation.

While America, Canada, and Britain, though not totally dismissing the idea, jointly stated that further studies and observations were needed to establish that relationship, Italy, Singapore, and Brazil embraced the connection between HLA B66 and the number 666, based on the principles elucidated by Dickerson.

When the preliminary result of the HLA B66 study in Italy was leaked, the Italian parliament went into an emergency session to pass a bill calling for the construction of a massive prison in Milan to house the influx of the positive HLA B66, a.k.a. 666, inmates.

In Singapore, an abandoned army barrack built in 1941 that could house up to 100,000 troops was immediately slated to be converted into a holding cell to house the potential HLA B66 positive Singaporeans, so the government decreed.

A Brazilian government spokesperson had no comment when asked about the government reactions to the HLA B66 findings in Brazil.

A front-page newspaper article in Rio de Janeiro, *El Conquistador,* stated that the minister of interior would have a private conversation with the president and hopefully a resolution would be passed soon.

Meanwhile, back in Rome, church leaders were just concluding their seven-day, closed-door, lip-sealed conference. Leaked information, however, was posted on the Internet, which stated that the sessions were oftentimes contentious, and on one or two occasions, harsh words were exchanged.

At the conclusion of the meeting, however, an official joint communiqué made public through the wire services, televisions, and the World Wide Web stated:

"Recent events concerning HLA B66 have achieved one objective, and that is the start of serious dialogue between governments and religions. It also facilitated the coming together of different religious groups, and the reaffirmation of the existence of a Supreme Being, whom we all worship.

"To that end, therefore, we have concluded that further HLA B66 testing proceed with due diligence, and with an unbiased scrutiny. Beliefs, faith, and sometimes miracles, not magic, are the cornerstone connecting all religions.

"Scientific testing to prove or disprove one's allegiance to the Supreme Being, if it will ever come to that, is currently not prima fascia enough to qualify for sole association with God."

The communiqué concluded that science cannot and should not replace faith. It then warned all nations to remain vigilant.

# CHAPTER FORTY-SEVEN

"That thing sure looks just like my coat button," Dickerson exclaimed, while looking at the device that Pinkett had just shown her.

"It is made out of a button," answered Pinkett. "The good thing about it is that it can be made out of any size, shape, or color button."

"Why a button?" asked Dickerson. "Why does it not look like a pen, an umbrella, or a purse like you see in the movies?"

"We are not in the movies, and this is more serious than that. Besides, buttons are unique," answered Pinkett. "They have this spherical appearance, so it can emit huge spheres around you that are about five to six feet in diameter. It then bounces invisible beams off the boundaries of the spheres. The beams, when they shine on you and whoever is around you, are what we are picking up via satellite to make out exactly where you are, what you're wearing, whom you are talking to, and what both of you are saying."

"You sound like a physics professor," Dickerson smiled. "Where did you learn to be so smart?"

"Where? At the Central Intelligence Agency Academy in Langley, Virginia, that's where," Pinkett answered without hesitation.

"Do I have to wear the same button every day?" Dickerson asked, realizing that Pinkett was not in a jovial mood.

"No, I had them make twenty different versions to match twenty of your favorite dresses and suits."

"How do you know my favorite clothes?"

"That's my job as a lead detective to know these things," Pinkett stated.

"It will take several days to sew them all in," Dickerson observed.

"Not to worry," answered Pinkett. "We have two guys with us here in San Diego, and it will only take them about two days to fit all your clothes."

"How many of us are here?"

"What do you mean…us?"

"You keep using the word we…and us."

"We have quite a few field agents here, because we think something is about to happen."

"And if my intellect is right, I just might be in the middle of it all."

"Just might, not positively sure, but we are not taking any chances."

"Pinky," said Dickerson, looking her directly in eye, "do you think this will work?"

"Doc, this is top of the line," Pinkett answered in desperation. "I am staking my reputation on this. I also know you are a praying Catholic. So, pray a little."

"This is serious, isn't it?"

"Darn serious."

"Does the governor know?"

"Oh yes, he personally approved this project, and he made it possible so that I can be assigned to you."

666

Two weeks went by and nothing happened. Dickerson started expressing doubts whether anything might come out of this whole preparation thing.

Early Monday morning, the governor called to alert Dickerson that the United States government had filed an appeal with the State Supreme Court in Sacramento, California.

"The trial is set for the following Thursday at nine a.m., and if need be, may be continued on Friday but should last no later than three p.m."

"I will make myself available," answered Dickerson.

"We would like to be very well prepared," stated the governor. "This time, there will be testimony from various church groups who have called and want to lend their support."

"That's great."

"Also Pellagrini and Pinkett have been subpoenaed to appear and be cross-examined."

"Is that why she is in town?" Dickerson feigned.

"One of the reasons, the other reason I understood you have been briefed on."

"Yes, I have," answered Dickerson, learning how to be diplomatic.

Next day, there was a news report, out of Fresno, California, that between 100 to 200 demonstrators gathered in front of the Veteran's Administration Hospital on First Street to demonstrate opposition to mandatory testing. The demonstration so far had been orderly; but the mayor of Fresno marshaled the city's law enforcement agencies to be on high alert in case of any violent outbursts.

"What do you think of what's happening in Fresno?" asked Dr. Peter Millons as he entered Dickerson's office for their routine early-morning "cross checking" meeting.

It was 9:45 a.m., and Dr. Millons was forty-five minutes late, and as usual, Dickerson waited for his lame recurrent excuse.

"I don't know; I haven't given it a second thought," Dickerson answered. "So Pete, tell me, what's the excuse this time? You were supposed to be here at nine."

"It's my wife," Millons responded, face downcast.

"What? Is she sick?" asked Dickerson, a little concerned.

After some hesitation, Millons, still looking downcast in an almost apologetic voice, said, "You know, and everyone on this campus knows, that she sleeps around."

Dickerson had no immediate answer and was about to wing it.

"You don't have to answer, because I already know," continued Millons. "The worst thing is that she sleeps around a lot, not only with the residents but with any man she can charm."

"What are you saying? She is some kind of a nymphomaniac?" Dickerson asked.

*We all knew she was a nympho, but this is ridiculous,* thought Dickerson.

"In a sense yes, but that's not the bad news."

"What's the bad news?" Dickerson turned and look directly at Millons while bracing herself.

"I seriously believe that she had a hand in the string of killings off the San Diego River," Millons, looking intensely serious, confided to Dickerson.

"How do you know that?" a perplexed Dickerson queried.

"She admitted it when I confronted her."

"Why didn't you report her to the police?"

"Because I believe she needs help, and I don't want the kind of help that will result in her being incarcerated."

"What kind of help is that?"

Forehead wrinkled, Millons responded, "I…I don't know."

"Are you telling me this because you want her to be tested?" Dickerson surmised.

"Yes!" Millons answered without hesitation, and with a strange aura of excitement. "That way, we can ascertain for sure what type of help she needs."

"Okay, if that's what you want, go ahead and bring her in," Dickerson responded with resignation.

"She won't come in," Millons bemoaned.

"What do you mean, she won't come in? Have the authorities bring her in."

"She is in my van, right now, at the parking garage, refusing to come in."

Dickerson thought for a second, and then offered, "Do you want me to go talk to her?"

"Would you?" Millons pleaded.

"Sure, Pete, I will do that for you."

"No, don't go alone," Sergeant Ortiz uttered aloud, while watching the satellite monitor, on a stakeout from an unmarked police van parked at the corner of La Jolla Village Drive overlooking Highway 805.

"Don't worry," answered Detective Pinkett, the senior officer in the van, as she peered over the monitor. "He used to be her nemesis, but now they are the best of friends."

With that, Sergeant Ortiz continued to monitor their journey through the building all the way to the garage. At the third floor of the garage building, about two car lengths removed from the parked van, Dr. Millons reached into his pocket, pulled out some nuts, and began chewing on them.

"What in the name of…," exclaimed Sergeant Ortiz.

"Tell me something, sergeant," Pinkett screamed, dropping the *People Magazine* she was reading.

"We have a kidnapping in progress," screamed Ortiz over the police radio wave. "Dr. Dickerson has been forced into a black Mercedes SUV, while performing a Heimlich maneuver on Dr. Millons."

"Did you get the license plate?"

"No, I didn't think anything—" Ortiz started explaining.

"Sergeant!" screamed Pinkett. "You are not allowed to think anything here, just do your job!"

"Yes, ma'am," answered an apologetic Ortiz.

"Okay, switch on the audio. Let's hear what's going on."

There were two other men in the car, one driving, and the other in the passenger side. Dr. Dickerson was seated between a woman on her left and Dr. Millons on the right.

"Millons, what's the meaning of all this?" asked Dr. Dickerson, appearing calm, thoughtful, yet happy that she had agreed to wear the satellite button.

"You shouldn't have," Millons answered.

"Shouldn't have what?" Dickerson shrugged. "I didn't do anything to you."

"No? You just don't know how much damage you've done."

Sensing a deeper meaning than what Dr. Millons was expounding, Dickerson turned to the woman on the left side, and extended her right hand.

"Hi. I am Dr. Dickerson, you must be Mrs.…."

"Keep your hands in front of you at all times where I can see them, please," commanded the man on the front passenger side, as Dickerson attempted to extend a handshake to the woman whom she assumed was Mrs. Millons.

"Weapon," exclaimed Sergeant Ortiz.

"What type?" Pinkett asked.

"It's a 45 Magnum."

"Is the safety on?"

"Still on," answered Ortiz.

Driving south on Highway 805, the black Mercedes drove almost the entire length of the highway down to

Highway 905. The van then exited left toward Brown Field Municipal Airport.

Just about a mile before the airport, the car turned south again toward the Mexican border on a dirt road that looked like it had been hardly traveled.

Finally, making another right off the dirt road about two blocks east, a garage door on a two-storied house opened; The Mercedes drove in, and the garage door closed behind it.

With the .45 mm pointed at her back, Dickerson and the crew entered a dark room on the first floor. It was so dark that Dickerson could hardly see even her escorts. Suddenly a match was struck, and candlelight illuminated the room.

Sitting behind a dark oak table was a man in his early sixties, dressed in military attire, wearing dark rimmed spectacles.

*That's odd. Why is this man wearing shades in a very dark room?* Dickerson wondered.

There was an opened bottle of Courvoisier at the corner of the table and a half-filled glass of the alcohol in front of him. Sitting on the Lancashire chair, directly across the desk, Dickerson thought about Pinkett and the criminal element the nation had been after.

*Is this him?* Dickerson asked herself.

"My name is Mr. Abba Calabar, and these are my associates."

Dickerson looked at Millons.

*Pete…is an associate of this criminal element?* Dickerson pondered.

"I know what you're thinking," continued Mr. Calabar. "Yes, Dr. Million and his lovely wife have been with us for over ten years now, and yes, they are the disciples of the San Diego River."

"What disciples?" Dr. Dickerson retorted, "Is that what you guys call yourselves? I call them murderers."

"What are you trying to prove with this HLA B66 nonsense?" asked Mr. Calabar.

Straightening her sitting position on the chair while looking around the dimmed room, Dickerson sarcastically responded, "Well, since you want to know, folks like you and Dr. Millons over there have the stamped image 666 in their body and are therefore, as you call it, disciples of the devil."

"Aha, and what do you suggest be done to Dr. Millons, the 666 man?" asked Calabar with a mocking smile.

"Send him to hell," Dickerson answered without hesitation.

"How do you propose we do that?"

Dickerson did not answer, knowing full well that whatever answer she gave would be twisted by Mr. Calabar.

Sensing her dilemma, Mr. Calabar continued, "You see, you are no different after all. Send to hell those whom you disapprove of, the 666s, as you call them, and what do we do? We send six feet under those we disapprove of."

*Where are you Pinky, and your elaborate scheme for my rescue?* Dickerson asked herself, as she sensed her pulse racing. *Did they lose the signal in this remote area? They must be watching all this…or are they? Is it too dark in here, or have these people disrupted the signals?*

"What I'm going to propose we do…," Mr. Calabar was about to elaborate when suddenly, there was a thunderous, earsplitting, blinding flash. The candle went out simultaneously, and Dickerson could hardly hear the exchange of bullets.

She dove straight to the floor as she had been previously instructed to do in any circumstance like this, and covered her head with her hands. Just as quickly as it started, floods of light illuminated the entire room. Somebody was leaning over her, feeling for something.

She could hear echo-like sounds from a distance. She could not make out what the echoes was saying, then it dawned on her that the echoes were calling her name. She raised her head and opened her eyes to look at the echo, then another echo.

"She is alive," said the vibrating echo.

"Of course I am alive, you stupid echoes." Dickerson could barely say it aloud.

# CHAPTER FORTY-EIGHT

At the university hospital where Dickerson was kept overnight for observation, she woke up next morning and thought she had another nightmare. Pinkett was sitting on the hospital chair next to her bed. A dressing covering a throbbing pain around her left upper arm quickly brought her back to reality.

"Hi, Pinky. I did well, didn't I?" asked Dickerson.

"You were superb," Pinkett answered.

*Why does she still sound like she is talking out of a bottle?* Dickerson was puzzled.

Pinkett, realizing the anxious look on her face, quickly reminded her that her hearing would clear up by tonight.

"You were never in danger. Agent Watts, the man on the passenger side of the car, was watching you all the time."

"What about Millons? What happen to him?"

"He was killed in the exchange, and so was his wife."

"Mr. Calabar, did you get him?"

"He tried to kill you, but the bullet only grazed your left elbow. He was shot dead by Agent Watts."

"You guys are just as bad as the old KGB," commented Dickerson.

"We are here to serve and to protect," Pinkett answered.

"Seriously, thank you for looking after me," Dickerson whispered emotionally, with teardrops in her eyes.

"You're more than welcome. After all, what are friends for?" Pinkett sniffled, fighting back tears, and then squeezed Dickerson's fingers in reassurance.

6 6 6

At the State Supreme Court in Sacramento, California, at the corner of Folsom Boulevard and 5th Street, the aura of the day was everywhere. There were reporters, photographers, and onlookers blanketing the entrance to the building.

When Dickerson appeared, she was mobbed by reporters who wanted to know how she was feeling after her recent traumatic event that captivated the nation. She was, however, quickly escorted inside the courthouse by the California State Police and federal agents.

Facing the five court justices, the U.S. government again made it case for federal authority and control of the HLA B66 legislation.

The state of California star witness, Dr. Dickerson, who after recounting what happened to her the other day, announced that an emergency testing of the assailants showed them all to be HLA B66 positive.

She then strongly argued in support of mandatory testing, not only in California, but throughout the United States, an argument that the federal lawyers dismissed as post-traumatic stress syndrome.

Next, Pellagrini and Pinkett were cross-examined by the lawyers. They reported that close to 80 percent of the cases they had handled so far had tested positive, and that their correlative exercise strongly supported the assertions of Dr. Dickerson and Dr. Abramhoff. Pellagrini even sought and tested the old celebrated cases involving Joan Stead in Chicago; Alex Andalusia in Indiana; Martin and Stella Montgomery in Savanna, Georgia; Bill Stockton's remains in Atlanta; Dr. Lee Kwon Nsi and his gang in Indiana; Mr. Fleming and his Baton Rouge, Louisiana disciples; and now Mr. Calabar and his San Diego disciples.

All tested positive.

Various nationally renowned church leaders took the witness stand, at the request of the state of California, in strong support of mandatory testing. They methodically cited Dr. Dickerson's analysis with exploitive demonstration of her deductions and subsequent calculations for the conversion of HLA B66 into 666.

"They are still vicariously living among us today," argued Archbishop Joseph Meeks of the dioceses of Sacramento.

He pontificated that the second thousand years were upon us, and it was high time we finally seized the initiative and resolved that the hour had come for the beast and their disciples to be cast back to hell.

A week after the testimonies, the State Supreme Court ruled four to one in favor of mandatory testing. The United States government immediately filed an appeal for an urgent hearing at the United States Supreme Court.

# CHAPTER FORTY-NINE

The exotic restaurant, La Vallecito, on Prospect Street in La Jolla, typified the exurb of a California locale. Nestled in the middle of the trendy Prospect Street, it had its own glass-enclosed, beautifully designed valet parking.

It had always attracted movie stars and prominent business leaders. Lunch and dinner were by appointment only, and if a request was made for a seat on the outdoor, umbrella-decked seating overlooking the Pacific Ocean, patrons needed to be prepared to pay extra.

Always ready to enjoy a beautiful California sun and the cool breeze from the ocean, Dickerson remained a frequent customer of the restaurant. The owner of the restaurant knew Dickerson personally, and the waiters and waitresses were very familiar with her favorite dishes.

She had visited here several times before, both for lunch and dinners. The cool breeze from the ocean had a healing and soothing effect each time she visited the restaurant. Sitting at the farthest corner with an unobstructed view of the ocean, Dickerson would experience total body relaxation.

"This is beautiful," Pinkett marveled, breaking Dickerson's concentration.

"Yes, this is the place to be," Dickerson responded.

"You come here often, because everybody seems to know who you are."

"Not as often as I would like to," Dickerson answered, leaning her head back and closing her eyes to soak in the cool breeze.

"This is too ritzy for me."

"No, it's not that bad."

"Of course not, if I only made your income."

"What would you like to drink?" interrupted the waitress.

"Iced tea for me, with lime, no sugar," ordered Dickerson.

"Tonic water," answered Pinkett.

"Are you ready to order, or should I come back?"

"Give us a few minutes."

"What was that? Tonic water? Yuck...that bitter-tasting thing." Dickerson made a face like a little girl about to drink unwanted tonic.

"Oh, I love it," answered Pinkett. "It soothes and relaxes cramped muscles and joints, especially after a strenuous body use. You should know that, Doc."

"I never heard of that."

"Well, it's true. I'm a living witness."

The waitress came back with the drinks, served them, picked up a small notepad from her pocket, took their orders, and left.

"How is your arm?" asked the detective.

"It's okay, still hurts a little bit when I try to use it."

"Mr. Calabar had a gun with him, and he took a pot shot at your heart," said the detective.

"I thought you told me that nothing would happen," Dickerson queried.

"The agent had never met Mr. Calabar before. He infiltrated the San Diego chapter, and luckily for us, he was assigned to the unit that abducted you to meet Mr. Calabar."

"He had no clue that Mr. Calabar was packed. When the shooting started, his job was to eliminate Mr. Calabar while making sure that neither Dr. Millons nor the other fellow had an angle on you."

"You guys had it all figured out."

"Yes, after months of preparation."

"I could have been shot out there, you know."

"Yes, you could have," answered the detective after some hesitation, "that's why I suggested you pray. Apparently your prayers were answered."

"Thanks a lot. Tell me, Mr. Calabar…that was your man?" asked Dickerson, shaking her head.

"Yap, that was him," the detective nodded.

When Dickerson returned to the office after lunch, Abramhoff called to congratulate her on her successes in California.

"You are now a celebrity, and guess what? You are in the right state for that," Abramhoff joked.

"Well, thank you, David."

"I heard about your incident near the Mexican border. What was that all about?"

"I guess this guy, Mr. Calabar, a sub-Mediterranean looking fellow, somehow did not like my interpretation of the HLA B66, and it so happened that the police have been after him for a while," answered Dickerson.

"So he kidnapped you, while you were wired?"

"Apparently so, and the police have been following his movements for a while. They suspected that he might come after me. Why, I don't know. My suspicion is that it's because of my interpretations. Anyway, the Pellagrini-Pinkett people had that GEES on me. I was hooked up to this thing for over two weeks, then bingo. Mr. Calabar made his move, and the police moved in."

"You were like bait?" said Abramhoff clearing his throat.

"Yes, I was."

"Did you know that, or did you find out later?"

"I knew."

"Pinkett convinced you to do that?"

"Yes, she did."

"I don't know how you do it. Me, I am too much of a chicken for that kind of drama."

"You know something? Somehow, I wasn't even afraid."

"Some angel must have been watching over you."

"You might say that," answered Dickerson, thinking about her dream of the face on the car window. "How's Illinois with the mandatory testing?"

"We are waiting on California. Once it clears the Supreme Court; that will open the floodgate. Have you guys actually started testing in any locations?"

"Not really," answered Dickerson. "We are still on restraining orders from the U.S. government until the case is totally resolved."

"That's unconscionable, but what if the Supreme Court rules against your mandatory testing?"

"You know, I never even thought about that. We have been winning all these court cases that I am assuming it will just be a given," Dickerson answered reflectively. "I actually don't know what will happen if they say no."

"Let's just hope they don't," encouraged Abramhoff.

"As soon as the Supreme Court renders their positive opinion let's get together, Chicago or San Diego, to celebrate and plan the next move, because there is still the issue of what to do with thousands, or maybe millions, who might be positive," Dickerson suggested.

"Come to think of it, I have never been to San Diego before," answered Abramhoff, excited. "You, on the other hand, have been to Chicago two or three times."

"Oh, I will take you to this wonderful restaurant. It will take your breath away," Dickerson suggested.

"I am looking forward to it. Can I bring the wife and kids?"

"Please do," answered Dickerson, not giving it a second thought.

*Such a family guy, I didn't even know he was married,* thought Dickerson when she hung up.

The dean of the medical school called, asking for an audience with her. Wanting to get out of the office for a little fresh air, Dickerson strolled down the hallway, entered the elevator and exited at floor fourteen, then on to Dr. Matthew Gus' office.

"How are you feeling?" Dean Gus asked, as soon as Dr. Dickerson sat down.

"I am fine," Dickerson simply answered.

"Sit down, please," invited Dean Gus. "The reason I called to see you is that I want to personally thank you for all you have done for the university. Your impeccable research and the secondary benefits the university have enjoyed by your esteemed performance."

"Well, thank you," Dickerson smiled, while sipping on club soda.

"Two things I need to ask you." Dean Gus clasped both hands together.

*Oh, here we go,* thought Dickerson.

"First, you have been working on the HLA B66 for…?" asked the dean.

"Almost five years now," Dickerson reminded.

"During that time, you hardly have taken any vacation time," said the dean. "I am therefore suggesting that you take a paid sabbatical for a year, travel around the world and experience nature."

"Thank you very much, but we still have a lot of work left to be done," Dickerson smiled. "We are still waiting for the Supreme Court to clear the way for the mandatory testing, and when they do, I would very much like to get that project moving, since the governor has assigned me to be the medical director of the project. It is going to be a lot of work, you know, but I believe I can handle it, if that's what you are afraid of."

"Oh no, I know you have a great stamina for the job, but don't you think sometimes the body needs a rest?"

"I really appreciate your concern, but trust me, as soon as things settle down; I will take some time off."

"Okay."

"What was the second thing?" queried Dickerson, after the dean hesitated. "You said there are two things you wanted to talk about."

"Yes," continued the dean. "Few of the faculty members, not many, have expressed concern about…how should I say this…? How you are allowing your religion to supersede your research. They feel that your research may lose its objectivity. What do you think?"

"Who are these faculty members?" Dickerson asked with an angry tone.

"You know I can't tell you that," answered the dean with a conciliatory smile. "I really believe they don't mean any harm."

"They are just scientists like you," continued the dean, "and they want religion to be kept out of science as decreed by the Pope."

"You know I can't do that," answered Dickerson. "What I discovered was based on science, but with a deeper meaning and understanding. Religion is sometimes difficult for people to understand, and we were asked to use wisdom in our calculations. Dean, that's exactly what I did. There are things happening right now as verified by the Pellagrini and Pinkett Project, and more are about to happen. I can't stop now. Maybe this is destiny at work; I don't know. Ask Dr. Abramhoff; he will tell you."

With a huge smile on his face, the dean replied, "That's exactly what I thought you were going say. Keep up the good work."

# CHAPTER FIFTY

Tuesday morning, 6:30 a.m. in San Diego, as most Californians were barely waking up, in Washington, D.C., the Supreme Court reconvened. Several days of argument between the United States government solicitors on one side, and the state of California on the other, rested on nine Justices who would render their opinion on the mandatory testing issue.

"So what do you think is gonna happen?" Pinkett asked Pellagrini, as they sat in the U.S. Supreme Court building waiting for the justices to return.

"I am not a betting man, but if my hunches are correct, they are probably going to reject California's argument," Pellagrini responded, as he sat cross-legged, tapping his well polished shoe against the edge of the empty chair in front of him.

"What! What made you think that?" Pinkett was surprised.

"Didn't you watch Chief Justice Harris' body language as he listened to the arguments? He clearly was exhibiting signs of indignation as California presented its oral argument."

"I didn't perceive that at all. As a matter of fact, he smiled several times at the counselor from California," Pinkett observed.

"That exactly is the point," Pellagrini emphasized. "The smile was made as he sat back and listened, thumb resting on the jaw, the index finger near the temple, and the rest of the fingers covering the mouth. That's a bad sign in court. If he was leaning forward, hands clasped together while he smiled, I would give California the edge."

"Let me guess, this is one of your occult analyses?" Pinkett mocked.

"Keep watching," Pellagrini responded.

"In case you have forgotten, several states have legislation in place ready to institute mandatory testing once the Supreme Court renders their opinion."

Just as Pinkett was finishing her statement, the nine justices strolled out and sat on their benches. Chief Justice James Harris read the majority opinion.

"After thoroughly reviewing the Constitution of the United States, the various previous religious persecutions, and the wonderful criminal justice system in United States that has worked for over 200 years, the Supreme Court in a five to four decision has rejected the state of California's argument. We therefore urge the United States government and the state of California in particular to put in place a plan for total cessation of all mandatory testing."

As they were exiting the Supreme Court building, Pellagrini remarked, "Human behaviors are most often easily predictable." He then looked at a stunned Pinkett and smiled.

For the next several hours, all television stations in the country pre-empted their daily programming for an in-depth analysis of the latest Supreme Court decision. There were calls from various quarters for impeachment of the five justices that voted against mandatory testing.

Sensing a huge national unrest, the president immediately took to the airwaves and urged all Americans to remain calm. He reminded all that the United States of America is still a country where the rule of law, not anarchy, governed. He urged restraint from those who might use the Supreme Court decision to incite violence.

After the president's remark, Dr. Dickerson appeared in front of a huge television crew that camped outside the university administration building, to read a statement.

"We were truly disappointed at the Supreme Court decision against mandatory testing," Dickerson read. "We have shown beyond all reasonable doubt the associations between certain criminal elements and HLA B66. I have also postulated the association between HLA B66 and the number that stands for the beast. I would like to take this opportunity to thank the governor for his tireless efforts. I would also like to thank Dr. Abramhoff in Chicago for his dedication. He is such a brilliant man. I would also like to extend my deepest appreciation to the Pellagrini-Pinkett Project. They have truly opened our eyes. The HLA B66 issue is not dead, far from it. This is the beginning of our campaign, and I urge all good citizens to join our campaign. We all have been called, and it is up to us to answer that call. Thank you."

A statement also from Dr. Abramhoff was read on the networks expressing disappointment and dismay at the Supreme Court. It continued that it made the work of determining predestination all the more difficult, but nonetheless science would go forward and someday prevail.

# CHAPTER FIFTY-ONE

The campaign for the next president of the United States was gathering steam in several key states. The two candidates, tied up in several recent polls, were tirelessly searching for support from all fifty states. The battleground states were Florida, Pennsylvania, Missouri, Michigan, and surprisingly, New York.

President Steve McClellan, the Republican running for reelection, had labeled the challenger, Governor Betty Clayton, the Democrat from Ohio, a waffling liberal Democrat, soft on crime, weak on defense, and poised to raise taxes.

Governor Clayton, for her part, promised to restore discipline in government by reestablishing accountability, controlling run-away fiscal spending, and reestablishing American's pride overseas. Most importantly, Governor Clayton promised to dedicate her win and her first official duty as president, in an all-out effort to reverse the federal government ban on mandatory testing for HLA B66.

666

Two weeks after the Republican convention in Houston, Texas, two of the elder Supreme Court justices who voted against mandatory testing announced their early retirement from the bench. Associate Justice Jackson planned a retirement in January right after the presidential inauguration, while Justice Sandra Denver-Moose announced her retirement in mid-March.

The importance of the next president of the United States could not have been made any clearer. Governor Clayton, seizing the opportunity, declared that if elected president, America would again resume its leadership role in the international campaign for mandatory HLA B66 testing.

666

"How are you, David?" Dickerson called Abramhoff to finalize the arrangements for his upcoming San Diego trip. "I have booked you a suite with an adjourning double room at the Hyatt in downtown San Diego. I hope you like it."

"You shouldn't have, but thanks anyway," Abramhoff responded.

"It is close to the marina, in case you want to take the kids on a boat ride or sightseeing," Dickerson suggested.

"Oh, they would love it, and by the way, let me have Sabrina take care of all the finances," Abramhoff offered.

"Oh, don't worry about it; that's nothing considering what's been happening these days," Dickerson responded, letting out a big sigh.

"What...the Supreme Court ruling, or the presidential politics?" Abramhoff braced for Dickerson's volleys.

Ever since the Supreme Court ruling, Dickerson had become a vocal critic of the U.S. Supreme Court, its political influence, and the president's position in particular. She would sometimes call just to berate aloud, and all Abramhoff could do was listen.

"This is the first time I have been really excited and enthused about our presidential elections," an excited Dickerson responded.

"Who do you support?" asked Abramhoff, chuckling.

"Do you really have to ask? Of course I am 100 percent behind Governor Clayton, and she knows it. I just found a new love for governors, and…and with two Supreme Court justices retiring—mind you, these were the opposition justices, I believe we will be back in business big time if the governor wins. What about you? You sound subdued."

"She is not my adored candidate—after all, she is a democrat—but on this one particular issue, I will campaign hard for her and make sure she carries Illinois. Governor Roderick would kill me if he heard me say this."

"I will assume so. Isn't he the campaign coordinator for the president in the state of Illinois?"

"You got it."

"Listen," Dickerson interrupted with an air of excitement, "you know we totally forgot about that physician from West Virginia, the one with the special water from Peak Hole."

"Yes…Dr. Eugene Norfolk from West Virginia Commonwealth University. I remember him, and also don't forget about Dr. Dominic St. John in Boston with his blood transfusions," Abramhoff responded rather easily.

"How did you remember their names that easily?" Dickerson said, baffled.

"Because we have doctors here with the same exact names, only these guys are from Massachusetts both. But back to the fellow from West Virginia, what was your question?"

"Should we have a meeting with him, or possibly both of them, and investigate their claims of cures associated with the Peak Hole water and the blood transfusions?" Dickerson asked.

"Hmm…I would probably wait until after the presidential election to see which way the pendulum is swinging," Abramhoff answered philosophically.

# CHAPTER FIFTY-TWO

In Chicopee, Massachusetts, three decapitated bodies were discovered in the shallow southeast end of the Chicopee River, not far from the junction of Highway 291 and Fuller Road.

Two seventeen-year-olds playing with their Labrador retriever dog made the gruesome discovery. State, federal, and the Pellagrini Pinkett Project team were immediately notified. Intense investigation was launched.

The three late teens were all Latinos. Investigators questioned their mothers, their boyfriends, other friends, and relatives. It turned out that in a twelve-month period, their single mothers had all dated the same man. Lithuania Alvarez became the prime suspect in the investigation.

A search along Chicopee River west to the Connecticut River and east up to Palmer, Massachusetts, failed to yield the decapitated heads.

National news media swarmed Chicopee, Massachusetts, as Governor Clayton used the gruesome killings to make the case for national HLA B66 testing. Initial identification was problematic because of severe decomposition, but eventually all three bodies were properly matched.

Governor Clayton, on a campaign rally in Los Angeles, California, aroused the crowd, vowing that, "If elected president, my first order of business is to start the reversal process of the federal ban on mandatory HLA B66 testing."

Thunderous applause followed.

"And when vacancies do arise, as they certainly will, I will appoint judges to the Supreme Court who support our stand on mandatory testing."

More applause followed.

"Crime in the United States is at an all-time high, and the natures of some of these crimes are increasingly gruesome. Unless mandatory testing becomes the law of the land, criminals and criminals-to-be will continue to wreak havoc on you, your children, and your loved ones. Now that we have the means, we should not wait to see our relatives' mutilated or decomposed bodies all over the television, just like the family in Chicopee, Massachusetts, before we do something. If we continue with the president's current plan, we will always be behind the eight ball."

Prolonged applause followed.

The president's team immediately fired back, letting voters know that if elected president, Governor Clayton would use this unfair litmus test as an excuse to appoint liberal judges to the Supreme Court.

666

At the Pellagrini Pinkett Project Center, Mr. Alvarez's blood had undergone the usual HLA B66 testing.

"What was the result from that Massachusetts decapitation story? Sorry, I forgot the name of the town," asked Pinkett.

"You mean Chicopee, Massachusetts?" Pellagrini answered.

"Yeah, that's him."

"He tested positive, of course."

"You think he's guilty?"

"I know he is guilty, despite what he might say."

"Do you think this is a cult thing?"

"I don't know. The fact that their heads have not been found makes one think of a cult thing, but they are all late teenagers. I believe a sexual perversion has to be part of the story," Pellagrini analyzed.

A warrant was issued for the arrest of Lithuania Alvarez on suspicion of murder. Under intense police and Federal Bureau of Investigation questioning, Mr. Alvarez admitted knowing the young women, but still denied knowledge of their death.

He alleged that the young women made sexual advances at him, and he rebuffed them. With no solid evidence linking Mr. Alvarez to the crimes, he was released under monitoring by the Pellagrini Pinkett monitoring system.

Finally, the mother of one of the teenage girls came forward with damaging information. She claimed that she initially feared for her life, but after counseling, she was ready to testify.

At the police headquarters in downtown Springfield, Massachusetts, Mrs. Gonzalez, under oath, stated, "I dated Litu, that's what we call him, you know, for about ten months."

She did not make much eye contact, and incessantly fidgeted with the edge of her buttoned sweater.

"He corrupted my daughter. He was constantly buying her gifts…teenage girls, you know, they get excited with stuff like that."

"So what happened?" asked the detective.

"I knew he was sleeping with my daughter. You know, a mother knows these things. She was happy, so I didn't do nothing."

"Did your daughter confide in you about anything?"

"She finally told me when she became scared of him."

"What do you mean, scared of him?"

"She said that Litu warned her never to sleep with any other man. He made her swear…it was strange what he did."

"Why?"

"Litu pricked himself with a pin, squeezed two drops of blood in a cup of lemonade, and made her drink it. Then he told her that if she ever slept around or told anybody, her whole family here and in Mexico would be murdered."

"Why didn't you go to the police?"

"I was scared, you know." Mrs. Gonzalez made infrequent eye contact with the detective. "They have this gang called *Sin Aviso* in Chicopee, and we are all scared of them."

"Why are you scared of them?"

"They do things to people…I cannot say here, you know, as a warning to other people. I think Litu is a member of that gang."

"How do you know?"

"Well, he keeps making this phone call…ask his brother, Pedro, he will tell you. I think they are both in it."

Investigation of Pedro Alvarez, a pharmacist working at the Wal-Mart Drug store at the corner of Northampton and West Franklin Street in Holyoke, Massachusetts, helped provide much of the pieces to the puzzle.

Subsequent searches of Pedro's house on Lorraine Drive near Holyoke Community College led to the discovery of the three teenage heads, freshly preserved in three formaldehyde-filled glass jars. Pedro told investigators that Litu fabricated the preservation stuff just for sick pleasure.

Pedro tested negative for HLA B66, but the other four members of the captured *Sin Aviso* gang members tested positive.

666

At the third and final presidential debate, Governor Clayton made it clear that it was indeed the HLA testing that made it possible for the capture of Mr. Alvarez and the *Sin Aviso* group.

"If Mr. Alvarez was not subjugated to such an intense scrutiny with his positive HLA B66, the whole investigation would not have been a complete success," she argued.

The president countered that the current systems of checks and balances have always been effective and were still working well.

"It is the current system that flushed out the Alvarez *Sin Aviso* group and brought them to justice," he explained. "Mandatory testing, if made into law, will in fact subjugate innocent Americans to an unfair scrutiny."

On Election Day, the entire nation was glued to their television set all day long. During the late-night hours, there were multiple lead changes in the Electoral College vote, although Governor Clayton maintained a slim margin in the popular vote. It was not until midnight Mountain Time that Governor Clayton became president-elect of the United States.

# EPILOGUE

The United States of America, in collaboration with Argentina, France, Israel, Italy, Japan, Nigeria, India, North Korea, Philippines, Saudi Arabia, Scandinavia, South Africa, and Sweden instituted mandatory national HLA B66 testing.

The Pellagrini-Pinkett Center in Washington, D.C., became the international nerve center. Federal regional centers were set up in all major cities throughout the United States. Jim Pellagrini and Maria Pinkett were named federal co-coordinators, and Drs. Regina Dickerson and David Abramhoff were federal medical directors.

"What a long ride," observed Pinkett after all the routine set-ups were completed.

"It was worth it, won't you say?" Pellagrini responded.

"I guess."

"Oh…how I feel like Mr. Johnson," Pellagrini exhaled, sitting on the sofa, hands behind his head, eyes closed.

"And who is Mr. Johnson?" asked Pinkett with that curious look on her tired face.

"You haven't heard of Mr. Johnson?" a surprised Pellagrini asked, eyes and mouth wide open.

"No, I haven't."

"Oh, let me tell you," began Pellagrini. "This Church in Memphis, Tennessee, was packed with worshipers one Sunday morning, and the pastor was at the audience level preaching fervently. All of the sudden, the devil appeared on the pulpit. There was a mad dash for the exit. Everybody ran out of the church except for Mr. Johnson, calmly sitting two rows removed from the back. The devil looked around and noticed Mr. Johnson sitting calmly, staring at him, not flinching. The devil approached Mr. Johnson with an aura of fear.

"'Do you know who I am?' asked the devil, with a demonic voice.

"'Yap,' answered Johnson calmly.

"'You are not afraid of me?'

"'Nope.'

"'You know I can destroy you.'

"'Yap.'

"'You know I can make your life miserable in ways you can't imagine.'

"'Yap.'

"The devil became flabbergasted as to why this little seventy-year-old man was not afraid. Curiously, the devil asked, 'Why are you not afraid of me?'

"Mr. Johnson calmly looked the devil in the eye and replied, 'I've been married to your sister for fifty-two years.'"

Pinkett could not contain herself with laughter.

Just as it is harmful to drink wine alone, whereas mixing wine with water makes a more pleasant drink that increases delight, so a skillfully composed story delights the ears of those who read the work. Let this then be the end.

2 Maccabees 15:38–39